Hell's Gate

Hell's Gate

Michael Parker

ROBERT HALE · LONDON

ISBN 978-0-7090-8218-7

Robert Hale Limited
Clerkenwell House
Clerkenwell Green
London EC1R 0HT

2 4 6 8 10 9 7 5 3 1

*To my wife Patricia
who never lost faith*

Typeset in 10½/13pt New Century Schoolbook
by Derek Doyle & Associates, Shaw Heath
Printed and bound in Great Britain
by Biddles Limited, King's Lynn

CHAPTER ONE

BRITISH EAST AFRICA 1898
THE RIFT VALLEY

Reuben Cole watched his son David hold the rifle. The boy's blond hair was stained dark beneath the bush hat and small beads of sweat gathered on his forehead. Intense concentration was etched all over his face. Reuben turned and looked across the savannah at the gazelle that was grazing about one hundred yards from them. In his own hands was the Gibbs Farqhuarson rifle, the most powerful hunting rifle in Africa that could kill a charging buffalo at three hundred yards. He had it ready in case David failed to kill the gazelle, but only wounded it.

Above them the unseasonal clouds blotted out the sun, keeping the heat pressed in like a warm blanket. There was no breeze and the heat seemed to suffocate them. In the distance the rain blackened the sky above the horizon. Somewhere a train whistle sounded, carrying effortlessly through the air. Reuben heard it and looked at David. The boy never moved, his eyes focused on the gazelle. Reuben looked back at the animal as it lifted its head to the sound of the whistle. Satisfied there was no threat, the gazelle dropped its head and continued to graze.

David held his breath and squeezed the trigger. The rifle bucked in his hands and the gazelle dropped instantly. He cocked the rifle and held it steady, his eyes still focused on the gazelle. Then he relaxed and looked at his father with a self-satisfied grin on his face. 'Clean shot, mister,' he said.

Reuben smiled and put his hand on the boy's shoulder. 'Not bad for a twelve-year-old. Looks very good, David. It won't be long before you'll be wanting to use the Gibbs.' He stood up. 'Let's go see what you've bagged.'

David set the safety catch on his rifle and followed his father to where they had tethered their horses. He felt good, grown up. This had been the day his father had promised him for his twelfth birthday – to lead a hunt.

David was no stranger to shooting, and his ability with a rifle was never in doubt. But Reuben only let David hunt with him when their manservant Mirambo was with them, carrying a second rifle. There was no mother waiting at their farm for David to return to with his prize; she had died several years earlier, and Reuben had never remarried. It was something he kept reminding himself he had to do, to find David a mother. He just hadn't got round to doing anything about it. He would probably have to return to England to do so, but finding a woman willing to sacrifice herself to the savage climate of the Rift Valley would be difficult.

They reached the gazelle and Reuben lifted it up on to David's horse. David tied it securely and remounted. He felt a sudden thrill run through his body and the soft, blond hairs on his arms lifted in response. Now David was like the native boys; he had passed through to manhood with his first kill. He was now a man.

'Have you decided yet, Major?'

Joseph Grundy, chief administrator to the British East Africa Railway Company, was standing beside Major Kingsley Webb, commandant of the British East Africa Rifles in Nairobi. They were standing beneath a canopy, sheltering from the rain on the platform at Nairobi's railway station. Major Webb had a rubberized cape around his shoulders. He was a tall man whose features were a little gaunt, but beneath bright blue eyes they served to make him devilishly handsome. His hair was blond and had a natural curl to it. Shed of his uniform, Major Webb was a powerful man with a body honed to an almost arrogant perfection by years in the army. His current service in the inhospitable climate of East Africa had done nothing to lessen that perfection. And nothing to lessen his desire to serve except, perhaps, back with his regiment in Northern India.

'Have I decided what?'

'Whether to move the soldiers up the line.'

Grundy's concern was from a purely commercial standpoint. As chief administrator to the Railway Company at Nairobi (and quite literally governor of the camp), he was responsible for a conurbation of well over four thousand souls. Trade for the Company, which went hand in glove with construction, was of paramount importance. By now the Company should have been carrying fare-paying passengers along the entire length of the line from Mombasa on the east coast to Nairobi camp itself. This said nothing of the cargo, supplies, raw materials and the like which should now be forming a major part of the Company's two-way traffic. But because of political instability in Uganda, the proposed destination of the railway line, and the inherent vulnerability there since the Uganda Mutiny, troops were being brought in from India to fill the vacuum created in that country. As a result of which the army had slapped a ban on all civilian and commercial traffic while reinforcements were put in place. The few trains the Company had were now being used for troop carrying.

To add to the problem for Grundy, the rains had returned. Nobody knew why. The wet season had passed and now the lands should have been dry and dusty. But instead the rains were turning the earth into a quagmire, which bedevilled everything and anything that moved. And whenever the rain stopped, something that tended to happen with incredible speed, the sun transformed the railway camp into a hot, steaming Turkish bath.

The unpredictable weather also meant progress on the line was hauntingly slow. In good conditions the plate-laying gangs could lay track at the rate of one mile a day. But as the rains brought landslides and washed out large sections of the track, many of the gangs had to be diverted from the normal tasks to prop up and repair the line. Their progress was often reduced to little more than half a mile each day.

Webb considered his options. He had been doing little else all day. If they were unable to move the troops up to the railhead because the track was unsafe due to the rain, it would mean six hundred soldiers making temporary camp at Nairobi. Not to mention the pack animals travelling with them. Since the beginning of the Uganda Mutiny the previous year, they had witnessed the movement of almost twenty thousand soldiers and countless animals up to the railhead and into Uganda. It was difficult enough at the camp containing outbreaks of dysentery, malaria and other odious diseases without the added burden of the extra soldiers. Conditions in the camp, sprawled as it was over a large area, were almost primeval. They had but one hospital, which could barely cope. And with the drinking dens springing up, prostitution and the inevitable consequences of a burgeoning town, the influx of six hundred thirsty, sex-starved soldiers appalled even the most leviathan of minds.

Major Webb almost shuddered at the thought of it. The truth was that he didn't know the answer to Grundy's question; he would have to wait for the weather to relent and for the railway engineers to report on the condition of the track.

Reuben was about to mount his horse when he heard a sound like a small explosion. It rolled on for several seconds and the ground seemed to tremble slightly beneath his feet. His horse flared its nostrils and became restless. Reuben calmed the animal and mounted up quickly. He glanced over his shoulder, looking back at Mount Longonot in the distance as it towered over the Rift Valley. David leaned forward in his saddle and stroked the neck of his horse, calming it down.

'What was that, Dad?' he called, turning towards Reuben.

His father didn't answer him at first, but continued to study Mount Longonot. Then he shrugged and looked across at David. 'I think it's the railway engineers, doing some blasting.' He hoped he was right, but his heart told him otherwise. 'Not to worry, we'll get back to the farm. I'm sure Mirambo will be very pleased with your first kill.'

He pulled on the reins of his horse and David did the same. In unison the two horses moved off, heading towards Reuben Cole's farm in the Rift Valley.

High up the slope of the escarpment, watching from behind good cover, was Piet Snyder, a Dutchman whose catalogue of crimes marked him down as one of the worst criminals on the continent of Africa. His evil reputation was well-known among not just the burgeoning, white population in Africa, but most of the native Africans.

Piet Snyder was not just a convicted felon. He was a slave trader.

He slammed the telescope shut and smiled as Reuben and David moved off. Soon, he thought, he would have the prize he sought – and immense power.

Two short blasts from the train's whistle punctured the air again. They could see the iron horse now, rattling its way towards the station. It was an old Indian 'F' class, with a huge boiler dome above three large, driving wheels. Its cowcatchers and massive headlamps belonged to the American West, but here in Africa's wild tormented land, this diminutive giant provided all the guts and muscle that were needed to blaze a pioneering trail through the virgin bush.

The locomotive began to slow, its speed dropping noticeably. Despite the rain, heads appeared through open windows as the soldiers looked out in curiosity at Nairobi's colourless cluster of beleaguered townships.

As well as passenger carriages, there were also flat cars and cattle trucks. The flat cars were well loaded with weaponry and stores of all manner and description. And it was obvious from the baying coming from the animal wagons that there was a reasonable mix of horses and donkeys.

The arrival of the train seemed to bring everything to life. People began to appear from their hideaways where they sheltered from the rain and suffered the humidity in mumbling complaint. Porters began assembling on the platform and beside the track, their overseers patiently waiting before bellowing out orders.

The noise from the animal wagons increased as the occupants sensed the pending change and bellowed their approval. Or lack of it. Little black children ran laughing beside the train. They were laughing despite the rain, and as they ran, their tramping feet sent arcs of red mud into the air. And the rain began to slow to a simple downpour as if in deference to the general air of noise and excitement created by the train's arrival. There were more screams of delight from the children as great gouts of steam issued from beneath the wheels of the clanking locomotive as it ground to a halt.

Major Webb looked along the length of the carriages. By now it looked as if all the soldiers were bent on thrusting their heads through the open windows. From one of the carriages a young, fresh-faced army lieutenant stepped down on to the platform when the train stopped. He was carrying a dispatch case. He glanced up and down the length of the platform. With the lieutenant was a tall, elderly gentleman, who wore a long tailcoat over pinstriped trousers. He had a Panama hat on his head and, with the spats on his shoes, he looked quite out of place in the backwater that was Nairobi railway camp. This tall, elegant man was Sir Charles Ruskin, government administrator to the East African Railway Company and Joseph Grundy's boss. Together, Sir Charles and the young lieutenant walked along the platform to where Major Webb and Grundy were standing.

'Major Webb?' The young lieutenant spoke first. When Webb acknowledged him he smiled and saluted. 'Lieutenant Maclean, sir, your new adjutant.'

'Good morning, Lieutenant Maclean. Welcome to Nairobi.' Webb shook his hand after returning the salute. He then turned to the tall man and saluted him. 'Sir Charles, good to see you again.'

Ruskin smiled back. 'And you, Major.' He doffed his hat, and then he shook hands with Webb and Grundy. 'Damn rain,' he said, letting go of Grundy's hand. 'Seem to remember it was like this on my last visit to Nairobi, what?'

'Yes, but that was during the rainy season, Sir Charles,' Grundy answered lightly. 'We do have hot weather occasionally, you know.'

'Yes, and then it's too damn hot.' He spoke to Major Webb. 'Lieutenant Maclean has been extremely good company for me, Major. I believe he will be an asset to you.'

'Well, he will restore our complement of officers to two,' Webb told him a little acidly. It was not before time, either, he thought to himself. Lieutenant Maclean's predecessor had succumbed to malaria some three months earlier and was buried in the small cemetery beside the English Church.

'Oh, by the way, Major, I was asked to pass on a message to you.'

'What was that, Sir Charles?'

'Miss Hannah Bowers. She sends her apologies but cannot leave Machakos for a few days because her father still has church business to attend to.'

Major Webb thanked Sir Charles and tried not to show his disappointment. Hannah Bowers was the daughter of the Reverend Aubrey Bowers, chaplain to the British East Africa Company. It was almost an open secret among the British community at Nairobi that Hannah and Major Webb were very close, and everyone expected them to marry. But Hannah had refused to give him an answer to his proposal of marriage until her mother returned from England. Major Webb had hoped that Hannah would be on the train with news of her mother's impending return.

Webb turned to the young lieutenant. 'Nothing goes according to plan in this place,' he grumbled. 'Like I said, welcome to Nairobi.'

Despite the rain assaulting Nairobi camp, there was nothing on the escarpment, north of the Rift Valley where the sun burned down through a haze as the wind lifted the dust from the valley floor, funnelling it along the escarpment walls. Reuben glanced up and closed his eyes against the shimmering glare. He could feel the heat, trapped like liquid in the cradle between the hills. It enclosed him like a suffocating blanket. He removed his slouch hat and drew the back of his hand across his forehead. The sweat gathered and dripped from his brow. He jammed the hat back on his head and sighed heavily. The horse's ears pricked up, catching the sound and it moved restlessly beneath Reuben. He calmed it, rubbing his hand along its neck and urged it forward into a steady trot through the dry, savannah grass.

Ahead of him, high up on the slope, David rode effortlessly, his slight figure moving easily as the horse climbed to higher ground. It was almost as though the horse knew the air would be sweeter and cooler up there. Across the horse's back lay the body of the gazelle. Its beautiful, yellow coat with the distinctive black flash rocked crazily as David guided the horse through the coarse scrub grass that carpeted the slopes. Like his father, David was wearing a slouch hat. His blond hair hung beneath it in curls darkened by sweat. His young, strong arms were tanned

11

a deep, golden brown and he was wearing a heavily stained shirt over canvas trousers. He rode well forward in the saddle.

He pulled the horse up and looked back over his shoulder to his father who was now halfway up the slope. Below Reuben was a canopy of evergreen forest. They had skirted this and were now negotiating the escarpment, avoiding the outcroppings of rock and tumbling vegetation, as they moved towards the top. Reuben was barely two hundred feet behind him, but looked diminutive against the vast slope. David caught his father's upward glance and waved. Somehow this small gesture made him feel so adult; he felt he had achieved a status. He now believed he knew what it must be like for the young African boys when they bridged that challenging gap between youth and manhood. His chest swelled with a feeling of both pride and achievement.

As Reuben moved higher up the valley slope he was able to see dark, ash-coloured smoke rising above the distant hills in towering columns. The smoke drifted beyond the peaks of the volcanic escarpment. He had seen it much earlier that morning for the first time. It had puzzled him then, but now, together with the oppressive heat, it disturbed him even more.

The reason for Reuben's disquiet was that it was now the month of June, the time of the southeast wind known as the *Kuzi*, and the temperature should have been falling. Instead, the swirling, red dust was clamping the heat in, turning the valley into a devil's cauldron. Earlier it had been rain, unusual and unwelcome. Now it was this appalling heat. As he rode, Reuben could again feel distant earth tremors rolling like thunderclaps from beyond the cliffs of Hell's Gate, the brooding volcano once believed to be extinct: the towering Mount Longonot.

He dug his heels into the horse's flanks. There was a renewed urgency to reach the journey's end now; Reuben understood the portents too well. He had learned a great deal about the Rift Valley with its savage, yet breathtaking scenery; the strange but wonderful primeval rock formations and the heart-stopping volcanic disturbances. For five years he had struggled to build his farm which nestled in the cradle of the valley. It had been hard, daunting and backbreaking work. A battle against nature's intolerance, and he wanted nothing to threaten him or wreck those years of toil. Reuben feared for his home too. The house had been built high on the escarpment slope to catch the wind. It spread over an extensive plateau and afforded protection from the dreaded tsetse fly which spread its fever prevalently in the lower wetlands.

His thoughts were interrupted by a shout. It was David. The boy had cleared the high ground and had a commanding view of the valley and the farm. From his vantage point he could see a magnificent panorama marching away into the distance. Extinct volcanoes, incongruously topped with caps of trees, thrust their peaks up towards the blue sky. Mountainous wedges of rock tilted over at crazy angles. White pillars of salt rock eroded by centuries of wind formed grotesque shapes and stood erect like monolithic sentries. Whole swards of forest swept up into the distant foothills until their succulent shades of green merged with the duller hues of the rock. The view shimmered through the coruscating heat and a fine cloak of red and orange dust rose up to scatter the light from the sun. Beyond the awesome cliffs of Hell's Gate, which formed a natural barrier between the farm and the volcanic escarpment, stood Mount Longonot. It smouldered and rumbled like a glowering sentinel, coughing grey ash into the *kuzi* wind which carried it to lay a carpet of grey in the distant hills.

But the view was of little interest to David. As Reuben brought his horse to a stop beside him, David spoke in a rush, the words tumbling from his lips. 'Look. Father, in the valley – water!'

Reuben leaned forward, gripping the saddle horn. The leather creaked under the strain. He could see the water clearly. It meandered through the farm, round small hillocks and into shallow depressions. It flowed from the direction of Hell's Gate. He looked at it for some time before settling back into his saddle. David noticed the hard, fixed stare in his father's grey eyes.

'There was no water there when we left,' he said quietly. 'So why is it there now?'

It was a moment or two before Reuben could answer. Eventually he gathered up the reins. 'I don't know, David,' he replied. 'We'll have to find out. Come on.'

They cantered easily over the coarse grass, angling down the escarpment slope towards the valley floor. The presence of water on his land troubled Reuben immensely. If it remained during the dry season it would turn the farm into a quagmire when the seasonal rains came. As if to test his fears, another sound like a distant thunderclap shattered the sky above Mount Longonot. He shook his head in dismay and spurred his horse into a gallop.

They covered the remaining distance to the farmhouse at a steady pace, skirting the clusters of whistling thorn bush and acacia trees that grew at random, and putting the weaver birds to flight; their small, yellow breasts lost against the gold of the savannah. The body of the dead gazelle lurched precariously as David rode alongside his father.

Mirambo, the Kikuyu, watched them come like two insects scurrying across the landscape. He watched with feelings of relief and pleasure, his eyes brightening as he walked from the house. Some would have called him servant, or houseboy, but to Reuben he was a friend. He lived on Reuben's land with his wife and children, sharing the everyday tasks of the farm. Together they had built it, grafted hard at it and spilled blood for it. They were like partners in a great adventure, and Mirambo was never aware of anything between them other than a deep, abiding friendship. He waved as Reuben and David rode their horses into the high, thorned *boma*.

'*Jambo Bwana* Cole,' he called out. '*Jambo Sana* David.'

The red dust flew from the horses' hoofs into small, swirling clouds as they reined to a halt. Reuben slipped gratefully from the saddle and immediately released the girth buckle. Steam poured from his horse's flanks and white foam flecked its mouth.

'*Jambo* Mirambo,' he called back. He pulled the saddle from the horse's back and laid it across his shoulder. He nodded in the direction of the water flowing through the farm. '*Maji.*'

Mirambo nodded and his long ear lobes swung loosely. He raised two fingers. '*Mbili siku.*'

'Two days?' Reuben's forehead creased into a deep frown.

Mirambo pointed towards the column of smoke spiralling up from Mount Longonot. Reuben walked over and laid his hand on Mirambo's shoulder in greeting.

'*Kesho*, tomorrow. We shall go there tomorrow. But today. . . .' He left it unsaid and pointed down into the valley.

Mirambo's black face could not hide the look of impending

14

doom. He knew the search for the source of the water would be inevitable and likely to begin that very day. In his heart he knew where that search would take them. And in his pagan mind it carried them into the legends of Kikuyu folklore.

There was an excited shout, a clamouring of voices as Mirambo's children appeared from behind the farmhouse. They were running to see what great prize David had brought home with him. David had removed his saddle and laid it on the fence of the *boma*. Now he heaved the dead gazelle from his horse and dropped it on to the red earth with a mighty thud. For a moment the threat of the rising water was forgotten and the children began singing and shouting while David fussed around the dead animal. Mirambo flashed his teeth in a wide grin and walked over to him. He pushed his own children aside and studied the gazelle with care, making appreciative noises in his throat.

'What do you think, Mirambo?' David asked keenly, his eyes gleaming brilliant blue in the sun. 'It was an excellent shot.' He pointed to the mark where the bullet had entered just below the gazelle's ear.

Mirambo was pleased for the boy. He removed David's hat and ran his long, black bony fingers over his hair. '*Vyema, vizuri.*'

David whooped with joy and called over to his father. His face was vibrant and beaming. 'See, mister, Mirambo says it is excellent.'

Reuben's mind was too preoccupied to do justice to the occasion, but he tried manfully to respond to David's enthusiasm. 'So it is, David, an excellent prize. We are all very proud of you. But now we have more pressing things to attend to.' He turned away. 'Give the gazelle to Mirambo to skin for you,' he called over his shoulder. 'And bring your saddle into the *kibanda.*'

Mirambo lifted David's saddle from the fence rail of the *boma* and handed it to David. It almost dwarfed him as he carried it to the livery stable. Unlike his father, David had forgotten everything about the water and all its implications. The only thought that filled the boy's head was the sheer excitement of the last few days.

High up on the escarpment, again in safe cover, Piet Snyder watched through his telescope and smiled in satisfaction. Soon he would have the prize.

15

CHAPTER TWO

Major Webb relaxed in reasonable comfort in his dining chair. He was seated at the table in the private room of the Railway Club with his three guests. They had enjoyed a good meal and were now relaxing with port and cigars. The two waiters, both army personnel, had withdrawn and the talk was now of military and political matters.

'I find the army's decision to hold the rolling stock at Kilindi quite astonishing.' Joseph Grundy's opinion did not surprise any of them. 'My company is supposed to be operating a viable, commercial enterprise between Mombasa and Nairobi. I find it most difficult with the Army's heavy hand bearing down on us.'

'It's my understanding,' Major Webb told him, 'that your company is being compensated because of what is, essentially, a Government decision.' He looked directly at Sir Charles.

Sir Charles responded. 'I think you have to blame the foreign office for this,' he said. 'After all, they do tend to panic.'

'The army has never been its own master,' Lieutenant Maclean offered. 'Although I believe this decision would have originated from Army HQ at Machakos rather than Downing Street.'

'Could it not be that the army is simply accommodating government thinking?' Grundy put to him. 'Surely it was not the army's choice to flood Uganda with thousands of troops?'

Major Webb drew deeply on his cigar. He had the benefit of intelligence reports and the welter of information they offered. He wondered just how much these men understood of the situation. He suspected Sir Charles Ruskin knew a great deal, whereas Joseph Grundy's daily hours were devoted to the railway and its progress. Movement of soldiers and political sabre rattling were of little importance to him if they had no direct bearing on company progress and profits, despite their real effect. But the reality would have a far greater impact. The fact was that the exiled Bugandan leader, Mwanga, once Monarch of all Uganda, was massing an army of Muslims to fight against the British.

Mwanga first came to power in 1884 at the age of seventeen. Although he had been educated by Catholic missionaries, his elevation to the throne had been a bad mistake. When James Hannington had been appointed Bishop of all Uganda, it had proved to be too much for Mwanga; Hannington was found murdered on the banks of the River Nile before he had set foot in his new diocese. Mwanga denied culpability, but the murder had his mark all over it. It was the one act that proved Mwanga's instability and sent alarm bells ringing through the corridors of power in Whitehall.

Mwanga was thrown in jail, but his time there was to be short-lived. The Kaiser's imperial Germany was now actively engaged in plotting to expand its empire in East Africa. Intelligence reports suggested that Mwanga was to be a key figure in this planned expansion and, unsurprisingly, he had 'escaped' from his jailers who happened to be under the control of the Germans.

Major Webb's concern was not wholly with events in Uganda, but of something much closer to home: Nairobi. Reports were coming in from his scouting parties of a migration of Masai and Wakamba tribes to the Mau Plateau, west of the Rift Valley. The incidence of raiding parties had increased dramatically. There were also reports that the raiding parties were being organized by a European, a Dutchman known as Piet Snyder. Snyder was a maverick, a renegade and an ex-convict. His crooked exploits in South Africa had earned him a fearsome reputation, a reputation that remained with him after he had been hounded from that country.

On his own, the presence of Snyder would have presented no real problem to the major. But the Masai build up was ominous in that it presented a buffer to the Railway Company, and therefore the government's progress towards Uganda – their ultimate goal. But it was all the more sinister if it was being orchestrated by a white man.

Webb's own appraisal of the situation, based on the intelligence reports, was that the threat came not just from the Masai, or the Wakamba, but from the imperial German government. But it was a fear that he could not express publicly because he had no real evidence to corroborate it.

'So, Major,' Sir Charles said. 'What are you going to do about it?'

Webb blew out a stream of cigar smoke. 'Do about what, Sir Charles?'

'This damn nonsense of holding the trains at Kilindi? Totally unnecessary in my view.'

Grundy liked that. Sir Charles was a powerful boss and ally to work with. He had practically skewered Major Webb with his directness, although Grundy knew he was only doing it for devilment.

Webb affected a contrite response. 'What can I do, Sir Charles? Machakos issued the order. Only they can rescind it.'

Sir Charles Ruskin leaned forward. His manner seemed just a little more serious. 'If this railway does not succeed, Major, there are plenty of people back in England who will rub their hands with glee. I can assure you of that.' He raised his hand and pointed his finger at the major. 'Mark my words; Salisbury's government will fall. He has a very small majority in the House and it wouldn't take much to topple him.'

'What is your opinion, Lieutenant Maclean?' Grundy asked him.

'What is my opinion?' Maclean repeated, hoping to gain a little breathing space while he considered his response. 'As a serving officer my loyalty is to my Queen, my country and my regiment.'

'Balls to your loyalty, young man,' Sir Charles cut in. 'What is your damn opinion?'

'My opinion would be of little value here, Sir Charles, in view of the short period I've spent in Africa.'

'Bloody man's a politician!' Grundy roared with laughter.

'Good,' Sir Charles bellowed. 'Three to one now, Major. You lose. Rescind the order!'

Major Webb laughed along with them. It was good, fairhearted baiting at the army's expense.

'You know, Sir Charles, if I could devote my time and energy to ensuring the trains run, then perhaps my task here would be a great deal simpler,' Webb declared a little more seriously. 'But I have a much wider and infinitely more difficult job to do here as you well know.'

'Yes, I accept that,' Sir Charles agreed, nodding vigorously. 'Something of a policeman's role though, wouldn't you say?'

Major Webb did not like the use of the word nor all that it implied. Although he was responsible for law and order in the region, it was Grundy's responsibility to police the Railway Company and its employees.

'I shall always see my role here as that of a soldier offering protection to all of Her Majesty's subjects.'

'And we've needed some of that lately,' observed Grundy.

Maclean looked up in surprise. 'Why is that, sir?'

It was Major Webb who answered. 'The natives, as they say, have been getting restless. Our patrols have been skirmishing with renegade bands lately. Nothing more than that.' He wished he had been speaking the absolute truth.

Maclean lifted the port and refilled their glasses. Grundy lit another cigar.

'Would you say there was a relationship between native aggression and progress on the line, sir?' Maclean asked the major.

Webb exchanged glances with Grundy. This time it was Grundy who answered for the major.

'If you take the railway line as a single entity then I'm sure we would agree; the tribes are as alive to commercial enterprise as any market man anywhere. The line brings goods, essentials and the like. They trade with us and, more or less, they leave us alone. So, more trade, more harmony and less aggression.

'From here all the way back to Mombasa,' Webb added for clarity. 'But beyond that we are still pushing into virtually uncharted territory. We also have the settlers to consider. Most of them have land concessions well away from the line. We have to protect them as well.'

'You have farmers in the Rift Valley, don't you?' Maclean asked Major Webb.

'Several,' Webb replied.

'Independent sort of bunch,' Grundy said.

Lieutenant Maclean raised his eyebrows. To a man of his station and upbringing, coupled with a paucity of experience in Africa, he couldn't understand how anybody could actually live so independently in such a hostile land.

Sir Charles nodded. 'But you still have to keep an eye on them.'

Major Webb shrugged. 'An Englishman and his castle still require our protection.'

The conversation went many ways after that and only a reminder of the time from one of them brought the evening to a close. The port decanter and two wine bottles stood empty, and half a dozen cigar butts lay crushed in the ashtrays. They were happy men as they walked out into the night air. It was a starry night. No rain. They were happy and content. And perhaps a little drunk.

Piet Snyder listened carefully, watching the black man's lips move with bewildering speed, picking out the words and turning them into a jumble of Dutch patois. He made sense of them and spoke to the man, articulating slowly, promising the prize that Mwanga valued above all else, above even that of a kingdom.

'Kabarega must be made to understand that this will be difficult, but it will be done. You must explain this to him,' Snyder insisted. 'And tell him his brother will be pleased.'

'My master will be at the gathering in ten days,' the black man replied. 'You will be ready?'

Snyder's mouth opened beneath the black beard. His teeth were yellow. He knew the black man's word was Kabarega's own. 'It is as certain as Mwanga being crowned king again.' He said it with apparent confidence, not trusting himself to admit that ten days was not enough time.

The black man smiled. He liked the sound of that word: king. It meant power. 'My master will understand the difficulties. There are always many soldiers.'

Snyder nodded and brushed his hand over his face. The flies moved away and buzzed briefly round his head before darting back into his beard again. 'The soldiers are not the problem.' He brushed at the flies again. 'It is the journey back. If the British patrols see us, they will act swiftly.'

20

'But not as swiftly as the Masai warriors.' The black man grinned again. Snyder thought he looked a slimy bastard, but he himself probably gave the same impression.

'Ten days is not much,' Snyder told him with a shake of his head. He held out his hand. 'Do you have a list of the demands?' The word was not right, but it was all part of the barter, the trade, and it amounted to the same thing.

The black man was carrying a bag of goatskin over his shoulder. He took a sheet of paper from it and handed it to Snyder. Snyder took the paper and spread it open on his knee. The writing was thin, but legible. It was also in Swahili, the common language of East Africa. It would have been difficult for a man speaking the coastal Swahili to understand the broken patois of the interior, but the written word was easily decipherable.

Snyder read through the document carefully. When he had finished reading it he looked up at the black man. 'I will take this to the imperial governor. He will draw up the formal document for his envoy to bring to Kabarega. In seven days,' he added.

The black man bowed his head and straightened from his squatting position.

'You have a great reputation, Dutchman. You will not let us down.' It sounded more like a command rather than an expression of faith in the Dutchman's ability.

Snyder watched him go. Ten days, he thought again. Not much time. If he moved swiftly he could have the document in the governor's hands and be back in the British Protectorate by dusk. With luck and good fortune on his side he would reach the Rift Valley the following evening. He pushed himself up from the log on which he had been sitting and turned to a tall Masai youth who had been standing patiently a few feet from him.

'I'll be on the Mau Escarpment two days from now. Wait for me there.'

The tall youth nodded and left. He ran with the unaffected ease in the characteristic stride so common to these fine young warriors. Snyder pulled himself up on to his horse, thankful that he had no need to run everywhere, and headed south, towards the next rendezvous, and to the next step in the expansionist plans of the German Empire.

*

As Major Webb and Lieutenant Maclean reached the platform, they could see Sir Charles Ruskin and Joseph Grundy already standing beside the waiting train. Smoke drifted up from the stack on top of the boiler. Steam whiskered its way from beneath the wheels. The line of carriages behind the tender was almost empty. Webb knew there would be some passengers on board, but not many. The army had raised no objection to fare-paying passengers travelling east.

Sir Charles greeted them warmly. 'Thank you for an entertaining evening, Major,' he said. 'And remember, it was three against one.'

Webb laughed. 'I'll sack my adjutant.'

Sir Charles and Grundy stepped up into an empty carriage.

'I'll pass your greetings on to the Reverend Bowers and his lovely daughter, Major. What do you say?'

'Thank you, Sir Charles, I would appreciate that. And could you make sure they return as soon as possible?'

'Of course my dear boy,' Ruskin promised. 'Have them back with you in a week's time.' He leaned out of the carriage window. 'If you have the damn trains running by then.'

Major Webb stood back, still smiling. There was a shout from the guard and a piercing blast from the train's whistle. A fierce jet of steam bellowed across the ground and the tiny engine strained as the carriages clanked on their couplings. Then, with a mighty chug and a slipping of the drive wheels, they were moving.

Webb saluted as the train pulled away. Then, suddenly, he felt a strange foreboding in his heart that stayed there until the train disappeared from view.

Mirambo shouldered the dead gazelle with considerable ease and sauntered towards his own small home where he lived about fifty yards from the main farmhouse, in what Reuben often referred to as 'that independent Kikuyu kingdom that had better not get any bigger'. It was a condition that Reuben made when Mirambo moved on to the plateau that his children would have to go once they had achieved their own independence. The last thing he wanted was a spawning Kikuyu nation on his doorstep.

Mirambo first met Reuben when he worked as a porter for him

during Reuben's trek from Mombasa to the Rift Valley. David was only a baby. Although it was unusual for a native to leave the security of his own homeland, unless working as a porter on expeditions into the interior, Mirambo had fallen into the lure of working with the white *'bwanas'*. He soon found the stories were fabrications put about by the *bwanas* themselves in order to disguise the real hardships and deprivations that would have to be endured. Mirambo also learned, to his bitter resentment, of the disease and hunger that were to become his constant companions. Of the burning, trackless deserts and wilderness; the intense cold at night up in the mountainous highlands and the insufferably dark, dank forests that fought you every step of the way. He had seen the ravages of disease brought on by the tsetse fly and debilitating swamp fever. He had known the savage fury of tribal attacks. Lived with it, suffered from it and hated it.

But the one thing Mirambo feared the most, above all else, were the despised slave traders who spread their odour of death and fear across the entire continent. They came from the east, from Arabia, and from the west from a place they called the Americas. They came in large caravans that stretched from one horizon to another in a chain of human indignity, misery and suffering.

Mirambo had seen all this with his own eyes and had experienced the stink of fear restricting the breath in his throat. It was an intolerable sore that ate its way into the heart of Africa, denuding it of its youth, its potential and its lifeblood – men, women and children, even babes in arms. It mattered nought to the slave trader. Nothing mattered to the traders except to sell their human cargo of abject misery into the stinking slave markets of Mombasa and Zanzibar, or cast them into the hold of a funereal ship for them to be damned to hell across some raging sea.

It was against this background of fear and uncertainty that Mirambo unwittingly laid the seeds of his fate, when he agreed to remain in the Rift Valley and work with the white *Bwana* Cole.

CHAPTER THREE

The Reverend Aubrey Bowers pulled a handkerchief from his sleeve and dabbed lightly at his brow. Hannah watched and worried a little about her father's ability to withstand the heat here in Machakos. He had joined his daughter out on the terrace of Sir Charles Ruskin's home, but it was quite clear that he found the temperature just a trifle high. Hannah realized that he was more comfortable back at Nairobi in their villa, built on the high ground to take advantage of the cooling breezes that often swept up the hill in the early afternoon.

'Are you all right, Father?' she asked.

'Yes my dear,' he answered quickly. 'The service this morning, I should think. Don't worry, I'll be fine.'

Bowers had conducted the service that morning at the small Episcopalian church in Machakos. It had been well attended and he had expressed his delight at the growing number of black faces in the congregation. As chaplain to the Railway Company, he tried to visit Machakos as often as he could. After all, it was his church. Something he would always regard as a spiritual monument to the advance of Christianity. He had laid the first brick and toiled hard with willing volunteers to bring the small house of God to the relative splendour it now was. 'You could pass this church through the door of Saint Paul's Cathedral,' he would often say, 'but you could never accuse it of having a small heart.'

They had returned from the service for lunch, after which the reverend had taken a nap. It was now mid-afternoon and they were being entertained by Lady Ruskin while her husband, Sir Charles was expected to arrive later that day.

'I wonder if Charles will be able to help you,' Mary Ruskin asked aloud.

'Well, if Charles cannot, nobody can,' Bowers declared and pushed the handkerchief back up his sleeve. 'I really have to be back in Nairobi by next week. Sunday, in fact.'

'Well, I'm sure something will turn up.'

Bowers laughed. 'You sound like Mister Micawber, Mary.'

'He was an optimist,' Hannah told him. 'It's what you should be.'

He smiled at her. 'I have my faith, my dear. That makes me an eternal optimist.'

They all turned their heads when they heard the sound of footsteps on the boards of the terrace. It was Sir Charles. He removed his hat and deferred to the ladies, then sat in a chair beneath one of the parasols.

'Well, Aubrey, it's bad news I'm afraid,' he said to the reverend. Lady Ruskin poured him a glass of home-made lemonade, which he took gratefully. 'No more trains for at least a fortnight.'

Bowers sagged visibly. 'Oh, but that's ridiculous,' he complained. 'There must be one train at least?'

'Apparently not. It's this damned emergency in Uganda,' Ruskin answered. 'It's putting an appalling strain on our resources. The trains have to wait at Mombasa.'

Bowers shook his head and a deep frown creased his brow. 'Why do they have to keep the trains from running?'

Hannah, who had been watching her father with some amusement, spoke up. 'You know why, Father dear,' she said. 'The trains are needed there to bring the soldiers in when they arrive from India.'

Bowers looked at his daughter as her hand touched lightly on his. He closed his fingers gently round hers and smiled warmly. 'The troops are still a thousand miles away, my dear. All we wish to do is travel under a hundred miles to Nairobi. A train could have us there by evening.' He glanced at Sir Charles. 'And be back in Mombasa by tomorrow.'

'If it didn't break down,' Lady Ruskin added, throwing a mischievous look at her husband. 'But aren't the trains your responsibility, Charles?' she asked.

'Yes, but the army has pulled rank.'

Bowers looked taken aback at this. 'You mean young Major Webb carries government support on this? Even though you are their most senior administrator in the whole of East Africa?'

Hannah's eyes moved quickly at the mention of the Major's name.

Sir Charles explained. 'Whitehall dictates military policy, Aubrey. I am informed, naturally, but only as a matter of protocol. And because Major Webb is the ranking officer in the field, as it were, it is he who implements that policy.'

'But surely Charles,' Lady Ruskin put in, 'military headquarters here in Machakos issued the order?'

'Not in this case,' he replied. 'The order has come from Whitehall.'

'It all sounds rather confusing to me,' she said with a lift of her shoulder. 'So, this is a military decision?'

'Well, yes. Political decisions are not readily admitted, are they? And of course, commercial considerations are not too relevant at the moment. You know,' Sir Charles continued suddenly, 'apart from all the reasons why things should or should not happen, there is rather a fine balance to be maintained. Major Webb is the man in the middle, so to speak, and does have a difficult job to do, which I think he does rather well, in fact. He is highly regarded where it matters.'

Hannah's father glanced at her. His eyes lightened. 'I think my daughter would agree with that, wouldn't you Hannah?' He chuckled and turned away. 'Sometimes I think he must be the only officer at Nairobi.'

Hannah could feel her face warming, as a blush spread to her cheeks. 'Major Webb has an adjutant, Father, you know he has.'

'As a matter of fact, Hannah,' Sir Charles said to her, 'Major Webb was rather keen for you and your father to return to Nairobi as soon as possible. I'm sure, if he could have done, he would have arranged for at least one train to be at your disposal.'

Hannah thanked him. 'It doesn't surprise me that he wouldn't do it,' she added. 'Major Webb would always put his duty first. But I'm sure you know that.'

'I do, my dear.' He patted her hand.

Lady Ruskin placed her hands on her lap in a gesture that signalled the end of one conversation and the beginning of another. She looked across the table at Bowers. 'That means you will be staying here with us, Aubrey, until Charles can arrange something.'

Sir Charles shot her an enquiring glance. He thought he had made his position perfectly clear; organizing trains was not within his area of jurisdiction.

Bowers was shaking his head. 'That is most kind of you, Mary, but I cannot stay any longer. I have decided to leave for Nairobi first thing tomorrow.'

Lady Ruskin was astounded. She sat back in her chair. 'But that's preposterous, Aubrey, you simply cannot—'

'I've made up my mind, Mary,' he interrupted. 'I have already missed one Sunday at Nairobi, and I do not intend missing another.'

Sir Charles looked mortified. 'Surely you don't intend travelling on foot?' His eyebrows were raised in an incongruous gesture. 'Aubrey, the whole idea is absolutely ridiculous.'

Bowers put his hands together in a small, supplicant gesture. 'Heavens above, no, Charles. We'll take horses and porters,' he assured him.

'But you haven't trekked for years,' Ruskin argued. 'And besides, it's damned uncivilized.'

'Charles,' Lady Ruskin protested. 'I do wish you would moderate your language.'

'I'm sorry my dear,' he apologized. 'But so it is: damned uncivilized.'

Lady Ruskin threw her hands up in despair. Hannah smiled to herself.

Bowers tried to reassure his old friend. 'Trekking never stopped me when I first came to Africa,' he told him. 'I know I was a great deal younger then, but I'm not exactly an old man.' Bowers was sixty, but age had never been a concern of his.

Sir Charles wanted to argue further, but guessed there wouldn't be much point. 'Well at least hang on for a day or so, Aubrey,' he urged him, shooting a quick glance at his wife. 'Perhaps I will be able to arrange something after all.'

Bowers thanked him. 'You're a poor liar, Charles, but I do thank you for trying. I cannot wait any longer. I've no wish to be absent from my flock for too long,' he explained.'

Lady Ruskin turned to him. 'Oh Aubrey, you do exasperate me. With the number of Sikhs and Muslims you have at Nairobi, it's a small wonder you have any flock at all.'

Mary Ruskin had often expressed wonder at Bowers' decision to conduct his pastoral duties at the railhead camp when he could have led a far more genteel life, and more fitting in her opinion, at Machakos. As chaplain to the East Africa Railway Company, Bowers had that right, but always argued that the rewards of administering to a community that included over two hundred soldiers, a European contingent and well over two thousand Indian workers was sufficient reason to remain with the railhead camps as they were established along the line. Although he accepted that once the Company moved its headquarters to Nairobi, for that was the intention, he might consider remaining there permanently.

He smiled benevolently at Lady Ruskin. 'I know you don't mean that. God's church welcomes all manner of men and women.'

'That might be so, Aubrey,' she responded. 'But the vast majority of them will not even be aware of your absence.' She reached out and clasped Hannah tightly by the hand. 'At least you will stay here with us, won't you, my dear?'

Hannah replied without hesitation. 'I'm afraid not, Lady Ruskin. While my mother is away in England, my place is with my father. I shall return with him.'

Lady Ruskin threw her hands up in horror and looked to her husband for support. 'Charles, can't you persuade her?'

Charles arched one eyebrow and regarded Hannah with an affected air of a schoolmaster about to administer some sound advice to a pupil. 'I think it would be better if you remained here with us, Hannah. And it would also help if you persuaded this silly fool of a father of yours to do the same.'

Bowers said nothing. He knew his daughter's dislike of shilly-shallying and wavering decisions, as well as her sense of filial duty.

'You have both been very good to us these last few days, Sir Charles,' Hannah told him truthfully. 'And I do realize you have our safety and happiness at heart, but my father has made his decision and I shall return with him.'

'Well, Aubrey,' he said disconsolately to Hannah's father. 'The decision appears to have been made. The least I can do is make every effort to ensure your complete comfort on this mad business. So, how can I be of help?'

Bowers pulled a watch from inside his coat pocket and checked the time. 'Well, could you arrange horses and porters for me? I would like to leave first thing in the morning.'

Sir Charles tried once more to dissuade him. 'Look, Aubrey, surely you can wait just a few days more?'

Bowers shook his head quite firmly. 'No, Charles, I've made up my mind. I want to be back in Nairobi next Sunday. If we leave first thing in the morning, we should be back by Saturday evening. If we delay any longer I doubt that we could cover the hundred miles by then.'

Sir Charles studied his old friend for a while, wondering if it was the thick skin of the holy man that made him so stubborn. He decided it was.

'Let's hope you are right,' Ruskin answered wistfully. Then he straightened and stood up. 'Well, you stubborn old goat, the least I can do is see about gathering this little expedition of yours together.'

'Thank you, Charles,' Bowers said. 'I shall be a lot happier knowing I'm on my way back to Nairobi.'

The sun was well up when Reuben and David led the horses out of the *boma*. The descent to the farm was gradual and usually afforded a pleasant outlook. But now the view was marred by the red, swirling dust. Running through the centre of the farm was a wide, shallow ditch. At its deepest it was about ten feet. During the wet season the ditch would flood to a depth of about three feet. It caused no problems for Reuben. At strategic points along its length, Reuben had constructed small bridges and dug channels to provide irrigation where it was needed.

He sat on his horse, contemplating all the possibilities for a while. David was beside him while Mirambo, who chose to walk rather than ride, stood ahead of them.

'Is the water coming through Hell's Gate?' Reuben asked, still looking down into the valley.

Mirambo rolled his eyes up from beneath his eyelids. 'I did not go there.'

Reuben understood Mirambo's native fear of the legends attached to Hell's Gate, so he did not labour the point. 'How far did you go?'

'Edge of farm.'

Reuben scanned the valley. 'What are the animals doing?' Although they were on cultivated land they were still surrounded by wild, untamed country; any unusual behaviour by the wildlife would indicate something quite out of the ordinary.

'Some still come to seek water,' he shrugged, 'but they are afraid.'

Reuben nodded, satisfied for now. They continued their descent to the bottom of the valley.

The wind became hotter as they got nearer to the farm. The dust thickened and the heat seemed to radiate from the ground in tangible waves. The sweat was now running freely down their bodies. Mirambo's black skin glistened where the red dust had not stuck to his flesh. But for Reuben and David, in their heavy cotton clothes, the dust reached into their deepest crevasses, uncomfortable and cloying. Reuben took a patterned handkerchief from his pocket and tied it round his face to mollify the effects of the dust. David followed his father's example. Mirambo simply put his hand over his mouth.

When they reached the water's edge, Reuben slipped down from the saddle and stepped into the ditch. The stream was flowing rapidly and he could feel it piling up against his legs with some strength. It answered his worse fears. He turned towards the northern end of the valley and gazed upon the scene that had so often filled him with awe.

In the distance the rising bastions of Hell's Gate stood like two giant castle keeps. On either side the land rose sharply to lofty hills that circled the devil's kingdom beyond that native legend spoke of. He knew he would have to go through there. Although he scorned Mirambo's wild stories, he still felt a chill slither down his spine at the prospect of passing between those towering cliffs while Mount Longonot snuffed and roared from its lofty pinnacle beyond.

He pointed along the valley. 'It looks like it's flowing through Hell's Gate.' He paused. 'Mirambo!'

The Kikuyu felt his whole body stiffen at the prospect of going anywhere near the devil's kingdom. The old native superstition stole up on him and squeezed his heart.

'I want you to remain here on the farm with David,' Reuben told him.

Mirambo's body quickly relaxed, but David's stiffened in protest.

'But Dad, I want to go with you.'

'There is a great deal of work to do here, David,' he told him. 'Mirambo will need your help.'

'But mister—' The protest fell from his lips; but it was of little use. Reuben had already turned away. The dismay on David's face was clear to see. His usually bright features had buckled into a surly frown. He knew there was no point in arguing with his father. 'When are you going?' he asked.

'I shall go now.'

'How long will you be?'

Reuben climbed out of the ditch. 'I reckon I'll be back before sunset tomorrow,' he said. 'Until then, you take care of Mirambo.'

The smile on Reuben's face cracked David's dour expression. He grinned at his father, pulled his horse round and waved goodbye. Mirambo smiled more from relief than anything else; he was happy to accompany David back to the farm.

Snyder had ridden hard to reach his vantage point high up on the valley side. Although he incurred little risk when in the German Protectorate, here, well inside the British Protectorate, the risks were great. But so too was the prize.He was concealed from view by a backdrop of wildly rampant thorn bush. He thought about the ten days he had promised the black messenger. Kabarega would not wait. So much depended on his plan, and his promise, succeeding. He had to show Kabarega, and through him, Mwanga, that his promises could be kept. Mwanga was fickle and temperamental, and was likely to throw a tantrum and refuse to cooperate. And without Mwanga, the plan would fail.

He saw Reuben and David come out of the *boma*. He sat up, jamming the telescope to his eye. He followed them carefully as they walked down the slope towards the edge of the farm. The black had joined them. He looked closely at David and asked himself where else in this kingdom of black gems would a man find a jewel so rare? Where would the men with black hearts and black skins find such a prize? They had spoken of the boy with the hair of purest gold and not been believed. Now Snyder would deliver this golden jewel to them and place it in their hands.

'A young, white skin for a kingdom,' he said to himself. 'Soon, Mwanga, he will be yours.'

He stood up and shoved the telescope into his saddle-bag and mounted up. Within minutes he was gone, while below, Reuben and David went about their business with Mirambo. Unobserving, unseeing and unknowing.

Reuben reached Hell's Gate in well under an hour. He had spent some time checking for possible points of diversion, considering how best to do it and how long it might take. The stream had not risen to any great degree which gave him some small comfort. The western depression had proved disappointing. He had ridden over there and found a land bar cutting it off from the water. Digging through it would have proved too much for his meagre resources although he would have attempted it if it had been necessary.

As he approached the narrow entrance to Hell's Gate, he could feel the wind funnelling towards it. The heat coming up from beneath his feet seemed to intensify with the wind. In the mouth of the gorge he could see steam jets hissing from the ground and from large cracks on the lower edges of the cliff faces. The steam was quickly dissipated however by the strong wind piling up in the mouth of the gorge, but beyond that it was swirling so thickly it was like a fog.

The gorge should have been mild and quiescent, like a sleeping giant, a relic from the volcanic past. But the vibrant sounds beneath it filtered upwards and shook the ground in a gentle, shuddering rhythm. Reuben urged his horse forward and they disappeared through a cloud of swirling steam. Beside him the cliff wall rose up until it was lost from sight. Small stones and shards of rock clattered down the gorge to land around him. Where the wind cooled the stream, a water line had formed along the cliff face and condensed droplets of moisture twinkled in the shafts of sunlight that penetrated and blazed against the rock.

Reuben dismounted and picked his way carefully along the wide ledges which were no more than a continuous jumble of rock smoothed by timeless erosion. The gorge shelved quickly into a narrow gully through which the water tumbled. In the cliff walls, huge cracks had appeared. They zigzagged upwards and disappeared into a blur each time Mount Longonot rumbled.

As he worked his way deeper into the chasm, the heat intensified, becoming almost insufferable. The small stones which clattered down beside him were no danger to him but they disturbed the horse which kept shying and trying to pull away from Reuben. Its nostrils flared and its eyes blazed in fear. It pulled, wanting to break free from Reuben's strong hold.

It was inevitable that Reuben would begin to doubt the wisdom of his decision to follow the water course, and it crossed his mind to turn back and ride up over the escarpment to the other side of Hell's Gate. But that would have taken hours and he did not feel inclined to chance that route. It was possible that the water had sprung from a subterranean source inside the gorge. So he pressed on, shoving doubts and indecision to the back of his mind.

The surface changed constantly. From slate grey lava rock it changed to black obsidian; rock that had been subjected to intense heat and forged in the devil's own furnace, rock the colour of midnight that could cut through a man's leg with the ease of the keenest blade. In stark contrast to this jet-black rock, smaller patches of lighter coloured ground gave sanctuary to tiny clusters of pink flowers. And, totally oblivious to conditions inside the gorge, were darting swifts, flashing black and white against the dun-coloured surface, tracing incredible patterns. Below them the water dragged the colour from the soil and turned the colour of blood.

Reuben had no time to stare and wonder at the natural wildlife inside the gorge. The walls seemed to close in and overwhelm him. The booming sounds from Mount Longonot echoed from the satanic land, rolling and twisting into a Hadean symphony, clattering along the gorge to brush against the wind and jar the obsidian rock and granite walls, threatening to wrench them free and send them crashing into the raging waters below.

The steam continued to hiss loudly around him, mushrooming up into damp, vaporous clouds. The horse bucked and pulled, its hoofs lashing out, slipping ominously on the wide ledge. Reuben entreated the animal and clutched tightly at the bridle in an effort to keep the animal's head down. The muscles in his arms tightened and locked against the leather, biting hard as his shirt stretched taut against his arms, while the effort of the fight against the struggling animal brought the veins out like tendrils on his neck.

Reuben began to lose heart as the combined onslaught of the gorge and the animal's fear threatened his progress. But he hung on grimly, fighting them both, his determination to succeed ever pushing back the thoughts of capitulation. As each minute passed, so the struggle waned until, perceptibly, the gorge began to soften and relent. The horse calmed too, sensing the danger was behind them and, together, they were allowed to pass in safety. Mount Longonot still challenged them from its lofty pinnacle, but the gods were being kind now. The sheer walls began to fall away into gentle, sloping hills. The steam cooled and disappeared by the time Reuben reached the northern entrance to Hell's Gate, and the wind lost its strength as the valley opened up before him, beckoning him into the devil kingdom that Mirambo so ingenuously feared.

Craggy peaks, long dormant, rose above a lush valley which gave sustenance to clusters of acacia trees and succulent grass. Green solanum bushes bubbling with an abundance of yellow buck apples contrasted sharply with the tall leonotis plants that stretched their long necks above the grass. At their tops were delicate blooms of red flowers, some bending beneath the weight of tiny, shrikes perched deftly on top. Whistling thorn bushes, capped in a mantle of thatch fashioned by the busy weaver birds abounded everywhere. All around him nature's palette seemed to spring up in amazing splendour above the golden savannah. But the most startling of all was the towering finger of rock that rose majestically out of the valley floor. It stood incongruously on its own against the vegetation. This pinnacle of rock was called 'embarta' by the Masai. It meant 'horse' and stood guardian over the entrance to Hell's Gate.

Reuben had seen this before, but only from the heights of the eastern escarpment which looked down on the northern entrance to Hell's Gate. The view had never failed to impress him and always seemed to reveal some new facet of its wonderful character.

The wind that had funnelled so viciously into the southern entrance to the gate lost much of its force as it spilled out into the open valley. The dust was gone now and Reuben's handkerchief hung limp and forgotten around his neck. He studied the course of the stream, breathing freely. A natural depression, an ancient water course, brought the water down towards Hell's Gate from the far end of the valley in the north. It flowed beneath the western shoulder of Mount Longonot which, to Reuben, meant one thing: it was coming from Lake Naivasha, the highest lake in the entire Rift Valley. His hopes vanished there and then. It looked certain that the volcanic upheavals of the last few days had somehow opened up the ancient water course that had once flowed from Lake Naivasha. And that meant the end of his farm and the years of work and hardship he had put into it, for there was no way he would be able to stem the water flowing from the lake.

He resigned himself to a last, forlorn hope that he was wrong, that the lake was not the source of the stream. He climbed back on to his horse and headed towards the northern end of the valley.

Snyder rode hard, leaving the Mau Escarpment behind and heading for the relative safety of the German Protectorate. He had seen Reuben ride away and David returning to the farmhouse with the black man. He was not aware of the dilemma facing Reuben; that was not his concern. But what did concern him was his own promise to Kabarega, by way of the messenger, that he would deliver the prize in return for Mwanga's co-operation.

Snyder pulled up beside a *kopje* where a small group of Masai warriors, a *ruga-ruga,* was waiting. The young men were dressed for battle, wearing feathers and red clay. One of them stood up as Snyder approached. Snyder dismounted.

'We go now,' he told the young Masai warrior. He pointed south. 'We go to the valley beneath the Mau Escarpment. In the

35

morning, before the sun rises we will attack the farm, take the children and the golden boy.'

The young Masai nodded and called to the others. He motioned them forward with his arm and said something to them which Snyder did not understand. Then he turned to Snyder. 'We will wait for you at the Mau Escarpment.'

Snyder nodded and watched as the *ruga-ruga* moved off, running at a steady trot. Then he allowed himself a smile.

By tomorrow, he thought, the prize will be in my hands.

It was quite early the following morning when Hannah and her father left Machakos. Sir Charles had engaged three porters for the relatively straightforward journey to Nairobi. They were responsible for the baggage mules, which carried the Bowers' luggage and camping equipment. Hannah and her father rode on horses. Aubrey Bowers had no qualms about tackling the journey. He was a man of great faith and was quite looking forward to it. Hannah viewed it speculatively as another fascinating aspect of life in the Dark Continent, but still wished her father had not been so stubborn.

They had nearly a hundred miles before them when they left Machakos and by midday had covered the first ten. There was no reason then why they should not reach journey's end in Nairobi by Saturday night.

Reuben sat on a rocky outcrop chewing a strip of dried meat. The valley spread below him in a panorama of shapes and colours. Behind him Mount Longonot still poured columns of grey ash into the sky. The slim column reached several hundred feet before it was flattened by the high, strong winds to form a strato-cumulus pattern in the blue sky. The dust drifted over the shores of Lake Naivasha, bringing an early dusk to the vast expanse of water.

Reuben had climbed to a clear vantage point to study the possibility of shortening his route, hoping to track the water by sight, but his attention had now been drawn by the incongruous appearance of the Uganda railway line loping its way across the uneven valley floor. The line came over the eastern escarpment by way of the southern shoulder of Mount Longonot. From there it descended into the valley in a long, shallow gradient that seemed to cling precariously to the steep, angular slope until it spilled out on to the valley floor. From there it swept majestically towards the main depression through which the water was flowing. The engineers had constructed a trestle bridge to carry the track over the depression. The bridge was about four hundred yards long and much of it cleared the ground by a few feet. But where the ground fell away sharply, it put the height of the central span at about one hundred feet.

The bridge had been beautifully constructed by a crosshatching of timbers neatly locked between massive piles driven deep into the earth. These formed the main supports for the pillars. The whole structure looked very imposing but at the same time bizarre and incredible in such an alien environment. The track crossed the bridge and continued its snake-like progress around high ground and *kopjes* towards the western escarpment where it was lost to view in the shimmering heat.

For all that Reuben was fascinated by the whole concept, the vision and skills that had gone into the construction of the line, his mind kept coming back to the bridge. It looked monstrous as it straddled the depression. Strong and capable, it was tough enough to withstand anything. The soft lapping of the waters against the lofty pillars held no immediate threat. But if the water became a raging torrent it could undermine the tenacious hold of the deeply driven piles and bring the whole framework crashing down into the river below.

He threw away the strip of biltong and worked his way back down to the water's edge, moving towards its source somewhere on the higher ground. The signs of some unusual upheaval were clear as he moved towards the higher ground. He was moving parallel to the valley sides and the soft, rolling curves began to break up as he worked his way closer to Lake Naivasha. Slabs of rock had thrust up from beneath the earth to expose new, virgin soil. Trees had canted over at crazy angles and others had toppled as though pushed by some giant hand.

He dismounted from his horse and walked slowly, carefully avoiding the holes and small crevasses. He kept to the water course now, and when it disappeared into some cavernous slash in the ground he was still able to hear the sound of the rushing water in its subterranean plunge.

His breathing became more laboured and the strain was telling on his legs as he climbed over the disturbed ground following the uneven course of the water. At times he had to leave his horse tethered so he could negotiate some deep cleft before continuing his climb towards the lake.

The sun touched the horizon briefly before plunging rapidly from sight. Reuben paused and looked round, listening carefully. He was fairly close to his destination, but the enclosing darkness meant he would have to camp for the night. He found a flat pan of land, free of long grass and decided to spend the night there.

As darkness finally cupped its hand over the bush, Reuben sat beside a small fire, drinking tea. The flames danced before him, throwing shadows and keeping out the chill as the vast, empty sky sucked the last vestiges of warmth from the land. He thought about the farm and what might happen if he was unable to defeat the threat of the rising water. If it destroyed everything he had worked for, his future in Africa would be lost. And so would David's.

He sat with his legs drawn close to his body. The sounds of the night began to creep up on him. If the farm failed they might have to return to England, but to what? Reuben had burned his bridges by coming to Africa; there was nothing left for him back home. The death of David's mother had been a terrible loss, but possibly worse was the knowledge that David could not really know the joy of having a mother in his life.

He made up the fire, piling on the wood so that it would not need rekindling, and climbed into his bedroll. Sleep wouldn't come at first and he lay there thinking. He wondered again if, for David's sake, he really should return to England and find a wife. Love would not matter; the important thing would be to find a woman he could live with, take as his wife and, more importantly, one who could learn to love David as if he were her own flesh and blood. The doubts, indecision and thoughts drifted through his mind until at last they faded and he fell asleep.

Major Webb did not keep Sergeant Bill Ord waiting for long. One thing he had learned throughout his army service was the need to have the trust and respect of his men, particularly his senior non-commissioned officers.

Sergeant Ord was waiting outside the major's office when the door opened and Lieutenant Maclean ushered him in. He saluted Major Webb and waited.

'Good morning, Sergeant Ord. Ready to go?'

'Good morning, sir. Yes; the lads are mounted up.'

Maclean nodded his satisfaction and slid a sheet of paper across the desk. 'Just have a look at this, will you? And tell me what you think.'

Bill Ord studied the paper. It was an intelligence report filed by a previous patrol. It was standard practice for each patrol leader to write a report after the patrol had returned; usually nothing more than a diary. In some cases the men leading the patrols were not always equipped to compile a comprehensive report, and the writing and grammar could be very elementary. But the content was what concerned Major Webb, not the style.

Bill Ord put the report back on the major's desk. 'Snyder's about then?' he said, arching his eyebrows. 'I can't see him doing any business here, sir. And we've had no reports of the natives being taken off anyway. But he must be up to no good. He knows we'll pick him up if we find him in our territory.'

'That's what bothers me,' Major Webb admitted. 'He has no business here, so why has he been seen here?'

'All we can do is keep our eyes and ears open, sir.'

'While you're doing that, I want you up north of the Mau Escarpment. Go by the railhead first, track northwest from there. Try to be back here in three days.'

'Yessir!' Bill Ord saluted and left the room.

When the sergeant had gone, Maclean turned to Webb. 'Looks a good man, that one,' he offered. 'What's he like?'

Major Webb said nothing for a while, just simply stared ahead of him. After a short while, he answered the lieutenant.

'I've known Bill Ord since I was a subaltern. My last commanding officer tried to commission him in the field, but Bill wouldn't have it. Said he wasn't cut out for it. Man's a damn fool; he would have made a very good officer.' He looked up at Maclean. 'If you find yourself in a tight corner, you want men like Bill Ord with you.'

Maclean noticed that Webb had referred to the sergeant as

'Bill' and remarked on it.

'Can't help it,' Webb answered. 'I find it difficult enough to address him by his rank when I am obliged to.' He stood up. 'Now, I think it's time I took you round Nairobi and introduced you to its less likeable side.'

Maclean hurried out with the Major and found himself hoping he would never find himself in a tight corner and have to rely on men like Sergeant Bill Ord.

Reuben awoke quickly the following morning as the sun was just beginning to show above the horizon, bringing its span of blue and orange to chase away the night. He set about making the fire again to brew tea and cook some porridge. Then he found a fresh water hole to wash the sleep from his body. He broke camp and was well away as the sun rose above the hills. Climbing in the cool, morning air was invigorating, putting renewed energy into his steps, and within an hour he had reached his objective.

Reuben found he could not easily absorb the sight that lay before him. He stood fascinated and unbelieving, rooted to the spot by a scene of such awesome power and majesty that he felt mortally insignificant. The upheavals in the ground that he had witnessed on his climb to the top of the long slope had culminated in a enormous, open crevasse. The earth had literally been torn open to reveal two opposing faces. The distance between the high point of these two faces was about sixty feet. Sandwiched between the crevasse was a granite wall, sheer and daunting. A massive split ran from the top of the wall down into the yawning chasm. At the bottom, another split slanted away at an angle, coming to within thirty feet of the summit. And from this near vertical gash in the new cliff face, the waters of Lake Naivasha hurtled with mind-shuddering power, into the virgin gorge below.

Reuben stood there witnessing the power of nature over all things. Clouds of spray flew up from the gorge below, born from a cacophonous display of might and energy. The spray ballooned over him and settled into a fine mist, lanced through with all the colours of the rainbow. Water ran from the edges of the gorge in small rivulets, spiralling down the slope to gather in the hollows and depressions, throwing up haloes of colour which arched upwards and curled over as if bowing in deference to the lake itself.

'My God.' He uttered the words almost reverently, as though he feared offending the forces that had carved such a spectacle of frightening omnipotence. It was not difficult to imagine the formidable pressure behind the rock if it weakened and surrendered to that pressure. It was too terrible to contemplate.

He turned his head away, looking down into the valley and far away to his left to where the water was flowing. If the rock gave, nothing would be able to withstand the driving cataract. Everything in its path would be smashed and hurled aside. And the basin in the valley would become just another lake.

It was some time before he was able to grasp fully the devastation caused by what must have been an earthquake. Out here in the wilderness it would probably have gone largely unnoticed. But while it affected nobody, who was there to show concern? Except, perhaps, himself? Standing on that rocky pinnacle looking down at the havoc below, he could see his future was inextricably tied to whatever decision the Railway Company might make. If they found it expedient to dam the water, his farm could still be saved. If, however, they chose to abandon the valley, it would be the end of his farm.

He turned away from the spectacle and made his way down the craggy slope to where he had tethered his horse. It was time to return to the farm. He knew that he could cut his journey by riding over the eastern escarpment. If he rode quickly, he could make the farm by late afternoon. Tomorrow, he decided, he would ride to Nairobi and talk to the Railway Company.

He swung up into the saddle and glanced up at the sky. He offered up a silent prayer that others might intercede and stem the flow. It was all he could do. He tugged at the reins and headed for the escarpment heights, leaving the roar of the falling water behind him.

The buzzard held the warm air beneath its wings and drifted gently on the wind. Curling the tip of one wing it rolled over and soared majestically into a sweeping curve. The wind tugged at its feathers and checked its downward spiral. With delicate skill it floated on the wind until it found another upward drift of warm air, trapping it beneath its wings so that it rose steadily again. The sky above the bird was clear and blue, lending it freedom, allowing it to exhibit all its skills as it moved in graceful symmetry, weaving invisible patterns above the landscape.

Reuben watched the flight of the buzzard with a sense of detachment. He had seen it all before and gave it little thought. He was close to the farm now. The ride over the escarpment had been swift and unhindered, and there had been little to occupy his mind except the rising water. Then something stabbed at his mind and he checked the horse in mid-stride. There were several buzzards, not just one. The horse moved restlessly beneath him as he looked down into the valley. He could make out the farmhouse. It all seemed quiet. No movement. No sign of activity. He nudged the horse forward, a feeling of unease settling in his stomach.

Something was wrong. There was no smoke from the chimney or from Mirambo's own cooking fires. In the warm, still air he should have been able to hear the sound of Mirambo's children playing. But no sound of laughter carried across the valley slope. There was nothing; just an unedifying silence.

He pushed the horse forward into a canter. As he reached the edge of the plateau, he was able to make out a kneeling figure. Beneath it was a shapeless bundle. The kneeling figure was rocking back and forth, head bowed, swaying gently.

It was Mirambo.

Reuben drove his heels into the horse's side and reached the house at a gallop. He flew from the saddle before the horse stopped and ran to where Mirambo was crouched over the sprawling figure of his wife. The poor man had neither the strength nor the will to look up as Reuben dropped to his knees beside him. The woman was dead. Her head almost severed from her body. Her blood had flowed into the dust and dried in a dark, flowering stain.

Reuben took Mirambo firmly by the shoulders, urging him to look up. What was left of his face where the knives had slashed was unrecognizable. A great wound was visible across his chest. Reuben knew he would not live. He released him gently and the poor man prostrated himself across his wife's body.

'Who did this?' he asked softly.

Mirambo's jaw moved but the sound was just a hoarse rattle

in his throat. Reuben leaned closer.

'Mirambo, who did this?' His teeth clenched and he hissed the words at him again. 'For God's sake, who did this?'

The mouth moved again, trembling with great pain. Reuben leaned close so that his ear touched the wetness on Mirambo's lips. The voice was fading, the life drifting from him quickly.

'Please, Mirambo. Please!' Tears had formed in Reuben's eyes and now began to flow on to his cheeks, there to mingle with Mirambo's blood.

Mirambo spoke again, dragging the sound from deep within his injured chest. The word formed into one, explosive cough.

Reuben sank back on to his heels, his face drawn into a mask of horror. He laid Mirambo down, his head shaking in utter disbelief. Mirambo had told him what had happened in an unintelligible babble. But one word had come through. One word that Reuben understood. One word that carried the stink of death.

Snyder!

A hollow feeling spread through Reuben's chest and dived into the pit of his stomach, swirling round until it clawed its way into his bowels. Snyder the Dutchman who had fled from the Boers in the south and, by ingratiating himself with the Masai people, had formed small, wandering bands of warriors known as a *ruga-ruga*. He had led attacks on other tribes, plundered their villages and raped their women. Snyder was a parasite, a growth – a man whose name was synonymous with every appalling crime a man could commit in the wild continent that was Africa.

Reuben scrambled to his feet, concerned now for David. His heart told him he would not find his son, or Mirambo's children. The small, flat plateau of land around him was deserted. He ran towards the farmhouse, calling out as he ran, his eyes searching frantically. Reaching the house he raced up the few steps to the terrace, his boots clubbing the boards, the sound hammering into his brain. He threw open the door. The house was silent, lifeless. It was as though its soul had departed. Despite the warmth outside, there was a chill that sent a shiver racing through his heart. He called out.

'David, where are you?'

If he paused to listen, it was but for a moment. The panic drove him through the house in a blind, rushing torment. Doors were thrown back, cupboards wrenched open, coats tossed aside, curtains torn down. Any place that might conceivably hide a frightened child was torn apart in a manic fury.

He ran from the house, desperate for some sign that would tell him where David might be hiding. He dashed into the *boma*, scattering the frightened horses. He searched frantically through the livery stable, calling constantly in a forlorn hope that David might answer, all the while refusing to believe in his heart what was obvious.

He ran down the slope to the farm, still calling. He cast about, appealing desperately for his son to appear. He searched through the crops and the ditches, running along the borders until his lungs cried out for him to stop. But he couldn't. Reuben could not stop; he had to run and run and search and search until it was physically impossible to run anymore. When he stopped, he sagged to knees in the awful realization that it was hopeless. David was gone; taken by the slave traders.

Reuben went back to the farmhouse, fighting tears of despair. Mirambo lay dead across the prostrate body of his wife. He dropped to his knees and lifted his head, cradling the dead Kikuyu's face in his hands. Mirambo's blood seeped through his fingers.

'Oh, my poor friend. How you must have fought.'

He buried Mirambo and his wife together as the sun dipped towards the distant hills. He dug the grave deep so that neither the jackals nor the hyenas could get to their bodies. He said a Christian prayer over the small patch of ground and committed their souls to the safe-keeping of whichever pagan god their beliefs cherished.

Reuben rode away from the farmhouse the following morning with a Winchester rifle slung across his back. The long barrel of the Gibbs poked its nose through the toe of the bucket holster. He carried a water bottle, some money, a bed roll and a little biltong. He also had his remaining horses with him to leave in a livery stable in Nairobi.

He stopped at the top of the escarpment and looked back. The sky was empty now. The farmhouse was dead. He closed his eyes tightly and squeezed back the tears, turning his horse so he would not have to look again. Then he dug his spurs into the horse's flanks and set off along the road to Nairobi Camp.

CHAPTER FOUR

David awoke to a confusion of sounds and near darkness. He could hear voices. Someone was shouting. There was urgency in many of the voices, but little anger. He sat up, lifting his hands to his eyes and immediately felt the restraining yoke of chains around his small wrists. He clutched at the chain, bewildered, his drawn face puckering into a frown. Then the awful truth of his situation dawned on him and his heart sank. He looked round and could see other children. Like him they were chained and waking from an exhausted sleep. There were many children. David searched for Mirambo's, but it was difficult to pick out their black faces. He remembered the fear when Snyder had arrived with his raiding party at the farm. He recalled the screams of Mirambo's wife and how she had been cut down, and how bravely Mirambo had tried to defend her.

A movement in the shadows caught his attention. A tall figure was moving among the children, urging them to wake, harrying them. His voice was clipped and monosyllabic. '*Angalia! Kijani!*'

The children started to cry and suddenly David felt his own tears gathering at the corners of his eyes. He fought them back, determined not to show weakness. He thought of the previous day again. It had been very brutal. They had been forced to walk until darkness brought them to this place. They had been given no food and only a few sips of water. Now his belly cried out and his tongue felt like a growing serpent.

'*Maji,*' he cried out. '*Lete maji!*'

He heard the big man's voice, the white man. 'Who cries for water?' Snyder walked over to David and knelt over him.

'I want water,' demanded David. 'And I'm hungry.' He looked

45

into Snyder's big face, holding his gaze.

Snyder's lips compressed into a smile so that the pink of his flesh could be seen beneath the full, dark beard. David could smell his rancid breath. He took David's small chin between his fingers so that the skin puckered. 'Still some spirit, eh?' He laughed. The man was unknown to David, but he had heard accents like that at the railway camp. The accent of the Boer. 'Mwanga will like that, my golden one. You will be his favourite.' He let go of David's chin and stood up, calling out to others David could not see.

The children were eventually given some food and water. David recognized one of the young Masai warriors from the attack at the farm. Although his hatred of this young man burned like a fire inside his chest, his anger was set aside when the drinking bowl was offered. David remembered how his father always boiled their drinking water and warned against supping from rivers and streams. David's thirst shut out this warning and he drank greedily until his thirst was quenched. Then the awful, brackish taste prevailed and he cast the bowl aside.

It was not long before Snyder was railing at the Masai to get the children up and moving. Although the children had been given something to eat, it had been very little and the hunger pains still gnawed away.

They moved out and David could soon feel the sun on his back. The wretched line of children trudged on under the watchful eyes of their Masai captors. Snyder rode at the head of the column, seemingly oblivious to them. Then, quite suddenly, he turned and spoke to the Masai. Although he spoke in Swahili, David was able to understand him. Snyder pointed ahead and gestured, telling the Masai guards that he was riding on to the encampment because he wanted to be there when Kabarega arrived. He then spurred his horse and rode off.

David gave it little thought. He had never heard of this man, Kabarega. His thirst returned, but his hunger surged above it. The other children were openly complaining and crying. There were ten in the line. David was the only white boy. He could tell they were moving up on to the Mau Escarpment. The sun was still behind them, which meant they were moving west. David had often studied simple sketches of Africa with his father as he had tried to grasp the sheer enormity of the Dark Continent. From that scant knowledge he knew they were heading towards the place often referred to as the 'interior'. To the place he had heard his father call the 'Jewel of Africa'.

They were heading west, towards Uganda.

Nairobi plain was known by the Masai as *Nakusontelon*. It meant 'the beginning of all beauty'. It was bisected by a small river the Masai called 'sweet water' and it was here, several years earlier, that a survey team from the Royal Engineers declared that it would make an ideal site on which to establish a rail camp.

The railway line entered the plain from the southeast and ran through the area used for engineering sheds, rail workshops and shunting yards. It continued its way through the sprawling, embryonic town of huts and tents, past the army camp on its eastern side and left the plain by way of the northwest. Along the western flank of the plain was a line of hills topped with a flat crown of acacia trees. It was here, in the area affording prime living conditions, that the Company had built brick homes for its senior officials. The hills overlooked the conurbation of life that was an enigma in the fiercely protective tribal kingdoms of Africa. So many different people of so many different creeds and religions whose nationalities and colour were as foreign to them as they were to Africa, fused into an alliance of common purpose; to extend a life-giving arterial line into the very heart of this massive continent.

It was raining when Reuben reached Nairobi. Not hard as was often the case during the rainy season, but a thin, slanting rain. Reuben might have wondered why it was happening. Why it was raining now. But the changes wrought upon him and the country he had learned to love brought about a philosophical response, and he accepted it as such.

It was the middle of the morning. The sun, which had now disappeared, had dried the ground sufficiently to warm the rain hitting the ground, turning the moisture into a fine mist. It hung a few feet above the red earth so that the camp was partly shrouded in a steam bath. Reuben followed the road between the railway line and the river until he came to the station.

Reuben tethered the horses and walked into the warm interior. It smelled of fresh paint and new wood. Hanging from the ceiling a large fan cut silently through the air, moving the warmth about. The European distinction of the place struck him as odd in a land where the contrasts were made by nature itself. He allowed himself a few moments to dwell on the march of progress before finding somebody in authority. It was an Indian clerk.

'I want passage to Mombasa,' Reuben told him.

The request was met with surprise, which quickly turned into a patronizing expression. 'There is no passenger service yet. In two, three weeks maybe.' He held out his hands. 'Sorry.'

'I'll go freight,' Reuben declared. 'I'll pay my way.'

'I cannot do that,' the clerk told him. 'You must get permission from somebody in higher authority.'

Reuben hurried from the station, his mind fixed on David and the need to secure a passage to Mombasa. He had lost his temper with the railway clerk and had kept pleading that he had to find his son, but the clerk remained resolute and stone faced.

'You need permission from a higher authority,' he kept saying.

Reuben swung up into the saddle and rode the short distance to the administrative offices of the East African Railway Company. The man he had been told to ask for was Joseph Grundy, company administrator.

Grundy's office was large without being too grand, but it fitted his status within the hierarchy. Reuben did not equivocate even though he was surprised at being seen so readily. He had expected a much longer wait. After introducing himself he came straight to the point. 'Mister Grundy, I have to get to Mombasa urgently and I am told there is no passenger service. I need your authority to travel freight.'

Grundy looked over the top of his spectacles at Reuben and shook his head. 'It isn't me personally who issues the authority, Cole; it's my office.' He asked Reuben to sit down. 'But I will see if I can at least arrange something for you.' Reuben thanked him and sat down and tried to calm his nerves.

Then Grundy dropped the bombshell: 'But you must understand it won't be for a week or two.'

The colour drained from Reuben's face and he sagged visibly

in the chair. 'I have to go today. I have to get my son back!'

Grundy's hand hovered over the desk. 'I'm afraid that's impossible. There are no trains leaving Nairobi in the foreseeable future. Certainly not for at least a week.'

It was far too long for Reuben. If he had any hope of catching Snyder, he had to reach Mombasa sooner than that.

'I was under the impression that trains ran from here fairly regularly.'

Grundy nodded. 'Well, to a point that would normally be true. But the crisis in Uganda has put its own restrictions upon us. We have already moved several thousand troops up to the railhead. There are more to come but they are in India. Consequently our entire rolling stock has been ordered to Mombasa to await their arrival.'

Reuben knew very little of the 'trouble' in Uganda. He shook his head and frowned. 'I'm afraid I don't involve myself in affairs much beyond' – he made a sweeping gesture with his hand – 'well, beyond my home. And what news I receive from England,' he added.

'So you have nothing here at all?' Reuben asked.

'Nothing apart from sufficient rolling stock to ferry men and equipment up to the railhead.' It was clear to Grundy that Cole was under some strain. 'What is so important that you cannot wait a week or so? Do you really have to get to Mombasa as soon as possible?'

'Absolutely vital.' Reuben did not want to go into details about David with this stranger, but he did repeat that he wanted to get his son back.

'Well, you could try getting to Machakos and seeing what help you get there. They might have something.' He shrugged apologetically. 'Not much help I'm afraid.'

For a while Reuben sat there saying nothing, just staring at the man sitting behind the desk. Nothing could hide his utter disappointment and dismay. Now he was left with no alternative but to do as Grundy had suggested; there was no other way. He had to reach David.

He thanked Grundy and left, making his way from there to the European bazaar. It was a small collection of stores, which provided all manner of goods and services to a ready market.

There was also an Indian bazaar a short distance away providing for the huge Indian contingent in the camp.

He purchased enough provisions for his journey to Machakos and then took his horses to the livery stable. He kept his own horse, selling the others to the stable owner. He neither knew nor cared how much they might cost to buy back. If indeed he would ever want them back. His only thought was for David.

He left immediately. Nairobi held nothing for him now; his business lay further to the east. He had a few hours of daylight left and was determined to put as much distance between himself and Nairobi before darkness fell.

So Reuben continued his journey, but in the opposite direction to that in which Snyder's Masai were taking his son.

Sergeant Bill Ord was thinking about the dubious comforts of his tent back in Nairobi when he saw a lone horseman in the distance. He called his troop to a halt and lifted a small telescope to his eye. The troop corporal, Joe Hillier, came up beside him. Ord kept his eye pressed firmly to the telescope for some time.

'I wonder,' he muttered under his breath. He handed the telescope to the corporal. 'What do you think, Joe?' he asked.

Hillier studied the moving horseman as carefully as he could. The heat shimmer lifting from the ground made it difficult, but not impossible. After a while he lowered the telescope and looked at Ord. 'He's a long way off, sarge, but it looks like Snyder.'

Ord grunted with a mixture of satisfaction and puzzlement. 'Aye, that's what I thought.' He rubbed his chin. 'But what's the beggar doing out here?'

'Shall we go after him?' Hillier asked, snapping the telescope shut.

'No,' Ord replied. 'Major's expecting us back today.' He looked up at the sun. 'Like as not it'll be midday before we get back.' He let his eye settle on the disappearing horseman in the distance. 'Any rate, we'd never catch him.'

He put the telescope back into its leather case. The last thing he wanted was another foray into the bush, and he was quite sure his men didn't want it either. There were better things to do than go chasing lone riders who just happened to look like Snyder. Could be anybody, he told himself. He took up the reins and ordered the troop to move on. They rode on for a little while, each with his own thoughts. Bill Ord was nothing if not a conscientious man, and he hadn't missed the strange look his corporal gave him earlier. It began to trouble him that he might be accused of failing in his duty if he didn't follow up a chance like that. Whether the failure was his own or not, the decision not to go was his alone, not a collective decision by his men. And he knew, deep down, he had made the wrong one. And it didn't help to have an astute corporal like Joe Hillier riding alongside casting knowing glances at you.

He called the troop to a halt again and turned to his corporal. 'OK, Joe, take Taffy with you. Just find out where he is going and report back.'

Hillier smiled. It was a broad, knowing grin that spread right across his face. 'Right, Sarge.' He pulled on the reins and turned his horse round. 'Come on Taffy,' he shouted. 'Let's find out what that Dutch bastard is up to.'

The brightness was beginning to fade after his first full day in the saddle and Reuben was thinking of making camp quite soon. He would have liked to have kept riding, but he knew that was impossible. He needed the safety and comfort of a campfire, and his horse needed resting too. He was riding along the old caravan route. To the north of him lay the railway line; impotent as far as he was concerned. Ten more minutes or so, he reckoned, and he would have to stop and make camp. He kept going, thinking of David.

Soon he could hear voices. He stopped and listened carefully. The air was quite still and the sounds carried easily to his ears. He heard a woman laugh with unmistakable clarity. There was a sibilant quality in the sound. It was a cultured, English sound. He rode on until he saw the flickering light of a camp-fire.

Hannah and her father were talking and laughing. She glanced up quickly when she heard the sound of a horse's footfall. The sight of a lone horseman riding towards them startled her for a moment. She drew her father's attention to Reuben's approach. Bowers looked a little surprised and concerned, but stood up as Reuben rode into the camp. Reuben brought the horse to a halt, touched the rim of his slouch hat and climbed down from the saddle. He introduced himself.

'Good evening. I'm Reuben Cole,' He removed his hat and held it casually at his side. 'Would you mind if I share your fire tonight?'

'But of course not,' Bowers effused. 'Join us by all means Mister Cole. I'm Aubrey Bowers, by the way, and this is my daughter, Hannah.'

Reuben nodded his head at Bowers and then turned towards Hannah. 'Miss Bowers.' He slipped the girth buckle and pulled the saddle from the horse's back.

'You're from Nairobi, sir, aren't you?'

'Yes. I'm chaplain to the East Africa Railway Company,' Bowers explained.

'I've heard of you,' Reuben said over his shoulder, 'but we've never met.' He dropped the saddle to the ground. 'If you'll excuse me, I'll take care of my horse, then I'll join you.'

'Would you care for some tea?' Hannah asked. She stared into his strong, handsome face. Although she had never seen him before, Hannah detected an ease within the man, a confidence that came from someone born with an instinct for independence. Someone who had control over his own destiny. She felt herself warm to him intuitively.

He smiled at her and she smiled back. 'I would love some.' He pulled the Winchester rifle from where it was slung behind his back and grabbed the stock. The rifle was like a toy in his hands. He led the horse away and Hannah watched him go. She watched him for a while, not moving. Eventually her father spoke to her.

'Hannah?' She looked round. 'You were going to make the gentleman some tea.'

'Yes,' she answered briskly. 'Of course.'

Reuben returned and took the tea from Hannah. In the fire-light he could see she was extremely beautiful. The flickering shadows across her face did nothing to hide her beauty. He sat opposite her and lifted his cup in a silent toast.

'Something to eat, Mister Cole?' She asked him.

'Please, don't trouble yourself. And call me Reuben.'

'It's no trouble, Cole,' Bowers answered. 'We'll have one of our porters get you something.'

'In that case, Mr Bowers, thank you.'

52

The food arrived, meagre fare but filling. Reuben was glad he did not have to worry about getting his own food. They talked as he ate.

'How come you are travelling on foot, sir?'

'No trains.' The reply was simply stated, but still had impact.

Reuben suppressed a smile. 'Yes, I heard. They are holding all rolling stock at Mombasa to ferry troops to the railhead. Is your business in Nairobi so urgent that you are obliged to trek all this way with your daughter?'

'I believe there is always some urgency in God's work, Cole. I have to be back at my church by Sunday.'

'It's risky, you know.' He waved his hand. 'Travelling like this.'

'We are our Lord's children,' Bowers replied airily. 'He will protect us.'

'Wish I had your faith, sir. And what about Miss Bowers?' He turned towards Hannah. 'Are you happy with the Lord's protection?'

Hannah wondered if Reuben regarded them both as a little mad. Probably, she decided. 'My father's duty is to his church. To his parish. Mine is to my father. I insisted on returning with him, so faith has little to do with it.'

'But fate has,' Reuben replied.

Hannah looked puzzled. 'Fate?' she asked.

'Or destiny,' Reuben told her. 'I believe our paths are already mapped out for us; our destinies. The trick is to know your destiny so that you can take a measure of control. Make the path easier, so to speak.'

'An interesting thought,' Bowers observed. 'So, what is it that keeps us in Africa? Faith or fate?'

'Well, in your case, sir, I suppose it must be faith,' Reuben conceded. 'But in mine? Destiny.'

'And who shares that destiny?' Hannah asked him. 'Are you out here on your own?'

Bowers shot her a quick glance.

Reuben shook his head. 'No, my son David is with me.' The words tumbled out before he could stop them and he had to force out the next few words. 'He is at home right now.'

'In England?' Hannah asked.

Reuben clutched at the unexpected straw immediately. 'Yes,'

he lied quickly, 'He's with his aunt.'

'And where is his mother?' Hannah asked tentatively.

Reuben breathed a deep sigh. Not because of Hannah's question, but to stop himself thinking too much of David's fate. 'His mother is dead. She died several years ago.'

Hannah and her father both looked appalled. 'Oh my goodness, we are sorry,' Hannah said for both of them.

Reuben held up his hand. 'It was a long time ago,' he offered by way of an explanation.

'And your son, David. Will he be coming back?' Bowers asked.

Reuben's eyes hardened. 'Oh yes, he'll be coming back.'

'What is he like?' Hannah asked.

Reuben put his mug to his lips and drained it. He didn't like the way the conversation was going but he knew he would have to satisfy their curiosity. It was only natural they should ask about himself and David, but he did not want to burden them with the horror of David's kidnap. He decided the only way out was to make his excuses and withdraw as soon as possible. 'He's a fine boy. He loves it out here. He has a passion for horses.' His voice drifted a little, becoming vague. He checked himself. 'Look, I hope you don't mind, but I would like to get some sleep. It has been very nice talking to you both and I do thank you for your hospitality, but I have to make an early start in the morning.' He put his mug down. It was the third cup Hannah had poured for him. She looked disappointed but said nothing. Her father echoed her thoughts for her. Most of them anyway.

'Such a pity,' he said. 'Just as we were getting to know you.'

Reuben smiled. 'Ships that pass in the night, sir? Still, perhaps we'll get a chance to meet in Nairobi one day. The four of us.'

Hannah spoke. 'Would that be destiny or fate, Reuben?'

He looked into her eyes. Behind them, in the light from the fire, he saw something. Was it hope? Or his own imagination? 'Destiny, I hope.'

Hannah lowered her eyes from Reuben's steady gaze. 'That would be nice. We shall look forward to it.' She felt her cheeks redden and was thankful for the firelight.

Reuben got up and shook Mr Bowers by the hand. 'I don't expect to be here when you rise in the morning, so I'll say my goodbyes now. And thank you both for everything.' He looked at Hannah. 'Goodnight, Miss Bowers, I hope we shall meet again.'

When their eyes met, Hannah felt as if she was looking deep into his soul. The sensation beneath her chest was extraordinary and a little confusing. She watched him pick up his saddle and move beyond the fire until his shape was almost lost amongst the dark edges of their camp. She didn't notice her father watching her. Nor the smile gathering on his lips.

'Well, my dear,' he said after a while. 'Perhaps you and I should think about retiring too. Home tomorrow.'

Hannah blinked a few times. 'Yes, Father, of course. Home tomorrow.'

She sounded thoughtful and Bowers thought of Reuben, destiny and ships that pass in the night.

The following morning Reuben steered his horse back on to the old caravan route before any of them were awake. The air was fresh and it was that time of day he enjoyed most when nature was working, bringing the bush back to life again. He rode swiftly, knowing the horse would not suffer in the cool of the early morning. Soon he would have to slow the pace when the heat of the sun dominated everything. But, with luck, he would make Machakos by nightfall the following day.

He had been on the trail less than an hour when he saw runners in the distance. There were six men in a single line, about a mile from him. He stopped the horse and pulled a small telescope from his saddle-bag. He lifted it to his eye and the figures jumped into life before him. Blurred images gradually took shape as he twisted the focusing ring. They were moving at a steady, rhythmic pace and he could see the bright flashes of colour contrasting sharply against the lion's mane headgear each runner was wearing. They were heading west. He lowered the telescope and became very thoughtful, staring obliquely at the running men. 'Masai,' he said to himself grimly. 'But what the hell are they doing this far out?' Masai country was beyond the Rift Valley, well to the west, but Reuben had heard of Masai raiding parties reaching fifty miles or more from the Masai heartland.

He brought the telescope to his eye again, thinking of David. He wondered if this could be the same group that took David and

Mirambo's children. If so, where was Snyder? He wondered if it was possible that they had transferred the children somewhere further to the east. Perhaps Snyder had joined up with other slavers. He lowered the telescope, tapping out a tattoo with his fingertips. Incongruously, this gave Reuben some hope. If it was the same group and he could track them and capture one of the runners, perhaps he could force the man to take him to David. It meant backtracking and going over ground he had already covered. It was a gamble, but he had to try. And he still had time.

He snapped the telescope shut and pushed it back into the saddle-bag. Then he pulled the horse round and turned back the way he had come; back in the direction of the Bowers' camp.

Hannah woke late that morning because she had not slept too well. On retiring to bed she had found she could not get Reuben Cole out of her mind. His effect on her had been quite disturbing under the circumstances, although, when she had allowed her mind to think freely, she had to admit to herself that it had been pleasant. But what troubled Hannah was that her thoughts of a man she barely knew, a complete stranger too, offended her sense of propriety. Her association with Major Webb, a man who had always conducted himself in the most exemplary fashion and of whom she had grown quite fond, had almost reached its inevitable conclusion. Hannah was looking forward to seeing him again, and she knew that feeling would be reciprocated. So why, despite her efforts to think of Major Webb before she slept, could she not get this man, Reuben Cole, out of her mind?

Her father was already up when Hannah appeared from her tent. She kissed him lightly on the cheek and wished him good morning. 'I'm going down to the stream to wash,' she told him.

'Well do be careful, my dear,' he warned her. 'Take a rifle with you.'

She laughed lightly. 'I might manage to shoot myself in the foot with it. Or hit a tree perhaps.' She kissed him again. 'Don't fuss so, papa. I shall be fine.'

He made a tutting sound with his tongue. 'Very well, but try not to be too long.'

Down at the stream, her father's warning was the furthest thing from her mind as she scooped up a handful of water to her face. She was screened from the camp by a thick copse of trees and thorn bush. They cut off all sound from the camp and gave her a feeling of privacy. She had removed her cotton blouse and her reflection shimmered in the water. The morning air brushed lightly against her skin, prickling her arms and shoulders with goose bumps. Her bodice stretched taut across her breasts which she could feel as she stooped forward. She wished she could peel off her long skirt and heavy undergarments, stand naked in the water and let the cool air caress her. She looked longingly at the water and felt an overwhelming compulsion to plunge in and cleanse herself of all the dirt from the bush.

She had a comb in her hair, which she pulled free, and ran her fingers through the auburn tresses, shaking her head with each movement so that her hair tumbled across her shoulders. It flew gently like reeds bending in the wind and she could feel the soft warmth of the early morning sun bathe her face.

She thought of Reuben Cole, the stranger with the straight nose and firm mouth that revealed a set of fine, white teeth when he laughed. His smile was warm and disarming. She closed her eyes and visualized his face: lean and tanned beneath a tangle of dark hair. She recalled its ruggedness, honed by the harsh African climate. A small, tingling sensation lingered on her flesh as she thought of him and his soft, grey eyes. Something behind those eyes cried out and she wanted to cup his rugged face in her hands and feel his flesh against hers.

She placed both hands in her lap and knelt there quietly, thinking of Reuben. Her thoughts flew in wild, uncontained abandon. She was shocked by her own recklessness, but was unable to resist the sensuous temptations of her mind. So much so that she did not hear the soft pad of feet on the hard ground as the young Masai warrior stole up behind her. She sucked in a deep, hard breath as a black hand whipped over her face and clamped her mouth shut. Hannah reached up instinctively and grabbed the savage's wrist. He pulled her back towards him and brought his other hand round with such force that it seemed to crush her breasts. She jerked upwards and groaned in pain. Suddenly she was lifted off her feet and thrown to the ground. The fall jarred her and drove the breath from her body. She screamed and opened her eyes.

The young Masai stood before her like an apparition from hell. His head was covered in an old, lion's mane headdress. He was laughing and his eyes were wild and bright with lust. Another young man stood a few paces from them, encouraging his Masai comrade with an eerie, ululating cry from deep within his throat.

Hannah looked quickly from one to the other, her mouth open in horror. She pushed herself to her feet in a desperate hope that she could run from them, but her attacker threw himself forward and spun her round. He tore wildly at her bodice, ignoring the fierce blows Hannah was aiming at him, until he had ripped the garment away. As Hannah's breasts spilled from the torn garment his eyes widened on seeing the soft, white flesh and deep, brown nipples. He sprang forward to seize her, drawing her in quickly, pressing his body close. Hannah tried to kick him, lunging wildly, but the tight folds of her skirt restricted her movements and she lost her balance. She tried not to fall, but the weight of the Masai was too much and she crashed to the ground, the young savage on top of her. She struck out at him blindly, flailing him about the head and body, screaming at him. But her blows were like those of a child and only seemed to increase his amusement and pleasure. He cackled something towards his friend who laughed and goaded him on. Then Hannah caught the foul smell of his breath and her stomach knotted in revulsion and she vomited. She could smell the stink of the wretched bile as it seeped between their bodies.

The Masai threw his head back in astonishment and looked down at the yellow liquid dribbling from Hannah's lips. She lashed out at him again, fighting fiercely and clawing mercilessly at his black flesh. Her nails sunk into his skin drawing small, red trails of blood. As Hannah fought, she sobbed hysterically. The tears rolled down her cheeks to mingle with the vomit on her face. She kept shaking her head from side to side, screaming and calling for her father, her voice cracking with the spasm of crying that had taken hold of her.

The youth seemed to snap suddenly out of his apparent surprise and he whipped his hand sharply across Hannah's face. The pain lanced through her head and she could taste the blood in her mouth. She screamed in terror as the youth jumped up and stood over her. His penis was disgustingly erect and wet from the lust within him. He reached down and grabbed her hair, pulling her towards him and working her face against the hard flesh. She sobbed pitifully, begging for mercy and pleading that he leave her alone. He shouted something to his companion and made a gesture to him. His warrior brother laughed and lifted the cloth that was bound around his waist and showed his massive penis, grasped in his hand. The young man attacking Hannah threw her head back and tore the remains of her bodice from her. She was now naked from the waist up. He leaned forward and tried to push his penis into Hannah's mouth, then he moved so that his genitals were pressed hard against her lips. His companion was going crazy, dancing round them in some kind of trance-like dance, holding on to himself and brandishing it like a staff, eager to take his turn with Hannah when his evil partner had finished.

Hannah twisted her face this way and that, clamping her mouth shut but sobbing at the same time. She had no strength left to fight the brute and the smell of him was so revolting that she could do little else but retch continuously. Then she felt unseen hands tugging at her skirt and she knew the ultimate, degrading act was about to be committed. The youth lifted his head up and reached down to pull Hannah's skirt above her waist when a shattering explosion took half his face away. His head burst open like a ripe fruit splattering blood and matter all over her. Hannah screamed violently as the dead Masai fell on her. She kicked out savagely, filled with horror and terror, and pushed the pariah from her.

Reuben burst through the bush, dropped the Gibbs to the ground and cocked the Winchester. The other Masai went rigid with fear and turned to run, but instinct told him he would never make it. He reached down to Hannah who was lying on the ground terror stricken, and hoisted her up so that she hung from him like a rag doll.

Reuben called to her. She did not respond so he called again. Although she lifted her head, she seemed to be overcome with mortal fear; she went berserk, struggling wildly and screaming in abject terror.

Reuben shouted at her. 'Hannah, open your legs!'

She did not respond so he shouted again. The Masai was holding her like a shield to protect himself as he edged away from Reuben. Each step took him closer to the protective screen of the thorn bush.

Reuben screamed at Hannah, putting strident urgency into his voice. It cut through to her senses and she could now see who it was pointing a rifle at them. She spread her legs beneath the long skirt. The material stretched taut and Reuben could see the outline of the savage's thigh beneath it. He aimed for the bulging shape and squeezed the trigger.

Hannah felt the impact as the bullet thudded into the fleshy muscle. The youth screamed out in pain and dropped her. Hannah crawled on all fours like a baby, hurrying to get away from him. He made a grab for her but as his fingers closed on the folds of her skirt, Reuben shot him again. He collapsed and Hannah broke down completely, sobbing like a frightened, demented child. Reuben lowered his gun and looked at the forlorn figure of Hannah. She was half sitting, half lying on the ground. Her clothes were in tatters, her hair hung lank and matted round her face. Blood flowed from her mouth to mingle with the remains of the Masai's face. This sordid mess was laced with vomit and lay on her breasts and shoulders, and stained the remains of her clothes. Beside her lay the two bodies of the young men. One of them still had his lion headdress on. The other's had been shot away. The whole scene was like something from an abattoir.

Reuben went to her. She was trying to control her convulsive sobbing. He picked up the tattered bodice and draped it carefully round her shoulders. She looked up, her eyes questioning; bewildered. How had it happened? Why? He knelt beside her and drew her in close, not speaking. The stench of bile stung his nose and he turned his face away. He could feel the tremors running through her body and he knew she was inconsolable. It was some time before Reuben thought about her father. His eyes had been searching continually for signs of the other Masai, wondering if the sound of gunfire would bring them running. Or perhaps they would flee. He couldn't understand why they had attacked the camp. Wanton savagery perhaps? Had Snyder put them up to this, he asked himself? The Masai called themselves the 'children of *Ngai*', the Masai god. But this was devil's work.

He got up and retrieved the Gibbs. He loaded it and swung it over his shoulder. Then he searched the area until he was satisfied the other Masai had fled. Finally, with tentative steps, afraid of what he might find, he made his way to the camp. The three porters were dead; nothing could be done for them. In the middle of a small clearing, sprawled beside the cooking fire, was Hannah's father. Reuben's heart sank and he hurried across to the supine figure. He knelt beside him and noticed immediately the blood on his face. It ran from an ugly swelling in his scalp. Bowers was not dead, but he was unconscious and his breathing was very shallow. Reuben slipped his hand inside the reverend's waistcoat to feel for a heartbeat. It was barely perceptible, but at least it was there. He decided to leave Bowers and get back to Hannah.

Outwardly Hannah was calm when he returned. The torn bodice was in place and water from the river had gone some way to restoring her modesty and rid her of the more pungent reminders of her encounter. Her lips were swollen and there were several light bruises and contusions on her face. Her eyes were red and sunken, like dark cavities against the pallor of her skin. Her blouse lay neatly folded beside the water where she had left it. Reuben picked it up and brought it across to her. He held it out. She took it and laid it round her shoulders, pulling it close to her body. He could see her hand was shaking.

'I don't know how to thank you.' Her voice faltered, threatening to crack up. 'If you had not . . . that savage. . . .' She stumbled on the words, unable to say what was in her mind. She tried but the thought of repeating it, summoning up the vision, just choked the words back. Suddenly her whole body shuddered violently and she covered her face with her hands. 'Oh God, it was horrible.'

Reuben reached forward and she allowed herself to be pulled towards him. He held her close, just offering comfort. Suddenly she pushed herself away.

'My father,' she gasped. 'Why hasn't he come?'

She knew that the sounds of her screams and the gunfire would have brought her father running. She looked beyond Reuben towards the camp, knowing he had just been there. He had come back, alone. The fear grew instantly in her eyes. She knew something had happened.

'No,' she cried. 'Not that.'

'Don't worry,' Reuben reassured her. 'Your father will be fine. I've seen him.'

Hannah pushed herself away from him and scrambled to her feet. 'I must go to him.' She tried to run but her legs caved in beneath her and she stumbled forward. Reuben caught her and lifted her up into his arms.

'I will carry you,' he said.

They were both immediately aware of their closeness. Before, when he had been comforting Hannah, it was the caring of one person for another. Now, in the intimacy of this contact, the warmth from Reuben's body flowed into her and she could feel the hard strength in his arms, firmly locked beneath her. Despite the trauma of the attack, Hannah found a disturbing sensuality in his touch, which was impossible to deny. It frightened her to think there was something lurking beneath the surface. Something atavistic and irrational. In other circumstances she might have welcomed it, but now she had to shut the feeling out.

'Let me walk?' she asked. 'Please?'

Reuben looked steadily into her eyes for a moment. He didn't move or say anything. For a while he too had sensed that subconscious pleasure. Hannah's softness seemed to envelope him so that he was surrounded by it, and there was nothing else around them. It was fleeting and momentary until he let her down gently and they walked together back to the camp. When she saw her father, Hannah cried out and ran to him. When she reached the prostrate clergyman, she almost fell upon him. Reuben found something soft, came up beside Hannah and placed it beneath Bowers' head. He then told her he would fetch some water. Hannah examined her father carefully, her own suffering forgotten. Apart from the nasty wound on his head and graze marks on his face where he had fallen to the ground, she could find nothing else wrong with him. When Reuben returned with the water, she bathed and dressed her father's wounds. He regained consciousness for a short time, looked at her and smiled, then closed his eyes again.

'My father needs a doctor,' Hannah said. 'Thank goodness there is one in Nairobi.' She looked up at Reuben. 'The porters

will have to make up some kind of stretcher. My father is in no
fit state to ride a horse. Would you—?' She stopped when she saw
Reuben shaking his head.

'I'm afraid they're dead, Hannah.'

She turned her head away as though she was unable to decide
what to do or say next. 'We must get him back to Nairobi.' She
could see uncertainty in Reuben's eyes. 'You will help me, won't
you?'

He didn't answer immediately.

'Please?' she begged him.

Reuben knew he had no choice. To leave Hannah alone with
her injured father would be to condemn them. But to help would
be to jeopardize his own quest to save David. He felt his whole
world collapsing around him. Damn you woman, he thought.
Damn you and your father to hell.

'Yes,' he said reluctantly. 'I will help you get to Nairobi.'

CHAPTER FIVE

They saw Nairobi through a curtain of rain. It came down like iron rods, beating the sodden ground and turning it into a quagmire. The glistening railway track was lost from time to time as water poured across it in oily torrents, snaking like a twisting serpent. Thousands of tiny bubbles burst on the surface into little fountains, marching ahead of them like rows of soldiers.

Hannah shivered continually. The hat she normally wore had become useless, so she had discarded it. Now her auburn hair hung in lank, spiralling wisps around her face and clung to her neck and shoulders. The bruising on her cheeks was duller, but still contrasted vividly with the pale colour of her skin. Her clothes were like wet rags, divesting her of any dignity.

Reuben rode behind her. He had constructed a sledge for her father and this was tied to the chaplain's horse so that it canted up at an angle. The strong, side staves were tied to a point on the saddle and were heavily padded so they did not abrade the horse's flanks. The whole thing dragged behind the horse. Bowers had lapsed into a semiconscious condition, waking only occasionally. This troubled Hannah deeply, and she was aware of the need to get him to a doctor as soon as possible. His head lolled from one side to another, jerking with the movement of the sledge across the ground. Hannah had tried to protect her father's head by covering it, but, like her own hat, the cover had become useless and had been thrown away. Although Hannah worried about him constantly, she knew there was nothing they could do now until they reached Nairobi.

From time to time she would look ahead at Reuben. His broad back seemed to be hunched disconsolately. She felt an overwhelming compassion for him and her heart ached each time she recalled what he had told her. No man should be asked to make the choice he had been forced to make, she reminded herself constantly, and she thanked God Reuben had agreed to help her.

They came to the river, greatly swollen now because of the rain, and kept to its western side, following the railway line towards the foothills that flanked the camp boundary. Between the line and the river were orderly rows of tents and wooden huts. Amongst the tents were the remains of cooking fires and empty pots, having long since lost the battle against the teeming rain. The tents were stained at the bottom edges with red mud, adding an irregular patchwork of discordant colour. Inside the tents the occupants absorbed themselves in whatever pursuit they could to while away the hours until the rain stopped and they could resume the day to day routine of their lives.

Reuben followed Hannah alongside the living area, attracting curious glances. There was some life in the deluge: tethered goats bleating weakly against the rain, their stuttering cries unheard against the noise of the downpour. Bedraggled chickens scurried away from the horses' hoofs as the red mud was scooped before them into great, looping arcs. A shrill blast of a train whistle carried clearly across the plain. It was followed by the noise of escaping steam as a train shunted somewhere between the engine sheds. There was a faint but distinctive sound of metal striking metal; the chink, chink of a blacksmith's hammer blows on an anvil. It filtered through the drumming tattoo of the rain on canvas.

The need for a doctor was foremost on Reuben's mind and he called a halt outside the Railway Club. He dismounted and went inside. He stopped in the entrance lobby and the rain dripped from him to form small puddles on the polished floor. A houseboy acknowledged him with a slight bow of the head and disappeared somewhere. Within a few minutes, the club secretary, Harold Whiting, appeared. He glanced disdainfully at Reuben, but his expression changed when Reuben explained what had happened. He spoke only of the attack on Mr Bowers.

'We shall be taking him up to his house,' Reuben told him. 'I would be obliged if you could arrange for a doctor to attend him there as soon as possible.'

Whiting agreed immediately, his eyes darting from Reuben to Hannah who was clearly visible through the high entrance doors. He looked concerned. 'I shall send someone for Doctor Markham,' he promised. 'And I shall have a carriage brought round, have Mr Bowers off that awful thing,' he added as an afterthought.

When it arrived they transferred Hannah's father to the relative comfort of the open carriage. Reuben thanked Whiting for his help. The club secretary expressed his concern and fervent wish that the chaplin would recover. He held an umbrella over Hannah as he spoke, an ineffective gesture in the pouring rain considering Hannah's already sodden condition.

Hannah thanked him and climbed up on to the carriage next to her father. 'And could you have someone pass a message to Major Webb?'

Whiting dipped his head quickly as Reuben looked round at Hannah. 'It shall be done,' he told her. 'Right away.' He then hurried back into the club, not bothering to watch them go.

Reuben picked up the reins of the two horses and tied them to the carriage. He clambered up on to the seat and goaded the horses into an easy pace. Behind him Hannah cradled her father's head in her lap. The horses slithered in the mud, but finally they got the wheels turning and the carriage moved off. Reuben glanced around at the drab, colourless city of tents and shook his head; he had never expected to return to this godforsaken place without his son. He flicked the reins in frustration and guided the horses towards the road that would take them up the hill and to the Bowerses' family home.

Major Webb fingered the report that lay on his desk. He stared at Sergeant Ord who was sitting opposite him, waiting patiently, and leaned back in his chair. It creaked and the noise rose above the sound of the rain drumming on the windows. Although it was daylight outside, an oil lamp burned on Major Webb's desk.

'How long do you expect Corporal Hillier to stay out?'

Bill Ord considered the question for a moment. 'Shouldn't be too long, sir. Like as not he'll be back tonight.'

'He won't go after Snyder?'

Ord shook his head vigorously. 'Told him not to, sir. Having the

Dutchman back here won't tell us what he's up to. Just follow and report back, that's what I said.'

Webb accepted that. He knew Sergeant Ord had a fine grasp of the situation. He could be blunt and laconic, but he wasn't stupid. And he was quite right that nothing would be achieved by capturing Snyder. Not yet. Webb tapped the report again. 'What do you make of this Masai build up?' he asked.

Ord breathed in audibly. His chest swelled. 'Could be just a gathering of the tribes. Bit unusual I must admit.' He looked at the Major and arched his eyebrows. 'Without inside information. . . .' He shrugged and left it at that.

'Could they be planning a campaign?'

'It's possible, sir,' Ord admitted. 'You know the Masai; if they can't fight against other tribes, they'll organize battles against themselves.'

'Is that what you really think, Bill? That they are planning some self indulgent lunacy against themselves?'

Ord shook his head solemnly. 'No, I suppose not. My instincts tell me they are up to no good.'

Major Webb had every reason to trust his sergeant's instincts. They had known each other a good many years. Webb had been a subaltern when he had first met the dour Yorkshireman, and had relied on the man's judgement many times since then. He knew Bill Ord regarded their relationship as something special, but more importantly, they both had the utmost respect for each other.

'So what do you think?' Webb asked him.

Ord pulled a pipe from his pocket and held it up in front of him. Webb nodded. He filled the pipe and lit a taper from the oil lamp, then put the flame to the rosewood bowl. 'I think they are here to stop us.'

The smoke drifted up, spiralling into the light cast by the oil lamp. The rain spattered against the window. For all the world they could have been in England.

'But we are not a threat,' Webb contended levelly.

'Aren't we? It will be their land we're going through. They will see that as a threat.' He jabbed the pipe stem softly towards the Major, making his point.

'It isn't their land, Bill.' Webb was being a little mischievous in suggesting that. 'Not by right, anyway.'

'Masai need no rights. You know that.'

Webb glanced out of the window at the rain. He well understood how the Masai had no regard for boundaries; the earth was
theirs to wander and graze cattle at will. It was their claimed
birthright and one which they had often defended in bloody
combat, vigorously and successfully.

'I have to agree with you, Bill,' he said, turning away from the
window. 'But the railway is running northwest, away from their
land.'

Ord chuckled. 'Show them a compass. It doesn't matter to
them where it points. That's where their land stretches.'

Webb leaned forward. 'So where does Snyder fit in?'

'If he's got anything to do with the build up, then he means us
bloody harm.' He scowled and drew heavily on the pipe.

Webb became thoughtful for a while. He knew more than the
sergeant, but not knowing the finer points did not preclude Bill
Ord from making shrewd guesses.

'They could stop all troop movement into Uganda,' Ord put to
him. 'Wouldn't need to be for too long.'

Webb's eyes focused on him. 'Why?'

'You'd only need a three-month hold up here and those bloody
coolies would up sticks and move back to India.'

Webb had no professional interest in the Indian work gangs
employed by the Railway Company other than his professional
duties as a soldier to protect them. But the assessment of Ord's
had not been far from his own view. If the Indian workers
decamped back to India, the line would probably close down. And
an act of that magnitude would lose them Uganda: no railway, no
expansion. It was as simple as that. He was about to answer
when there was a knock on the door. At his call a young soldier
stepped into the room and came up to attention.

'Major Webb, sir. Message from Mister Whiting at the Railway
Club. Miss Bowers and her father have been attacked and are
being taken up to their home by a farmer. Could you come right
away?'

'What?' Webb exploded from his chair, which toppled and
crashed to the floor. Sergeant Ord sat there stunned. 'What the
blazes were they doing. . . .' He stopped and looked at Sergeant

Ord as if wanting an answer. He then looked back at the soldier. 'What happened?'

'I'm sorry sir, all I know is that a farmer brought them in. They have both been attacked.' He shook his head. 'I don't know any more.'

The muscles in Webb's jaw stood out as he clenched his teeth in an expression of contained anger. 'I'll go up right away. Thank you, Private, you may go.'

'Would you like me to come up there with you, sir?' Ord asked him.

'No thanks, Bill.' He picked up the fallen chair, setting it down carefully. 'You're off duty now. Just find Lieutenant Maclean and inform him of what's happened. Oh, and ask him to read your report.'

He went to the door and pulled it open. 'I'll see you in the morning. First thing.' He went out, closing the door behind him.

Bill Ord sat there in the relative quiet and noticed that, even though it was raining, Major Webb had left his cape behind.

The Bowerses' home was a sprawling bungalow overlooking Nairobi. It nestled in its prime position on the hill among the other homes built for the senior officers of the East Africa Railway Company. Reuben tethered the horses and lifted Hannah's father from the open carriage, carrying him carefully into the house. Hannah found some clean nightwear for her father and between them they managed to strip him off and make him as comfortable as possible.

When Doctor Markham arrived, Hannah took him through to her father. Reuben acknowledged the doctor, but decided to wait outside the house. It had stopped raining now and was pleasantly warm. For a while, Reuben was able to forget about the chaplain and think about Hannah. He marvelled at the way she had risen above her own, very traumatic experience, and coped with her father's needs. It was not difficult to understand why she had chosen to travel back from Machakos with him. She was obviously a devoted daughter.

He thought of David and was immediately stung with a pang of guilt that he had been distracted from his own goal. He felt that his present inactivity was inexcusable, one of indolent neglect and abrogation. For all that he felt this way, he knew nobody would have criticized him, even though it continued to play on his conscience. He promised himself he would leave as soon as he possibly could. Glancing up at the sky he judged there were a few hours of daylight left. He could make ready and leave within the hour. This time, nothing would distract him from his chosen course.

The sound of a rider approaching broke into Reuben's thoughts and he looked towards the sound. It was a soldier, an officer, and from his manner and uniform, Reuben presumed it was Major Webb. The major dismounted hurriedly, throwing the reins over the tethering rail and hurried along the path to where Reuben was standing. He stopped and removed his cork helmet, regarding Reuben curiously.

'Major Webb, I presume?' Reuben asked.

Webb drew himself up to his full height. He was an imposing figure of a man. He was taller than Reuben, good-looking, aristocratic and well refined. Against Reuben's hardness and chiselled features, he looked smooth and svelte. But behind the eyes was the same hardness and single-mindedness that marked Reuben's own character.

'Yes,' he answered. 'And who might you be, sir?'

'Reuben Cole. 'I brought Mr Bowers and his daughter home.'

'Ah, yes. You're the farmer. . . .' His words tailed off and he glanced at the house quickly. 'Is Hannah, I mean, Miss Bowers with her father?'

Reuben nodded. 'Yes. So is the doctor. Shouldn't be too long before he is through.' As Major Webb was about to move towards the house, Reuben put up a restraining hand, although he didn't touch Webb. 'Might be better if we wait until the doctor is finished. Don't you agree?'

Major Webb didn't care much for Reuben's manner; there was a suggestion of familiarity, which he found unsettling. Added to the man's dishevelled appearance it gave the major no taste for the normal courtesies he might be obliged to extend.

'I was informed that Mr Bowers and his daughter were attacked.'

Reuben nodded. 'Yes, Major, that's correct. But I arrived in time to scare them off.'

'Who? And how come you were there?'

'It was a Masai raiding party. I was on the old caravan road. I'd stayed at the Bowers' camp overnight but had left early. I saw the raiding party heading in their direction, so I went back.'

Major Webb stiffened at Reuben's mention of a raiding party. He had heard and witnessed untold horrors of Masai gangs. He suppressed a shudder and straightened his back. 'Most commendable of you. And brave,' he added, somewhat begrudgingly. 'How is Miss Bowers?'

Reuben thought it might be improper to explain exactly what had happened. He knew the details he had seen would have been quite unbearable for the Major, considering it was Hannah they were talking about. 'Oh, Miss Bowers is fine. Upset about her father, naturally.' He said nothing else and leaned up against the wooden balustrade while Major Webb paced up and down, his heels tapping out a slow beat on the wooden boards.

The front door of the house opened and the doctor appeared with Hannah. Webb went to her immediately. He took her hands in his. Reuben could see his expression registering shock as he looked at the bruises on her face.

'Kingsley, it's good of you to come.' Hannah looked pleased to see him.

His eyes moved quickly. 'Hannah, what in God's name were you doing on the old caravan road? You were supposed to stay at Machakos until arrangements could be made.'

'It was papa's decision, Kingsley. He wanted to return.'

His eyes searched her face restlessly. He wanted to ask her how she had suffered the bruising to her face, how she was and all manner of things, but the circumstances demanded that he asked, 'How is your father?'

'He will get well with rest,' Doctor Markham answered for her. 'It was fortunate that it was raining. Kept the insects quiet,' he explained. 'An insect bite wouldn't have done him much good in his condition.' He smiled. 'But he's a tough old goat and will get better with rest.' He looked at Hannah directly. 'As you will too, young lady.' The admonishment was precise as well as gentle, but quite clear; Hannah needed rest to overcome her injuries; mental and physical.

Major Webb looked at her with concern showing on his face. 'Hannah, tell me what happened,' he pleaded.

'It's nothing,' she told him disarmingly. 'Doctor Markham is just fussing.' She laid a hand on the doctor's arm and thanked him warmly. 'I will take your advice too, I promise.'

Doctor Markham placed his hat firmly on his head. 'I will call again tomorrow. Goodbye Hannah.' He nodded to Reuben and the major. 'Gentlemen.'

When the doctor had gone, Reuben took his leave of Hannah. 'I hope your father recovers. Some of that faith he has will help, I'm sure.'

A shadow seemed to pass over Hannah's face when Reuben told her he was leaving. Her eyes saddened and for a brief moment she didn't know what to say. She recovered her poise. 'Could you not possibly stay for some tea?' she asked hopefully. 'I know my father would like to thank you personally for what you did.'

Reuben smiled at her and looked over at Major Webb. 'You are in good hands now,' he said, turning back to her. 'And you know how important my business is to me.' He pushed his slouch hat back on his head. It was still damp from the battering it had taken from the rain. 'I'll come back another day. I promise. With David.'

Hannah felt her heart leap in anguish at the mention of David's name. She felt so desperately sorry and afraid for Reuben and his son. The torment Reuben had gone through, and must be going through even now, seared through her heart like a knife. She knew that to try to delay him further would be cruel and unjust. 'Thank you,' she said. 'For everything. And may God go with you.'

Major Webb seethed quietly at this little exchange. He thought Reuben was being far too personal for one who had only known the Bowerses briefly. And although he was relieved to see the man walking away, there was something he had to do. And as the thought entered his head, he wondered if he wasn't acting out of spite and jealousy. 'One moment, Cole.'

Reuben stopped and turned. Webb stepped down from the veranda and walked over to him.

'These savages that attacked Mr Bowers,' he began. 'You saw

them, naturally?'

Reuben answered guardedly. 'I saw some of them, Major. Why?'

Webb looked directly at him, searching for something Reuben could not fathom. 'If you could tell us exactly what you saw, it might help us to apprehend them.'

Reuben wondered if the man was being deliberately naïve. 'You're wasting your time, Major. This was a Masai *ruga-ruga*, you've more chance of catching dysentery.'

Webb bridled at the remark. 'I will interpret your information, Cole. Just tell me what you saw.'

'I saw nothing of significance, Major.' He looked beyond him to where Hannah was standing. 'Mr Bowers could tell you more. When he has fully recovered,' he added tartly. He touched the brim of his hat. 'Now, good day to you, Major Webb.' He turned to go, but Webb stopped him.

'Mister Cole, I am the Crown authority here in Nairobi. You are legally bound to cooperate with me. I find your remarks frivolous. I could detain you, you know.'

Reuben had no idea why the major was acting so churlishly, but he was smart enough to realize the situation could get out of hand unless he did something about it. Only his own acquiescence would restore the status quo. He could see the man was in no mood to be put off. He knew he had to be careful.

Reuben drew in a deep, slow breath to contain his rising anger. 'I was on my way to Machakos,' he began. 'I had stayed overnight at the Bowers' camp and left early this morning.' He paused. 'I saw the *ruga-ruga* heading in the direction of the camp. I knew Miss Bowers and her father were in no position to defend themselves if the Masai saw them. Probably couldn't rely on their porters.' He shrugged. 'I decided to turn back.'

'You are quite sure it was a Masai *ruga-ruga*' He laid emphasis on the words.

'No doubt about it. They were wearing headdresses and carrying shields and stabbing spears.'

For some reason not clear to Reuben, his words had a far deeper effect on the major than he would have thought possible. Webb became very thoughtful. 'Were they led by anyone?' he asked.

Reuben was curious. 'No, but I wouldn't have expected it. Why do you ask?'

Webb shook his head. 'No reason. What happened when you reached the camp?'

'It was like I said: I scared them off; went in firing the Winchester. My main concern was to protect Miss Bowers and her father.' He was lying deliberately to avoid distressing Hannah.

'Did you kill any of them?'

'Two. But not before they had murdered the porters.'

At this point Major Webb seemed satisfied. He nodded thoughtfully at Reuben. 'I presume you are about to recommence your journey to Machakos?'

Reuben nodded but said nothing of his plans to go on to Mombasa. 'I shall be stopping off at the Railway Club for a change of clothes and a meal,' he explained. 'Should be on my way in an hour or so.'

'Very well, Cole. Thank you for your co-operation.' He managed to make it sound a little trite. 'Come and see me when you return, will you? We may need to talk again.'

Reuben touched his hat. 'Certainly, Major, you can rely on it.' He walked to his horse and within moments was riding furiously towards Nairobi Camp.

Major Webb watched him until he was well out of sight with a growing conviction that he had scored a small, but very empty victory. In his heart he knew he had acted out of jealousy, miffed at Reuben's involvement with Hannah. He was a little embarrassed with himself for acting like a spoiled schoolboy cad. He shoved his feelings of guilt away and went back to the house.

Hannah took his arm and hugged it tightly. He placed his helmet on the hall stand and turned to face her. She looked up at him, her lovely face still pale and bruised. He lowered his lips to hers and kissed her.

When they drew apart, he touched her face lightly with the tips of his fingers. 'Will you tell me about this?' he asked.

She didn't answer him. 'Sit with papa, will you, Kingsley?' she asked. 'I have to bathe.'

Hannah gave him no time to answer. Webb watched her go and then went into the room where her father was sleeping. As he sat beside the chaplain, Major Webb listened to the sounds he could hear Hannah making, picturing each movement. He got up and paced the room softly. Then he picked up a book and flicked through its pages. He put it down. The sound of Bowers' peaceful breathing made him all the more impatient to be with Hannah. He stopped by the open door of the bedroom, looking absently towards the bathroom. He listened, so aware of her presence. It was spellbinding; never before had he been this close to her with nobody else around. Her father was forgotten while he stood there, framed in the open door. Suddenly the door opened and Hannah stepped out. She was drying her hair with a towel. As she stepped the few paces to her bedroom, her dressing gown flew open. Webb's heart almost burst from his chest. He saw her beautifully rounded breasts, tinted a delicate pink from the heat of the bath. Her flat stomach and small waist drew his eyes towards the slender arrowhead of delicate curls, pointing the way to unconscionable oblivion. But more devastating than the sight of Hannah's beautiful body, was the bruising and bright red weals that covered her flesh. Webb was no fool and he had seen evidence before of Masai rape. His heart sank with immeasurable sadness and anger as Hannah innocently revealed the savagery of the attack on her. He wanted to cry out, but he knew he couldn't, and within seconds Hannah was at the door of her room and closing it behind her.

It was some time before he heard Hannah's footsteps approach. She looked a great deal better. A touch of powder to her face had almost concealed the signs of bruising.

'How is he?' Hannah asked as she came into the room.

Webb stood up. 'He's still sleeping. He seems comfortable enough.'

'The doctor gave him laudanum.' She looked at her father tenderly, showing a natural concern. 'I do hope it helps.'

'I'm sure it will, Hannah.' He pulled at his tunic, fussing with it as a distracting preamble, reluctant to leave. 'Time I was away. My adjutant will wonder if I have misplaced my loyalties.'

Hannah walked him to the door. 'Will you be back later this evening?' she asked.

He agreed readily. 'Of course. I want to speak to your father, naturally. Oh, and I'll send some men out to where you were camped. Retrieve your possessions.' He picked up his helmet from the hall table. 'And I really should make an effort to locate the raiding party that attacked you. Cole has given me a small description. Not a lot, but it might help.'

'He's a remarkable man,' she said, just a little wistfully. 'He had such a terrible choice to make.'

They were by the door. 'What do you mean, Hannah?'

'He told me he was searching for his son. This was after he had saved us from those savages. He hadn't mentioned it the night before,' she said, shaking her head. 'But when I asked him to help me get my father back to Nairobi, he got into a terrible state. Such an appalling dilemma. That was when he told me.'

'Told you what?'

'About David, his son.' Hannah wasn't looking at Major Webb now. She was gazing out through the open door. It was as if she could see the events being re-enacted. Somewhere out there in the bush. 'A raiding party attacked his farm while he was away. They killed his servants and took the children. David too.' Webb could see tears welling up in Hannah's eyes. 'He found them gone when he returned to the farm. His manservant told him just before he died in his arms.' She put her hands to her face. 'It must have been so awful for him.'

Webb's face paled. 'Oh my God,' he whispered.

'He believes the man who took his son will take him to the slave markets in Mombasa,' Hannah went on. 'That was where he was going when we met him. So you see, he had to choose between protecting me and papa or going after his son.' She blinked away the tears and looked up at him.

Webb knew now why his small victory had been so hollow. He felt ashamed. 'So he's actually going to Mombasa? Not Machakos?'

'That's right.'

He stepped through the open door. 'You said: "The man who has his son". What did he mean by that?'

'I don't know,' Hannah answered truthfully. She could see something had disturbed him deeply.

'I have to go after him,' he said suddenly. 'I have to stop him.'

'Why?' Hannah asked. 'Don't you think he's done enough? Let him be.'

He shook his head. 'You don't understand, Hannah. Reuben Cole will not find his son in Mombasa.'

Reuben came down the stairs of the Railway Club into the lobby. He was wearing a dry change of clothes, which he had purchased from one of the stores in the bazaar and was feeling much better physically after lathering himself in a hot tub. Now he needed to eat before setting out on his quest again.

He wandered into the dining-room and ordered cold beef with bread and potatoes, some fruit and tea sweetened with honey. The tea was brought to him immediately and Reuben settled himself in a chair to wait for his meal. He had just started browsing through an old copy of the London *Times* when he heard the familiar sound of steel-edged heels on the floor of the lobby. He looked up from his paper as Major Webb asked for him by name. He detected a slight breathlessness in the major's voice which meant he had ridden hard. This worried Reuben because he felt it could only mean trouble. It crossed his mind to climb out through an open window, but before he could act, Major Webb walked into the dining-room.

'Cole!' Webb had his hand raised. Reuben debated whether to make a run for it there and then, but something in Webb's manner made him think again. Despite not wanting to see the man again, Reuben stood up politely, waiting for fate to deal the next hand.

'Good, glad I caught you.' He pulled a chair out and literally fell into it. Reuben sat down again. 'I need to talk to you. You're going after your son, aren't you?' The question was delivered without preamble. Reuben felt the flesh on his face draw tight. There was only one person who could have told Major Webb of his plan, and the only way he would find out why was to hear the major out.

'Yes, I am,' he answered steadily. 'What else have you been told?'

'That you are going to Mombasa. Not Machakos.'

He wondered what had possessed Hannah to say anything. 'Are you going to stop me?' he asked.

'No, but I believe your journey will be wasted.'

Reuben sat forward. 'Why?'

Webb's eyes flickered. 'Because you are counting on one man to do the obvious; the man who has your son.'

Reuben could feel little icicles touching the inside of his skin. 'You know who it is?'

Webb nodded. 'I believe I do. Yes.'

Reuben could see the rationale behind Webb's line. It was falling into place. 'The man you thought might have been leading the *ruga-ruga* that attacked the Bowers' camp?'

Webb's head bobbed again. 'Piet Snyder.'

Reuben was sitting forward, his body tense. He tried to relax and settled back in his chair, but the tension in his body kept his muscles taut. 'You know something that involves my son.' It was a statement.

At this point Webb raised his hands in supplication. 'I can't be sure,' he admitted. 'But what I do know is that you will not find Piet Snyder in Mombasa. At this moment he is heading west.'

Reuben sat up straight again. 'How do you know this?'

'One of my scouting parties saw Snyder this morning. They were returning from a patrol in the bush. The sergeant leading the patrol sent two of his men to track Snyder. They haven't reported back yet.' He paused, giving Reuben a chance to assimilate this information. 'Sergeant Ord reported coming across the remains of a temporary camp. Now, naturally Cole, I cannot say this is definitely connected with the disappearance of your son, but I've a fair idea it will be.'

Reuben's expression clouded considerably. If Webb's information was correct, it could only mean that Snyder was taking David and the other children towards Uganda, or somewhere deep into the interior. Perhaps to meet up with other slave caravans and sell the children there. In which case the chances of finding David would be remote.

'Did your patrol actually see the children with Snyder?'

Webb shook his head. 'No, but the remains of the camp indicated that a large party had stopped. And more pointedly, no signs of luggage or trappings were left behind.'

Reuben was now right on the horns of his own dilemma. How much of this could he rely on? Supposition mixed with a few facts. Was David going west or east? 'How can you convince me that my son is with Snyder when you admit Snyder was on his own? Perhaps he left my son with the Masai to take him east? Perhaps to sell on to another slaver?' He looked disconsolate, his mind in turmoil. Major Webb said nothing. Reuben went on. 'When I saw that raiding party this morning, I assumed that's what they had done. I wanted to catch at least one of them and wring the truth from him. Now I don't know. You tell me, Major, what should I do? Follow my own instincts and head east for Mombasa, or listen to you and search west in the interior?'

For a moment Webb was not able to look directly at Reuben. His eyes fell away and he couldn't find the words he needed to say. Words that Reuben would not want to hear. Suddenly he cleared his mind. What he was about to tell Reuben would not be pleasant, but the man needed to know.

'Have you ever heard of Mwanga?' he asked Reuben.

'Yes,' Reuben answered, wondering where all this was leading and what it might have to do with David. 'But only vaguely. Something to do with the mutiny in Uganda?'

'More or less,' Webb replied. 'When the Sudanese troops mutinied, Mwanga thought he saw a way to substantiate his claims as Kabaka, King of all Uganda. We chased him out of the territory. He fled into the German Protectorate. The Germans captured him and threw him in jail.' He shook his head and his lips drew into a tight grimace. 'So they claimed. However, Mwanga escaped and I have it on good authority that the German governor of the German Protectorate conspired with Mwanga's jailers.'

Reuben glanced at the clock on the dining-room wall. 'What has all this got to do with my son?' he asked testily.

'I'm coming to that. We know Mwanga is back in Uganda and is raising an army of Muslims to fight against us there. The German government want Uganda dearly and it would help their plans immensely if Mwanga were to succeed with his. That is why he was allowed to "escape" from prison.' Webb shuffled forward on his seat. 'Now, if the Germans can aid Mwanga in any way, they will. And because Mwanga's claim to be King over all Muslims is genuine, and there are twenty thousand of them in Uganda, the Germans are willing to pay him anything, any enticement, to throw his lot in with theirs.'

'Why my son?'

This was the moment Webb had been dreading. He took a while to consider his words carefully. 'Mwanga is a truly evil man. When the Arab slavers reach into Africa, they bring with them an obnoxious proclivity for sodomy. Mwanga has learned well. Although he has wives and concubines, he has an insatiable predilection for young boys.' He locked his hands together until his knuckles whitened then unlocked them again. 'Your David would be like a jewel among rough stones.'

The blood drained from Reuben's face. A deep loathing and repugnance filled him, crawling like a serpent into the pit of his belly. His eyes widened, reflecting the horror as the prospect of David's terrible fate bore down on him. 'Oh my God,' he whispered softly. 'Oh my poor David.'

Webb watched him crumble and was no less a man to admit he would not have handled that kind of news any differently. To see someone like Reuben Cole, who had already displayed such courage, to fragment like that, grieved Webb terribly.

'Cole?' He spoke Reuben's name quietly, almost afraid to speak too loudly in case he broke the man completely. 'You could still try to get your son back.'

Reuben lifted his downcast face, a disparaging look in his eyes. 'How, Major? Do I scour the African continent on my own?'

Webb ignored the cynicism. 'You could talk to Sergeant Ord. He might be able to help.'

Reuben doubted that. 'You said he didn't follow Snyder, so how can he be of any help?'

Webb could understand Reuben's doubt. 'Why not try? After all, he left two men to follow Snyder. When they return, we'll have a much better idea of where Snyder might be.'

Naturally, Reuben had never seen Piet Snyder, but was convinced that, given the chance of catching him, he could beat the truth from him. And it was at that moment that he knew he would not be going to Mombasa. 'Where can I find your sergeant?' he asked.

'Well, he could be in his tent.'

'And where might that be?'

Webb stood up. He was feeling a little better now that he was able to do something positive for Reuben. 'I will show you,' he said. 'Come on.'

They rode up to the army camp without speaking, each with his own thoughts. Reuben felt he had handed over his own destiny to Major Webb. He was reluctant to do so, but if it meant rescuing David, he was content to go along with it. Major Webb, however, wrestled with his own thoughts of Hannah. He could understand why she had shown such compassion for Cole, and that in itself could present a risk to their relationship. By helping Cole he was showing compassion too, and that could do him no harm as far as Hannah was concerned. He also believed that the odds were stacked against Reuben Cole finding his son and, indeed, surviving any confrontation with Snyder and his savages.

The main area of the army camp was fenced off to form an administrative compound and parade square. Outside this fenced area were lines of shallow tents. Pitched away from these tented rows was a single line of larger, more grandiose tents.

'That's where the Senior NCOs are, Cole,' Webb told him, pointing towards the separate line. 'Ask for Sergeant Ord in any one of them. If he isn't there, he may be in the sergeants' mess. That's in the compound,' he added. 'I'll leave you to it. If you need me, I'll be in my office.'

Reuben thanked him and turned away towards the tented lines.

Major Webb was still in two minds about Cole. His instincts told him that the farmer was a fine, upstanding man. Honest and brave. But he still held that niggling resentment towards him borne only out of the fact that he had won a great deal of favour in Hannah's eyes. He knew his thoughts were a churlish infringement upon his own self-discipline; the man deserved credit and he deserved help. But all Webb could feel at that moment was that he would be pleased if Reuben Cole was to disappear from his life all together.

He tethered his horse and walked into his office. There was no sign of Lieutenant Maclean. That needled Webb, unnecessarily, he had to admit, but he had wanted to find his adjutant around somewhere so he could get his mind back on to military matters. He threw himself into his chair and began rifling through the papers on his desk. Why am I getting angry? He wondered. Because of that bloody man, Cole. Here was a man who had brought some kind of glory upon himself and was earning maximum sympathy from Hannah. He was jealous. A sore that ate away at his heart because Cole represented a threat to him.

He shut out his personal thoughts and tried to concentrate on his paperwork. An orderly brought a signal in from Machakos.

'Request to lift train embargo denied.' He screwed it up and threw it into the waste paper basket.

'Too bloody late anyway,' he muttered angrily.

There was a knock on the door and Lieutenant Maclean entered. 'Hello, sir. How is Mr Bowers?'

Webb glared at him. 'Fine. Where have you been?'

'I thought I might discuss Sergeant Ord's report with him,' Maclean explained. 'One or two points I wanted clarifying.'

'And?'

Maclean shrugged. 'He wasn't there,' he said dismissively. 'I went to the Mess, and the lines. One of his chums said he would probably be in Abdullah's, wherever that is.'

Webb pulled a face and groaned.

'Problem, sir?'

Webb didn't answer directly. 'Did you see Reuben Cole?' Maclean's face was one of total incomprehension. 'Never mind,' Webb told him, remembering that Lieutenant Maclean had never seen Cole. He stood up and started buttoning his tunic. 'Don't make yourself comfortable.'

'Where are you going?' Maclean asked.

'We,' Webb corrected him, 'are going to Abdullah's. If Mister Cole finds Sergeant Ord in time, our journey will have been unnecessary. Otherwise. . . .' He didn't finish the sentence but left the office with Maclean trailing after him.

'He'll be at Abdullah's, sir,' the soldier told Reuben. 'Always likes to go on a bender after he's been out on patrol.'

Abdullah's was that kind of a place that springs up among any pioneering community, serving the needs of the people and making more money for the entrepreneurs than the pioneers they so 'selflessly' serve. Abdullah's was nothing if it was not colourful. Its bulging store of cloths, hardware, pottery, food-stuffs, herbs and spices livened up the drab streets of shanty huts and canvas tents, even managing to look imposing in its self-acclaimed grandeur among the squalor that was fast becoming Nairobi town.

Reuben steered his horse through the Indian quarter, squeezing between the narrow lanes of the bazaar until he reached the bold, emblazoned sign that declared he was outside Abdullah's

Emporium. Either through luck or shrewd judgement, Abdullah had built a drinking 'palace' adjacent to the European quarter. Still attached to the emporium, it crossed that invisible line between the two cultures and, while not embarrassing those of the Muslim faith, managed to quench the thirst of the most needy.

Reuben tied his horse to the hitching rail and glanced up at the remains of the day, wondering what made men drink at such an hour. He took the two steps up on to the flat boardwalk in one stride and pushed open the door.

The noise level barely wavered, neither rising nor falling when Reuben entered. He stood there for a moment, legs astride, hands on hips, looking around the packed room. It was an overtly – but unconsciously – aggressive stance, and caught the eye of one or two of the drinkers inside. Plain chairs and tables lent nothing to the dull interior. It was all very functional. Men filled the seats, intent on their chatter, laughing at jokes or complaining when a poor hand of cards was dealt to them. Some dark maidens languished among the men, draping themselves in the most provocative fashion, and smiling, their white teeth and pink lips flashing brilliantly against their dusky skins.

Reuben could see several soldiers occupying tables close to the bar. Their jackets had been thrown casually over the backs of their chairs. Others leaned against the bar, torsos propped up on elbows. The air was charged with the atmosphere unique to low-class drinking dens. The smell of beer and tobacco smoke was potent, and the noise of several conversations bubbled and burst into raucous laughter. The stink of sweat was pervasive in the powerful heat and mingled with the smoke, which hung in motionless palls above the unseeing heads of the drinkers. The whole tableau would have normally made Reuben turn and walk out. Instead he pushed himself through the narrow spaces until he stood behind the soldiers drinking at the bar.

'I'm looking for Sergeant Ord.'

No one responded.

'Any of you know Sergeant Bill Ord?' Reuben demanded.

Again nobody answered him.

'Are you all deaf?' he cried in exasperation.

Somebody turned his head and looked at him. Others followed. Reuben asked them again if Sergeant Ord was there.

'Who wants to know?'

The soldier was a little smaller than Reuben and quite stocky. His skin was the colour of tanned leather, which suggested much time spent out in the tropics. He sported a large moustache that had been waxed very carefully and rolled into fine points.

'Are you Sergeant Ord?' Reuben asked him.

'I asked who wanted to know.'

Reuben could feel several gazes burning into his back. The noise level in the bar began to subside and Reuben sensed a confrontation brewing. 'My name is Reuben Cole,' he answered levelly. 'Now, are you the man I'm looking for?'

The soldier shook his head quickly. 'No.' He looked at his comrades and burst out laughing, then turned his back on Reuben. His friends were all laughing at the little game and turned their backs too.

Reuben reached out for the soldier and spun him round. He was now at the end of his tether. Foremost in his mind was David and he didn't intend to let some little creep of a soldier have a joke at David's expense. Unfortunately for the soldier, he didn't know of the trauma Reuben was going through. A fist crashed into his moustache and sent him crashing against the bar and on to the beer-stained floor. Reuben stood over him.

'I asked a simple question.' The rage on his face was clear for everyone to see. 'All I want is a straightforward answer. Where is Sergeant Ord?'

The soldier had his hand to his face, which was beginning to swell. He looked up at Reuben. 'Bollocks,' was all he said.

As Reuben reached down to lift him to his feet, someone threw a punch at him. He saw it coming and ducked so that the punch flew harmlessly over his head. He straightened up, a snarl gathering on his face like a dangerous animal. The tension of the last few days was beginning to boil over and Reuben was not going to let anybody get the better of him. Wherever Sergeant Ord was, he had to find him, and these bastards were not going to stop him. He drove his fist solidly into the jaw of the man who threw the punch and sent him sprawling into a melee of arms and legs and crashing furniture.

The bloodied wax moustache surfaced and threw himself at Reuben. The cry uttering from his throat soared above the noise as he drove his fist towards Reuben's head. Reuben ducked and caught a staggering blow that had been aimed at his jaw from someone else. He felt the pain immediately but ignored it, and started swinging wildly at anybody who was within reach. His temper had broken in a wave of uncontrollable violence. He felt one fist connect with something hard and someone went down cursing. Then something soft followed by an explosive sound of escaping breath.

Two men jumped on Reuben's back, but he roared and straightened, throwing them off with considerable ease, and kept up the blows, thrashing whoever got in his way. Suddenly someone hooked his feet from beneath him and Reuben fell to the ground. Before he could move the soldiers piled in, leaping on to his sprawling figure. Reuben rolled over and arched his back, and with a superhuman effort pushed himself upright.

As someone was about to aim a kick at Reuben's head, a commanding voice curled itself around the sounds of the kicks and thuds and clattering furniture.

'What the bloody hell is going on?'

The soldiers, almost to a man, stopped instantly and sorted themselves out into some kind of shambling order. They all looked suddenly rather vulnerable and sheepish, nothing like the fighting men they had been a few seconds before.

Reuben straightened, his arms hanging by his side, hands still balled into granite-hard fists. He saw a man standing in front of a partially open door. He was wearing trousers and nothing else. Through the half open door it was just possible to see an unmade bed and locks of black hair adorning the pillow.

'I asked what's going on?' he bellowed again.

One of the soldiers pointed at Reuben. 'He started it.'

'And who are you, sir?' the man asked, not lowering his voice.

Reuben stood erect, defiant, his hands still clenched aggressively. 'My name is Reuben Cole,' he said. 'Are you Sergeant Ord?'

He took a moment to answer. 'What business is it of yours if I am?'

'If you are, then it's my business,' Reuben answered. 'Because you're the man I've come to see.'

Bill Ord closed the door behind him and took a step forward. He seemed oblivious to the fact that he was wearing only his trousers. 'State your business, Cole, although I've a mind to ignore you for disturbing me.' He looked beyond Reuben to the soldiers. 'The lads won't ignore you though.'

Reuben unclenched his fists and moved closer to the sergeant. 'I'm looking for my son. He was kidnapped four days ago.'

Ord shook his head. 'Nowt to do wi' me.'

Reuben moved closer still. He could see Ord tense. 'Snyder,' he said, expelling the word like rotten fruit from his mouth. 'He was the one who took my son.'

Ord's expression changed slightly. 'Well, why have you come to see me?' There was an equivocal tone to his question.

'Because you saw the Dutchman. You and your patrol.'

Ord stiffened immediately and his expression darkened. Reuben heard movement behind him. 'Who the bloody hell told you that?' Ord asked.

'I did!'

They all turned at the sound of this new voice from the front door of the emporium. Major Webb stood there with Lieutenant Maclean. Those soldiers who were still seated scrambled to their feet as Major Webb came into the room. He glanced disdainfully at the toppled furniture and negotiated his way past until he was standing beside Reuben. 'I suggested Mister Cole spoke to you, Sergeant.'

Ord acknowledged Major Webb's information with a slight nod of his head. He then spoke to Reuben. 'I only saw someone who looked like Snyder. Until Corporal Hillier comes back, we won't know who it was.' He was very non-committal. 'But I can tell you this; he had no boy wi' him.'

'But you found a camp, and from what Major Webb has told me, the right signs were there.' Reuben had to fight to keep his voice under control.

'What signs?' Ord asked.

'People. Children. All travelling light.' He could feel exasperation creeping into his voice at what he considered to be intransigence on Ord's part. He waited a moment. 'My son was kidnapped with three other children. Kikuyus. Their parents were butchered.' He clenched his teeth. 'Look! I have a choice; I can head for the slave markets in Mombasa and Zanzibar, and pray to God that I find my son, or I can go into the interior, the way Snyder was going. If I make the wrong choice, my son will be lost to me for ever.'

Bill Ord was a bachelor. He loved women. He loved soldiering. He had no time for children or family ties. His family was the army and he was his own man. He liked it that way. But he was also a man of sensibility, and in the same way that he knew how the men under his command were feeling, so too could he understand the torment Cole must be going through. But he knew that if Cole went after Snyder on his own, it would end in failure.

'You want me to influence your choice. Is that it?' Ord asked. 'And what if I'm wrong and the man we saw is not the Dutchman?'

'I will have to take that chance,' Reuben told him. He was thinking of Major Webb's revelation about Mwanga and young boys, and the longer it stayed in his mind, the more he believed the major was right. He had to go after Snyder. The sooner the better. 'Just tell me where I can pick up Snyder's trail. That's all I ask.'

Bill Ord weighed up the chances of Reuben finding his son against his own inertia. After spending time out in the bush, he was reluctant to leave the dubious pleasures Nairobi had to offer. To take Reuben to where they had seen Snyder would mean at least a whole day away from those pleasures. But if he did agree to take Reuben, he could leave him there, his duty done and his conscience clear. Then he thought of Corporal Hillier and Taffy. They had not balked at the idea of spending more time out there. No comfortable respite for them yet. The pros and cons of the argument whistled through his mind and brought him to the inevitable conclusion. He spoke to Major Webb. 'Do I have your permission to remount the patrol, sir?'

Webb allowed himself a smile. 'Permission granted, Sergeant Ord.'

Reuben felt his legs weaken, the relief was so overwhelming. He wanted to shake the man's hand and tell him how deeply grateful and indebted he was to him. But he knew, instinctively, that it would be the wrong thing to do. So he just thanked him. Later, he might be able to tell him just how thankful he was.

'It'll take time to provision up,' he told Reuben. 'And we'll not leave until morning. Lads'll not be happy till then.'

'They won't mind?'

Bill Ord stared at him, his eyes like hard stones. 'Oh, they'll mind. But they are my lads and they'll come.' He looked over Reuben's shoulder. 'Won't you lads?'

Reuben turned, following the direction of Ord's look. The wax moustache still had blood dribbling from it. A bruise on its owner's forehead was deepening in colour. Someone was nursing a bloody knuckle, which focused Reuben's mind on his own pain. Others stood with clothing torn, blood seeping into little florets on their heavy, cotton shirts. They stood dishevelled but, incongruously, menacing and under control. Reuben realized then, with a great deal of satisfaction, that if he wanted anybody on his side when he needed them, it would be this lot. He didn't have to say anything to them. No apologies for tearing into them. No contrite words. It was unnecessary. He smiled thinly and nodded his head. Bill Ord's men looked on indifferently.

'We'll mount patrol first light in the morning, Cole,' Ord told him. 'Be at camp gates. Now sir,' he said to the major. 'If you'll excuse me?'

Major Webb arched his eyebrows knowingly and dipped his head. Bill Ord dismissed himself, retiring the few short feet to the bedroom behind him.

'He's a first class soldier, Cole,' Webb said softly. 'But he has known failure like all of us.'

Reuben stared at him. 'I understand that. I'm no stranger to failure either.'

'I don't want you to build your hopes up too highly, that's all,' Webb warned him. 'If Sergeant Ord can be of help, he will. He'll do everything in his power, believe me.' His voice changed then, it became hard and demonstrative. 'But remember this, Cole; you are under his orders. If you do anything that jeopardizes or harms him or any of his men, I will regard it very seriously indeed. And your punishment will not be recorded on any army document. Do I make myself clear?'

'Eminently, Major.' In the circumstances Reuben knew he little choice but to agree. But he promised himself that nothing would prevent him finding David.

Nothing.

CHAPTER SIX

There were seven of them in the scouting party, including Reuben.There was a special bond between these men, Reuben found. It was something that came from spending months in the bush, living as friends and brothers, comrades in arms. Each acknowledged the other as his peer and equal. Reuben learned their names too. Wax moustache was Whitey. A satirical euphemism because he was almost as black as the natives. He had white hair, but very little of it. He was carrying the results of the evening fracas with Reuben. Albert had a sore head from too much drink and very little sleep. Jim was bruised, battered and the joker in the pack. Danny was the one, Reuben discovered, who he had thrown from his back; Edward, the one who had felled Reuben with a neat trip. He was cheerful and spoke endlessly about the black Amazon he had slept with. And finally, Billy, who had not joined the fight but remained glued to a hand of cards, and for most of the night judging from the way he looked.

They could all have been referred to as a motley bunch, just an assortment of odd characters. But within a short time, Reuben came to realize that a description such as that would have been wide of the mark.

They reached the Rift Valley before the sun went down, and they followed the railway line. Reuben looked north as they crossed the bridge. Mount Longonot was quiet. Beyond it was Lake Naivasha, unseen behind clouds. The river flowed one hundred feet beneath them in a benign, almost soporific manner. Reuben wondered what would happen if the rock holding the waters of Lake Naivasha gave way. He closed his mind to it and looked ahead to the west.

They camped for the night on the far side of the valley. Bill Ord told Reuben they had found what they believed to be the slavers' camp barely half a mile from them. It gave Reuben a feeling of closeness to David, just knowing he might have slept there a few nights before.

They broke camp the following morning and climbed up on to the Mau Escarpment, leaving the railway line behind. From there they crossed into the Kiambogo Hills to the place where Sergeant Ord had left Corporal Hillier and Taffy to track the man they believed might be Snyder. Ord's earlier plan had been to leave Reuben there, but the knowledge that two of his men were still out there brought about a change of heart.

'This is where we spotted Snyder,' he told Reuben. 'Where I sent my two men to track him.'

Reuben remembered Ord's promise to bring him this far. 'Will you be going back now?' he asked.

Ord shook his head. 'Not while Joe and Taffy are still out there.'

'How long will they stay out?'

Ord looked at him. 'For as long as they think necessary. But not for ever,' he added.

They picked up the trail blazed by the two men and their progress was reasonably swift, slowed only by the need to follow the axe marks hewn into the trunks of the trees. The patrol worked deeper and deeper into the forest until they came across the two men. They were sitting in a small clearing, smoking pipes beside a blazing fire. Their rifles were close to hand. As soon as they heard the sound of the patrol, they picked up their rifles and moved away from the fire into the cover of the trees. The look on their faces when their troop sergeant rode into the clearing with the others was a mixture of relief, surprise and bewilderment.

'What the bloody hell are you lot doing here?'

Sergeant Ord said hello to Joe Hillier. 'Surprised, Joe?'

'Yeah, but why?'

'Change of plan,' Ord remarked laconically. 'Got a brew on? We could all do with one.'

'Taff'll brew,' he said, pointing with the stem of his pipe. The

Welshman grinned and poured water from a water bag into his billy-can.

The patrol dismounted, tossing a few ribald remarks at their comrades and set about making themselves comfortable. Ord posted a guard with a promise to bring him a brew as soon as it was done. When things had settled down, he asked Hillier what progress they had made tracking Snyder.

Hillier looked at Reuben and wondered why he was there. 'Well, it was Snyder, as we thought. We tracked him to the Ndorobo Plain as far as the main Masai camp. Wasn't a lot we could do about that, so we decided to head back.'

'You didn't get very far,' Ord observed.

'That's because we saw this line of kids. All shackled and chained together.' He sucked on his pipe and blew out a stream of smoke. 'We followed them back towards the plain. We did think of attacking them. There was only a few Masai with them, but before we could do it they were joined by other Masai from the camp.' He shrugged. 'We should have done it as soon as we saw them,' he admitted apologetically. 'But we had to scout around first, make sure there was no others coming up behind.' He shook his head and was about to say something else but Reuben interrupted.

'Did you see a white boy among them?'

It explained why the patrol had come back with this stranger. He nodded his head slowly. 'Well, difficult to tell really. But there was a boy dressed normal like. I think he must have been a white boy. He had a slouch hat like yours.'

Reuben felt his senses swim and thought he was going to faint with relief. He had made the right decision. There was an agreeable murmur from the others, like a collective sigh, which brought a tingling sensation to Reuben's spine. Even the hardened Sergeant Ord was touched by it and he looked round at his men, smiling.

'Did they go into the camp?' Ord asked.

Hillier nodded.

'What are the chances of getting them out?' Reuben asked hesitantly.

Hillier removed the pipe from his mouth and shook his head. 'None at all, sir. It would take a regiment to free those kids.'

91

*

Piet Snyder pushed aside the bowl of thin, maize porridge and declined the offer of more. He was a big man with an appetite that matched his bulk, but here the relish for food had quickly deserted him. He was sitting inside a large hut, one of many inside a *manyatta*, a Masai village. Each hut in the village was a hastily erected framework of thorn bush covered with dung. It smelled abominably and attracted flies in their thousands. Snyder could barely tolerate the conditions while the Masai seemed totally oblivious to them.

Beside Snyder sat a tall, smartly dressed white man. His clothes marked him out as a European gentleman, in the style of a traveller to Africa. His nose looked eternally pinched from the pungent odour inside the hut. His name was Friedrich Gebauer, and he was the emissary of the German governor of the German Protectorate which bordered the Protectorate of British East Africa.

Apart from the general discomfort Gebauer was feeling, he had no wish to remain there a moment longer than was absolutely necessary. His presence in the British Protectorate was unofficial and unwarranted from the British point of view, and if the British found him there it could prove politically embarrassing both to him and the imperial German government.

Inside the entrance to the hut stood two Masai *elmoran*. These warriors were about eighteen years of age and resplendently dressed in goatskin cloaks. Their hair had been shaped into delicate pigtails, saturated in fat and red ochre. Around their waists were belts of goatskin from which hung huge swords. Their calf muscles were bound with ostrich feathers and they stood erect, their tall, sinewy bodies radiating pure, animal strength.

There were various mats scattered about the floor of the hut. At one end there was a pile of decorated cushions on which sat the elders of the Masai clans. But one man dominated everything. He was sitting upright on a Persian rug. His feet were tucked beneath him and his hands were placed reverently on his lap, palms uppermost. He wore a robe of purest white. On his head was a turban, which was also white. In contrast his skin was as black as night.

His name was Kabarega.

When Kabarega's guests had finished eating, he spoke to Snyder using the Swahili tongue.

'We have talked long and in much detail,' he began. 'Soon I must join my brother, Mwanga, in the north. He understands the draft of your terms as you understand his. Now, the final agreement. You have it with you?'

Snyder translated for Gebauer. When he had finished, the German coughed politely, touching his mouth with the handkerchief he had been clutching for some time, mostly to his nose. He produced a small roll of paper from a leather bag beside him. It was tied with a ribbon. He held it up for Kabarega to see.

'Read it to me,' Kabarega ordered.

Gebauer glanced hesitantly at Snyder who was watching the flies spiralling round the remains of his food. Already his plate was alive with them. He sensed Gebauer's eyes on him and he looked at the emissary. At this point, Gebauer began reading from the document while Snyder translated for the benefit of Kabarega and the assembled elders.

'His Imperial Majesty's German Government endorses the following terms of agreement between the People of Germany and Mwanga, King of all Bugandans. In return for Mwanga's co-operation with His Imperial Majesty's Government, it will assign to him such scheduled territories as are of predominately Muslim faith in Uganda. These territories will be autonomous and subject to Mwanga's religious patronage.

'Mwanga will be exonerated of all alleged crimes, and such records will be deleted. In return for his co-operation with His Imperial Majesty's Government, Mwanga will receive payment in any currency, precious stones or gold. Until Uganda is proclaimed a German Protectorate, he is afforded sanctuary from his enemies in any of His Imperial Majesty's Dominions in Africa.

'To afford the fullest protection to Mwanga's forces, he is to place said forces under the command of His Imperial Majesty's Military Commander in Uganda. To that end his forces are to cease all unofficial skirmishing and insurgent actions forthwith.'

Gebauer looked up. He was sweating quite profusely. 'The rest is just the formal closure to the document.'

Snyder sat back. The translation had been slow because Kabarega had interrupted many times, asking for several points to be clarified. He finally agreed the document was in order.

'Will Kabarega require a translation into his own language?' Gebauer asked the Dutchman. Snyder shook his head.

'The German translation is all he needs. Then nothing is lost from the original text.' He explained briefly to Kabarega what he had told Gebauer. 'Now that you are satisfied, Kabarega,' Snyder went on, 'we can send runners to the clans gathered on the Uasin Gishu plateau. Then our combined forces will number ten thousand. You will be in Uganda in ten days which will be the time to launch our attack on Nairobi. If the British try to reinforce their troops from Uganda, Mwanga's forces will be strong enough to hold them back.' He looked at Gebauer momentarily. 'Herr Gebauer will travel with you to Uganda under your protection. He will represent His Imperial Majesty's Governor and will offer the governor's respects and good wishes to Mwanga. Once Mwanga has signed the agreement, you will assign escorts to Herr Gebauer for his return to the German Protectorate.'

Snyder's autocratic attitude unsettled Gebauer, but not as much as the prospect of the next two or three weeks. Until he was back in the German Protectorate, languishing in the relative comfort of German civility, he would not be a happy man.

Kabarega turned and spoke to a tall, cadaverous Bugandan elder who had been standing behind him. They talked animatedly for some time. When the heated discourse ended, Kabarega turned to Snyder. 'We shall return to Uganda tomorrow.' He stood up. 'Now I would like to see the gift you have for my brother.'

Snyder got up and held his hand out towards the doorway. Kabarega nodded and beckoned his entourage to follow him from the hut.

The Masai camp consisted of a series of enclosures built around the outside of a large, open stockade. The long hut from which they emerged was inside the stockade. There was a fire burning not far from the hut. People were gathered round the flames, moving in unison to a strong, pulsating chant which flowed through their swollen ranks. They chanted to a rhythm which was beaten out by drummers pounding a tattoo on hollow logs. Dancers leapt into the air with incredible agility bringing shouts of approval from the good-humoured crowd. Much of this approval came from the young Masai girls who wore brightly coloured beads tied round their waists, the traditional belt of an unmarried girl.

Kabarega paid scant attention to the dancing and general high spirits in the camp. He followed Snyder and the escorting *elmoran* from the stockade. They walked to a hut which had been erected in a solitary position. This was an *osingiria*, a Masai prison hut. Kabarega's escort spoke to the guards who moved aside.

The smell inside was appalling; an overpowering stench of urine, excrement and animal dung permeated the air with such unbelievable oppression that they were all forced to hold their hands to their faces. Gebauer had no stomach for it and refused to enter the hut.

The only light that penetrated the interior was through a hole in the roof. It let some of the moonlight through. A lighted torch was produced by one of the guards and in the gloom it was possible to see several figures round the walls of the hut. Some were sitting forlornly, squatting on their haunches, resting their chins sadly on their knees. Others lay prone or curled up into the foetal position. In the sadness of their black faces, only the movement of their eyes showed a reaction to the visitors. None of them moved otherwise.

Except one.

He sat erect, his back against the wall and his feet thrust forward. He moved his head off the wall as they came in and brushed his blond hair back with a quick movement of his hand. Kabarega saw the gesture and approached David. He beckoned him to get up. David moved slowly, showing signs of stiffness. Kabarega laid his hands on him, feeling his arms and pinching his flesh. He looked into David's eyes and brushed his fingers gently through his blond hair, murmuring approvingly. He slid his hands over the small body and squeezed the tops of his legs. Then he slipped his hands into David's crotch. David pulled back quickly. Kabarega stood up smiling.

'You truly are a rare jewel,' he said in his own language. 'The white boy with the hair of purest gold. We were told it was so but did not believe it.' He turned to Snyder, switching to Swahili. 'You were right, *rafiki*, the boy is beautiful. Mwanga will be pleased. In fourteen days my brother will celebrate your attack on Nairobi and take the boy to his heart.' He looked at David once more. 'He will serve Mwanga well,' he said, and swept majestically from the hut.

Joseph Grundy pushed his spectacles up on to his forehead and rubbed his tired eyes. He had been battling with figures and statistics all day and was so weary he just wanted to go to bed. He looked up at the time and was disappointed to see there were still two hours left before dinner. Whatever his wife had arranged that evening, he doubted he would do justice to it. Grundy's post as chief administrator to the Railway Company was as much a political post as a career one. The success of the Company would probably be attributed to brilliant engineering skills and sheer determination by the work force. Failure would simply be laid at the feet of men such as he. Grundy was becoming fine-tuned to political opinions in England over the Uganda railway line as much as he was becoming fine-tuned to the military excursions into Uganda and the Sudan. They were all inextricably linked to the construction of the line and seemed about set to destroy each other.

As the build up in Uganda continued, so too did the threat to the line. He had no control over the military aspect of Britain's future in Central Africa, but the construction of the line was the backbone of Britain's expansionist plans, and Grundy was fast losing control over the Company's progress through no fault of his own. And that was a threat to those plans.

When the Railway Company was first formed, it had been known as the British East African Association. Its purpose was to develop British interests beyond Zanzibar and into the African interior. It was endorsed by the foreign office. Within a year it had a subscribed capital of £250,000, a royal charter and the name 'Imperial British East African Association' with its own flag and motto: 'Light and Liberty'. Within seven years the Association had been dissolved with debts totalling almost £200,000. Grundy had been instrumental in persuading the

British government to wipe out that debt in exchange for private assets held by the directors of the Association, which in essence, amounted to little more than the stock and some property in the Sultan of Zanzibar's mainland domain.

After being appointed administrator to the newly formed Railway Company, Grundy had worked tirelessly to show some creditable return for the government's – and private investors' – money. He had begged, borrowed and cajoled his way with each mile of track as it was laid from the port of Kilindi on the east coast to its present point northwest of the Rift Valley. But increasingly the government had usurped the Company's authority (having assumed the role, it must be said, of underwriter), by using the line as troop transport into the interior and placing an embargo on fare-paying passengers as often as it liked.

Slowly and inexorably the Company was driven deeper and deeper into debt. Progress was slowing down and investment by the government was appallingly low. Grundy knew that the German government was investing in their East African development at a rate two thousand times higher than the British. There was also a continuing cry back home in England to stop the line and ban all further expansion in East Africa. This clarion call did not surprise Grundy when he considered the figures that lay before him. This was the cost, not in pounds, shillings and pence, nor in rupees, but in human suffering. The indignity of living and working in such a pioneering environment was a terrible price to pay, even if such pioneering work was voluntary. But the treacherous climate so far that year had put four hundred men into the hospital tents with illnesses ranging from malaria, dysentery and ulcers to pneumonia. There had been many deaths. And for what? A desultory average wage of fifteen rupees each month, about one English pound, for the lowest paid Indian worker.

As the toll of sickness and death affected progress on the line, so too did it affect morale. There were often strikes, refusals to work overtime, absenteeism and drunkenness. The Company was like a monolith being assailed on all sides by a noxious, creeping attack of ill fortune, fate, government interference and war. And sitting astride this afflicted animal was Joseph

Grundy; the man in the highest place with the furthest to fall.

He decided he'd had enough for one day. He removed his glasses and folded them into his waistcoat pocket. After tidying up his desk he lifted a small pile of company mail which had arrived from Machakos two days before, but that he had been too preoccupied to sort through. He was surprised to see a letter addressed to the Reverend Aubrey Bowers. He didn't stop to wonder how the letter had turned up in his office, he just accepted it philosophically and pushed the letter into his jacket pocket. He knew he would be passing the Bowers' villa on his way home, so he decided he would drop it in. He bundled the remainder of the mail into his safe, checked there was nothing confidential left on his desk, and locked up for the night.

When Grundy arrived at the Bowers' home, he wasn't surprised to see Major Webb there. He was sitting out on the front porch with Hannah. He bade them both a very good evening and explained about the letter.

Hannah suggested he take it to her father. 'I'm sure he would love to see you.'

Grundy agreed, but said he wouldn't be more than a minute or two. 'Mary is expecting me for dinner,' he explained unnecessarily.

Hannah showed him through to the bedroom. Her father's eyes lit up when he saw the Company boss. 'Ah, Grundy, how good of you to drop by.' Hannah left them to it and went back out on to the front porch.

Major Webb was standing when Hannah returned. He sat down with her on the bench and took her hand. She smiled at him, then let her gaze fall away.

'Kingsley,' she started. 'What chance do you think Reuben Cole has of getting his son back?'

Webb had already found himself recounting the events of the previous evening. He was somewhat annoyed at her persistent questioning and tried not to show it. In truth he was worried by Hannah's natural concern over Reuben.

'Oh, I think he has a good chance,' he lied. 'Sergeant Ord is a good man.'

'But he doesn't know where his son is,' she pointed out.

He glanced down the valley to Nairobi camp, succumbing

slowly to the fall of darkness. 'No, Hannah, he doesn't know where the boy is, but Sergeant Ord will take him to the place where he last saw Snyder.' He looked back at her, hoping his affected sincerity showed in his eyes. 'I've no doubt Cole will trail him to a slave camp somewhere. Probably buy his son back, I should imagine.'

Hannah thought he was treating the matter far too lightly. 'It's rather a harsh thing to say. You're just trivializing it.'

'No, Hannah. This is a harsh country we live in. Men who choose to make their homes here must come to terms with it.'

'Oh, I think that's ghastly.' She looked cross with him. 'We should stamp out slavery. You cannot have people being obliged to buy their own children back just because it is a harsh country. It should be changed. Men like Snyder should be caught and thrown into prison. You should catch him, Kingsley,' she added pointedly.

He laughed gently and looked at her. 'You shouldn't worry your pretty head about such things, Hannah,' he told her. 'Men like Cole understand.'

'Don't patronize me, Kingsley,' she said angrily. 'I don't like it.'

'I'm sorry, Hannah, I did not mean to sound patronizing,' he reassured her. 'But there are facts of life that escape you when living, well' – he gestured around him, moving his hand round in a sweeping movement – 'living like this.'

'Meaning I should move down into Nairobi camp, is that it?'

'No, Hannah,' he said hurriedly. 'But you will see when you come to India that life is harsh there just as it is here. The British generally manage to live above it all. We live civilized lives and conduct ourselves accordingly. Like gentlemen.' He leaned close to her, closing his hand over hers. 'There are people just like Reuben Cole over there. They accept the harsh life and expect no escape from it. They will never change it. We will never change it.'

There was a polite cough and Grundy walked out on to the porch. Webb withdrew his hands from Hannah's and stood up. Grundy acknowledged him and spoke to Hannah. 'Your father asked me to give you this. It was with his letter.'

He handed her an envelope. Her name was written on it in beautiful copperplate handwriting. She recognized it instantly.

Her hand came up to her mouth in an exclamation of pure joy. 'It's from mother. Oh, how wonderful. Thank you, Joseph.' She stood up excitedly. 'Excuse me Kingsley, I must read this now. I won't be long.'

She ran from the porch and went to her bedroom. On her dressing table was a carved, ivory knife. She turned up the oil lamp and opened the envelope carefully, extracting the few pages inside. Then she sat at her dressing table and spread the pages out in front of her.

My dearest Hannah,

I do hope this letter finds you in the best of health. It is such a nuisance that we must wait several weeks before hearing from each other. I read in the newspapers of so much illness in Africa that I pray each day for your good health and your father's. And who knows? Even now you may be suffering from some awful calamity. But I shall put such thoughts from my mind and take a leaf from your father's book by trusting in God.

Now my dear, I do have some disappointing news for you. I shall not be returning to Africa for some time. My dear sister, your Aunt Jane, is so unwell that the doctor fears for her life. She is almost seventy, poor thing, and so frail. She has nobody, as you know, and I believe she will not last the year out. So, I have taken it upon myself to make her last few months as happy and comfortable as I can.

I think I am not being entirely truthful with myself, Hannah (or you my dear). Heaven knows there will be so much for me to do when Jane has passed on, as she surely will. What with the house and her business affairs, (just some investments our dear father left her). I sometimes think we were such a disappointment to your grandfather, Jane and I. He did so want boys. But he did look after us so. And of course the house will be mine after Jane's death. It was father's wish. So you see, my dear, I cannot see myself returning to Africa for a year or more. If at all.

At this point Hannah put her hand to her mouth and looked at herself in the mirror. She thought about Kingsley sitting outside, and Reuben Cole looking for his son. She lost herself in a train of thoughts for a moment. Then she shook her head and went back to reading her mother's letter.

Please don't be anxious my dear. By then it will be time for your father to retire. He has said he wants to retire in Africa, but I say that is a lot of nonsense; it is much nicer here in Brighton. He will argue of course, but don't all men? But I shall get my way, I know that (our secret, Hannah!). The money isn't a problem; your father has plenty of that. But of course, there is something which makes this decision so much easier. You and Major Webb will be married by then, won't you? I know you have been waiting for my return, you and Major Webb. He is such a nice man. And he will certainly become a very senior officer. Your father believes he will return to his regiment in India as a Lieutenant Colonel. I'm not sure what that is, but it sounds very important. You will make such a splendid wife for him. And you'll adore India.

Now you do understand what I'm saying, don't you Hannah? There is no need to wait for my blessing. Your father has told me how patient you've been. But no need now. You have my blessing. And please, please come home to Brighton to be married. Oh, I shall be so proud of you. I'm sure your father will be allowed to conduct the service. And of course, once your father is back in England, I just know I will be able to persuade him to stay.

There, now you have it. I do like making plans, don't I? But my remaining in England will not get in the way of your future happiness. Now you can announce your engagement to Major Webb. It will appear in the Gazette, *I think. Or The* Times? *Whatever, it will be so lovely.*

Hannah felt her earlier pleasure sliding away from her. She put the letter down and looked again at herself in the vanity mirror. Why aren't you smiling? she asked her reflection. Why aren't you dancing round the room with sheer joy and excitement?

Why are you afraid, now?

She did not read the rest of the letter, but folded it carefully and placed it in the drawer. Then she went back out on to the porch.

Webb almost jumped from his chair. 'Well?' His eyes were alive with anticipation.

'Well what, Kingsley?'

His expression changed. He looked puzzled and sensed something was wrong. He asked her.

'No, nothing wrong,' she answered, forcing a smile. 'Perhaps the nostalgia of England comes over too forcefully in Mother's letter.'

'Of course, it must be that.' He took her hand. 'Did your mother say when she would be returning?'

'No, Kingsley, she did not,' Hannah said truthfully. 'Perhaps she put that in father's letter.'

He looked disappointed. Hannah felt as though she had wounded him. She had no idea why she felt so melancholy, and it hurt her to see him downcast like that. She reached up and kissed him gently. 'Patience, my love.' She tried to add feeling and lightness to her voice. Stepping back, she smiled. 'Now, perhaps I should ask papa if he's ready for his bath.'

She left him there but instead of going to her father's room, she went to her own. She sat down at the dressing table, put her hands to her face and began to weep softly.

Reuben and Sergeant Ord were standing side by side on high ground overlooking the Masai camp. They were concealed by a small copse of trees. The rest of the patrol were lower down the slope with the horses. The size of the camp was staggering. Circular clusters of *enkangs* marched away into the distance until it was almost impossible to distinguish one from another. The sky above them was filled with the smoke from their cooking fires and, with little or no breeze to shift it, the smoke gathered in flattened blankets.

'How in God's name do we get in there?'

Reuben's question was rhetorical. Bill Ord was thinking along the same lines. He answered the question anyway. 'We don't. It's as simple as that.'

Reuben understood the sergeant's response. But for him there was no doubt in his mind that he had to find a way. 'My boy is down there somewhere.' His words were spoken quietly in a flat statement. 'I have to do something.'

'Cole, all we can do is watch and wait for something to happen.'

Reuben looked at him. 'And how long do we wait?'

Ord shrugged. 'How do I know?' he replied truthfully. 'If they are taking your boy to Uganda, they'll have to move him sometime. We'll just have to wait until then.'

Reuben did not need the truth. It was obvious. He wanted a chance to reach David, but chance was so unpredictable. The phlegmatic soldier beside him probably used chance but only if the dice was loaded in his favour. Until then, they would have to wait. Reuben searched around until he found a convenient spot on the ground to lie on. Then he took a telescope from his pocket and made himself as comfortable as possible. It was going to be a long wait.

Reuben kept the glass to his eye for almost two hours before something stirred him. Until then he had been quartering the camp looking for anything, any sign that might suggest where they were holding David and the other children. What Reuben spotted was an empty cart being pulled by an ox. The driver cajoled the lumbering beast through a series of obstacles, negotiating the thorn bush fences until it reached a hut, which had been erected in the centre of a small stockade. The driver brought the cart to a halt immediately outside the hut. It was then Reuben noticed two Masai guards outside the hut and little trip-hammers began sounding in his chest.

'Sergeant Ord! Quick!'

Reuben's excited voice reached Bill Ord's ears. He was sitting with the rest of the patrol just below Reuben's position. He got up and scrambled up the slope. 'What is it?'

Reuben handed him the telescope. 'I'm not sure. It may be nothing. Just take a look.' He explained roughly where he wanted him to focus the telescope. 'Outside the main stockade there's a smaller one. There's an empty ox cart outside it.'

Bill Ord kept the telescope pressed to his eye for some time. Then he suddenly thrust it back at Reuben. 'Look.' It was all he said.

Reuben's knuckles went white as he tightened his grip on the brass tube. He saw a straggling line of children emerging from the hut. At that distance it was possible to make out the slight figure of David. He had his slouch hat in his hand and his uncovered blond hair shone out like a beacon.

'There he is. Oh my God. . . .' Reuben's voice faltered into a sob and tears filled his eyes. He brushed them away angrily to clear his vision. 'He's there. He's there,' was all he kept saying.

Ord reached down for the telescope. Reuben could not see a thing now because he was so overcome with emotion. Ord watched as a group of adults approached the cart. He recognized Snyder but not the white man with him. He did note, however, that the man was incongruously dressed for the African bush. Kabarega was also there as were others who, Ord decided, were clan elders. He watched the children being loaded and chained into the cart. Suddenly he snapped the telescope shut.

'That's it, they're moving the children out.' He called down to the patrol. 'Come on lads, they're moving the children.' The soldiers scrambled to their feet. Reuben had wiped away his tears and came scurrying down the slope after Sergeant Ord.

'Now look, they are probably taking the children to Uganda,' he was telling the men. 'If so, it means they'll have to pass between Mau Forest and the Escarpment.' The hills beyond them rose up into a formidable barrier as if to reinforce the point. 'When they clear the plain they'll have to head northeast. We'll track them.' He pointed at two of the men. 'Albert, Danny, you scout forward. Shouldn't be too difficult.' He paused then and put his hand to his chin. He posed a figure of studied thought. A thinker. A planner. The others waited patiently but it was some time before he spoke.

'They'll have to cross rivers,' he said eventually. 'We'll get a chance there. Joe,' he turned to Corporal Hillier, 'I want you to go back to the railhead.'

The sudden change in thinking was totally unexpected. Reuben thought he saw a look of profound dismay coupled with complete surprise on the corporal's face.

'The railhead?' Hillier echoed. 'What for, Sarge?'

Bill Ord had been standing. He now squatted on his haunches. 'I figure it this way. We don't know how far we might have to go before we can stop them.' Reuben could see how the men hung on his every word and understood what complete loyalty meant. They were as one. 'If we are lucky,' Ord was saying, 'and rescue those poor beggars, we'll have to take them all. There's ten down there.' He pointed over the high ground. 'Can't leave any of them behind. And seeing as we only have eight horses, we can't let any of the little sods walk.' He moved a little, hammering the next point home with his finger. 'If anything goes wrong and we get a bloody *ruga-ruga* on our tail, we'd never outrun them. That's why I intend going straight for the railhead. It's the closest point.'

It meant following a route that would actually take them away from Nairobi. Hillier looked over his shoulder towards the east, beyond the Kiambogo Hills. 'That means you'll have to go over that lot.'

Ord nodded. 'Aye, I know, but it's a chance we'll have to take. So, what I want you to do, Joe, is get to the railhead and ask engineer in charge to hold train for us.'

Bill Ord knew there was always a train working up at the railhead. It was used to move the workers up and down the line and to shift materials. It rarely came back to Nairobi until the end of the working day.

'What about the coolie workers?' Hillier reminded him. 'They won't want to stay.'

'It's not a problem, Joe. Ask the engineer to have the train waiting for us by midnight tomorrow night. That'll give him time to get the men back to Nairobi.' He waited for Hillier to acknowledge it. 'Then,' he went on, 'if we don't show up tomorrow night, have him bring the train up the following night, and so on.'

'How long?'

'Couple or three days.'

'What if he won't do it?'

'Commandeer the bloody train, Joe,' Ord told him, raising his voice. 'And if he doesn't like it, get back to Nairobi and tell Major Webb. But whatever happens, I want that bloody train there, at the railhead, midnight. Got it?'

Hillier understood what odds they were up against. Getting the Company engineer at the railhead to co-operate in what was, to all intents and purposes, a military operation was going to be difficult to say the least. He thought it would be impossible. But what Sergeant Ord and the others were about to do carried all the risks. And he knew he had to have that train at that railhead. He looked at the others and gave them all a lopsided grin. It was almost an apology for not going with them. He climbed up on to his horse, wished them all good luck and rode off without looking back.

By following the lumbering ox cart and scouting ahead, it was soon clear to Sergeant Ord which route it would follow. He took the patrol on ahead until they came to a place where the river flowed out of the Mau Escarpment. It crossed a flat plain before disappearing into the forest. There were several rivers flowing out of the escarpment, but one, the Sissimdo, crossed the smallest gap, and the ox cart could only cross it in one place.

Sergeant Ord led the patrol into a part of the forest which was well ahead of the route he knew the ox cart was following. They moved into cover which gave them a good view of the river. The sun was behind them which meant the shadows of the trees were lengthening. To be seen from the river by a casual observer would prove almost impossible. Everyone settled down, and began the long wait.

Eventually the ox cart hove into sight. Reuben felt the hairs lift on the back of his neck when he saw it. There were ten guards walking in front and ten behind. Two others were on the cart; one was driving the oxen while the other sat among the children.

Sergeant Ord tapped Reuben on the shoulder. It startled him. 'You take the two men on the cart.' Reuben nodded and Ord motioned to three of his men. 'You three, wait until the leading group are in the water, then take them. Cole will take the two on the cart. I'll handle the rearguard.' He turned to Reuben. 'Remember, Cole, your boy and the children are important. Don't worry about us. Get the little ones into the forest and look after them.' He gripped his arm. 'Good luck.' He flashed a smile and vanished into the forest with the rest of the patrol.

Once they had disappeared it was as if they had never been there. Reuben was alone. Nothing disturbed the silence except his own breathing. He watched the ox cart intently. There was nothing else in Reuben's world now but the thought of rescuing his son. He could soon make out the little heads of the children rocking with the swaying motion of the cart. The guard sat at one end of the cart, oblivious to his little charges. Then he saw the distinct outline of David's slouch hat and his pulse quickened enormously. He wanted to race out there at that moment and rescue David. But he couldn't; he had to wait for Ord's men to start. He had no idea where they were.

Soon the ox cart reached the small crossing point at the Sissimdo River. The leading guards stepped gingerly into the water, glancing warily up and down its length. Reuben edged forward, out of the trees and into the long grass. As the last of the leading guards stepped into the water, he toppled. At that moment, Reuben heard the shot that had felled him.

Then all hell broke loose.

Reuben dashed forward, taking long, leaping strides over the long grass, shouting like the devil. The man driving the oxen swung round and reached into the boards at his feet. He pulled out an old musket, raised it quickly and fired at the screaming figure of Reuben. The ball sailed harmlessly by and before he had a chance to draw the long sword he was carrying, a bullet from Reuben's Winchester took half his shoulder away and any chance he ever had.

The children instinctively ducked as the bullets started whining through the air, but soon their youthful curiosity brought them back on to their knees and they bobbed their heads over the edge of the cart. As David's head popped up, the guard with them reached forward and grabbed David, knocking his slouch hat into the cart. The boy screamed in terror as the man drew a long sword from its scabbard and raised it high above his head.

Reuben stopped in his tracks, his mind racing. He was too far away to reach the cart before the man struck David with his sword. He dropped to one knee and sighted the rifle as the man forced David's head over the edge of the cart. His sword flashed briefly in the fading sunlight as Reuben fired. The bullet furrowed into the man's chest and he pitched backwards over the side.

David twisted himself up into a kneeling position. At first he wasn't sure what had happened. Not even aware that it was his father who had saved his life. But when he saw Reuben, his reaction was overwhelming. He screamed at the top of his voice but only unintelligible words erupted from his larynx and his eyes flooded with tears as the tension of the last few days poured from him.

Reuben saw his son's emotional outburst and felt his own emotions break loose. He lost control of them, laughing, crying, shouting. He saw the entire gamut of David's emotions: fear, excitement, bewilderment. He was close to the cart now, ignoring the gunfire going on all around him as he raced forward. David tried to leap from the cart but his chains held him firmly. Reuben reached the cart and leapt over the side. He bent low and swept David into his arms. David clung to him with such strength that Reuben thought his own ribs might crack. He kept repeating the word 'papa' over and over again, not letting go for a moment. Reuben wanted it to last, to savour it, but he knew he had to get the children to the relative safety of the trees.

The little black boys regarded him with wide-eyed fear as he went among them, searching for the point where the chain that shackled them was attached to the cart. He found the securing link and smashed it away from the wood with the butt of his rifle. Pulling the chain through the rings attached to the children, he jumped down from the cart and urged them to follow.

Reuben got the children to safety and turned his attention to the fight. He thought for a moment about helping the soldiers, but the fight was over. It had lasted barely two minutes. The total surprise and swiftness of the ambush had left Kabarega's men witless and outmanoeuvred; they had been overwhelmed quickly and comprehensively.

Seeing the soldiers riding back to him, and knowing it was safe to do so, he turned back to David and knelt beside him. David slung his arms around him. He wasn't crying now. Instead he kept moving his head back to look at his father as though not believing what he was seeing.

Reuben held him at arms length and shook his head in disgust. 'God in heaven, David,' he said, screwing his face up. 'What have they done to you?'

David just shrugged, still too shocked to say anything. Reuben pulled him close and held on to him. 'The best thing we can do,' he said in David's ear, 'is to get you all away from here as fast as we can.'

They gathered up the children and washed the filth from them in the river. Bill Ord took the oxen away and slaughtered them. He believed it would be better to kill them humanely than to leave them behind where they could be taken by lions.

The sun was settling into the lower half of the sky now, but there was sufficient warmth in the air to dry the children's clothes. Soon they were finished and heading for the Kiambogo Hills. Each of the men carried one of the children, while Reuben and Bill Ord carried two each. Reuben had David sitting in front of him. He held one arm tightly round the boy's waist and kept the reins in the other. Behind him sat one of Mirambo's sons, his legs spread wide over the rump of the horse and his spindly arms clutching Reuben's shirt firmly. He had his cheek pressed into Reuben's back and his little eyes were wide open and staring.

They could hear thunder in the distance. It echoed across the Mau Escarpment, beyond the hills, and for the first time they noticed darkening shadows of cloud mixing with the twilight. David shivered and Reuben drew him in closer. The wind stirred and veered off the hills, blowing in their faces, snatching the flimsy warmth from the air.

They rode in silence, climbing the sloping ground in a single column. Nothing stirred in the bush except the shrill, vibrant noise of the cicadas. The wildlife seemed to have deserted them. It was as if they could sense something was wrong. The thunder clattered into their silent world again and a ribbon of lightning slashed the sky beyond the peaks. Ten minutes more, Reuben thought, and they would have to camp.

The rain woke them the following morning. It hissed noisily through the trees and continued its deluge with unabated ferocity. There was no wind to muffle the noise of the thunder that clattered in the still air, its rumbling echoes fading away. They ate dried meat and drank tepid water from their drinking bottles. Within twenty minutes of waking they were on their way again.

The rain continued to hammer down at them. With each mile they were forced to climb higher as the ground became increasingly waterlogged. Progress was slow because of the many times they searched for better tracks. As the storm clouds drifted west towards Ndorobo, so the patrol continued to climb higher and the temperature continued to drop.

They pushed on doggedly, each keeping his own counsel. Reuben thought more and more about Lake Naivasha and that giant wedge of rock holding the waters back. How long, he wondered, could it possibly withstand the increasing pressure as the heavens continued to pour thousands of gallons of water into the lake's welcoming bowl?

Sergeant Ord thought about the railhead and his plan to get the children to safety before any pursuers could reach them. But the terrible conditions seemed bent on preventing them reaching the railhead by the end of that day. He was also becoming increasingly concerned for the children; they were suffering terribly from the cold and wet and already the soldiers had wrapped them in their blankets. The last thing any of them needed was to spend another night in the open.

Throughout the day they continually scanned the horizon behind them for signs of pursuit. None came and the daylight faded as twilight brought the first shadows of night. Sergeant Ord stiffened when he heard the hoot of a train whistle faintly in the distance. He pulled a watch from his tunic pocket. It was about the time that the track laying gangs would be leaving the railhead and returning to the advance camp. Some would inevitably go on to Nairobi. Would the train return, he wondered? It seemed so far away, another world. He glanced back at Reuben, checked his watch again and put it back in his tunic pocket without saying a word. He kept doing that; checking his watch at frequent intervals. He knew that if they missed the train, one or two of the weaker children might not make it through the night.

The clouds drifted away and the moon emerged in a white, candescent light. The ground levelled out until it broadened into a large plain. In the moonlight, they could see the dark silhouette of the train quite clearly in the distance. It was below them on the escarpment. It looked so small. Behind it they could make out the faint bulk of the box car. As they closed the gap between themselves and the train, they could see smoke drifting up from the stack on top of the boiler. There was no other sign of life.

They eventually reached the track and followed it, picking their way carefully through scattered sections of rail, large, wooden sleepers, and various impedimenta lying about. They approached cautiously but their arrival was announced by the sounds of the horses' hoofs clattering over rocks and discarded fishplates.

Bill Ord saw a movement in the shadows. He stiffened and felt his horse get restless beneath him. It whinnied softly as he tightened his grip on the reins. 'Who's there?' he called out.

A figure stepped out from the shadow of the train. He had a blanket draped over his shoulder. 'Thank God you made it,' a familiar voice cried. 'It's been a long wait.'

Corporal Joe Hillier stood grinning beneath the blanket. Sergeant Ord relaxed immediately and smiled for the first time in days. Someone jumped down from the footplate of the engine. Hillier glanced back over his shoulder as the man approached. He introduced the stranger. 'This is Mister Cameron, sarge. He's the engineer building the railway.'

Cameron smiled in the darkness. 'Well, not quite. But I do seem to spend most of my time at the railhead.'

Sergeant Ord got down from his horse. 'I must thank you for waiting, Mister Cameron,' he told him. 'We have some poorly children here.'

'Your corporal was very persuasive,' Cameron told him. 'I prefer to think I can go on building my railway with my limbs intact.'

Ord glanced knowingly at Hillier. 'Thank you anyway sir. Now, if you like, we'll get the children on board. I'll be staying here with my men. Mister Cole will travel with you.'

Reuben almost objected but realized at once it would be impossible for all of them to ride on the train because of the horses. And there was only one box car. He lowered David to the ground and dismounted. He handed the reins to Sergeant Ord.

The next ten minutes were spent making the children comfortable inside the box car. There were plenty of blankets, and Cameron had been thoughtful enough, probably prompted by Corporal Hillier, to bring food and water. Soon the young heads were covered and warm, gently nodding off into a safe world once more.

Reuben asked Cameron if he needed any help on the footplate. The Scot said he didn't but would be glad of some company.

Reuben shook hands with Sergeant Ord and the rest of the men. He told the wily sergeant there was no way he could express his gratitude sufficiently. It was only the darkness that saved Bill Ord from his blushes.

Reuben climbed up on to the footplate as Cameron was throwing logs into the fire. With the firebox door open, the heat blasted out. Reuben hadn't realized until then how cold it had become. Then the engineer kicked the firebox door shut and the change was incredible; it was as though the fire had never existed.

Cameron released the hand brake and wound the steam regulator open. He then released the steam brake and the engine gave a mighty shudder as the wheels slipped at first and then bit into the steel track. Reuben leaned over the weatherboard and held his hand up to Bill Ord and his men as Cameron took the train down the gentle gradient. He pulled sharply on the whistle several times. Its sibilant sound bounced off the escarpment into an empty sky.

Reuben was very happy; David was sound asleep in the box car and they were on their way home.

CHAPTER SEVEN

Major Webb felt someone shaking him. It was a soft, almost respectful touch on the shoulder. He opened his eyes.

'Sir, wake up.'

The hand shook him again. He opened his eyes further and he could see the weak, flickering light from the oil lamp.

'Major Webb,' the voice urged. 'Wake up.'

He pushed himself up on to one elbow. The soldier who was responsible for waking him backed off a pace and lowered the oil lamp.

'What is it?'

'We have a gentleman outside, sir. Says he wants to see you. He insists, like.'

'Does he now?' He sat up and rubbed his eyes. 'What time is it?'

'Just after two o'clock, sir.'

'Damn cheek,' Webb muttered. 'Who is it?'

'Says his name is Cole, sir.'

'Cole?' His hands dropped. 'Damn the man,' he muttered, 'I thought I'd seen the last of him. What does he want?' he asked irritably.

'Wouldn't say, sir. Like I said; he was most insistent on speaking to you.'

'Yes, he would be,' Webb said, more to himself than the soldier. He pointed to the oil lamp perched. 'Turn that up, will you?'

The soldier turned the wick up. Webb squinted against the glare as the soldier's silhouette moved aside.

'Where is he?' Webb asked.

'At the guardroom, sir.'

Webb sighed heavily. 'Very well, bring him here.' He saw no reason to get fully dressed just to go outside at Cole's behest. Neither was he in the right frame of mind to receive Cole; he felt quite miffed to think the man was back again.

'He has a boy with him, sir.'

Webb looked up sharply. 'A boy?' He could scarcely believe it. Not the same boy, surely? Not his son?

'Shall I fetch them both, sir?'

'Of course. Yes,' Webb answered testily. 'Bring them both.'

The soldier left and Webb sat on the edge of the bed for a moment absorbed in nothing more than the flame from the oil lamp. Then he shook his head and stood up. A water jug and basin stood on a wash stand. He went over to it and poured a little water into the glazed bowl. Then he splashed the water over his face, expunging the last vestiges of sleep from his mind. He dressed, pulling on a pair of uniform breeches and a shirt. A few minutes later there was a knock on the door. Reuben and David were ushered in by the soldier.

'Well, Cole. I must congratulate you on what appears to have been a tremendous success.' If the salutation was trite and affected, Reuben appeared not to notice.

'I could not have done it without Sergeant Ord and his men,' Reuben admitted. 'I owe you my thanks for allowing Sergeant Ord to remount the patrol.'

Webb regarded him obliquely. 'So, this is David.' He studied the boy. 'Fine looking lad, Cole, I must say. I will need to speak to him later, see what he can tell me about Snyder.' He turned his attention back to Reuben. 'And, of course, I will be speaking to Sergeant Ord. Is he with you?'

Reuben shook his head. 'No. I came on ahead.' He explained about the train.

'Damn good thinking,' Webb conceded. 'So, what brings you here?'

'The children.'

There followed a stony silence for a while.

'The children?' Webb repeated.

'I have the other nine children with me, Major. They need to be taken in somewhere.' Reuben sounded tired. 'After all, they are the army's responsibility.'

'And what makes you think the army should be charged with their care?'

'Major, it isn't what I think that's important. But these children were rescued by Sergeant Ord's patrol; your men. And I was under his orders. Remember?'

Major Webb's face dropped a little when Reuben made an indirect reference to his threat when agreeing to let the patrol go out again. 'I see what you mean,' he said and recovered his poise. 'And have you any suggestions?'

'Well, at the moment they are all sleeping in the box car.' He shrugged loosely. 'I imagine they will be quite happy until the morning. Perhaps you could put a guard on them for now? Make a decision later.'

Webb smiled grudgingly. 'Yes, I could do that. Although goodness knows what I will do with them tomorrow.'

At that moment Reuben neither knew nor cared. He was physically and mentally exhausted. The trauma he had gone through rendered him incapable of benevolent thought towards the major's new predicament. Consequently he was totally unmoved by Webb's apparent show of indifference. 'I'm sure you'll work something out, Major,' he told him.

Webb nodded absently. 'Perhaps I will. But having presented me with nine children, perhaps you can tell me how?'

'No I can't, Major. Or would you rather we'd left them with Snyder?' he retorted enquiringly.

'That's an unchristian suggestion, Cole, which you know is not true.' Webb sounded suitably contrite. 'But to be woken in the middle of the night with this problem isn't something I associate with soldiering.'

'Perhaps not, but it's a fact and has to be dealt with,' Reuben said a little sternly. 'And you are a resourceful man, Major. I'm sure you'll find a way.'

Webb leaned against the edge of the table. He could see young David looking at him without expression. It was a poor show for a man in his position to act so waspishly in front of the boy, but he couldn't help his feelings of antipathy towards Cole.

'Very well, Cole, leave it with me,' he agreed. 'I'll put a guard on the box car and follow it up in the morning.'

Reuben muttered his thanks and turned to go.

'What will you do now, Cole?' Webb asked. 'Return to the farm?'

Reuben stopped. 'Yes. Why?'

Webb glanced meaningfully at David. 'In view of recent events, I thought you might have chosen not to.'

'It's our home, Major,' he replied simply. 'We are going back.'

Noble sentiments, thought Webb. 'When will that be? Tomorrow?'

'In a day or so. I shall call on Miss Hannah and her father. I promised I would take David to see them.'

Webb stiffened involuntarily. 'Well, don't linger too long, Cole. I shouldn't like that.'

Reuben sensed a challenge there. He could, perhaps, understand it in view of how prominently he himself now figured in Hannah's life. Any man wishing to ingratiate himself with a woman as beautiful as Hannah could do no better than to save her life. And he was no fool; it rankled with Major Webb. Still, there had been a suggestion of rebuke, and he could not resist a small put down.

'I'm sorry you feel that way, Major. But I will linger with Miss Hannah for as long as she allows.'

'It would serve no purpose, Cole,' Webb answered hurriedly. 'Miss Hannah and I are betrothed.' It was hurled like a stone and struck with as much force.

'I didn't know,' Reuben replied, genuinely surprised.

'No. It is something Miss Bowers and I have decided not to announce until after her father has fully recovered.'

Reuben took David's hand. David had never known his father to do that before. He had often held David's hand, but only in response, never as a gesture.

'You have my congratulations, Major,' he told him. 'I hope you'll both be very happy.' He went towards the door and opened it.

'Say nothing of this, Cole. Please,' Webb added. 'I did promise Miss Bowers.'

'Yes, of course. Goodnight.' He pulled David gently through the open door and closed it behind him.'

After they had gone, Major Webb slumped down on the bed. He wondered why he had acted like a spoiled schoolboy. And why he had lied.

Despite his very late night, Reuben woke early. The light from the window framed the drawn curtains and lit the room as if it were broad daylight. In that transitory moment, he wondered where he was and why he had woken in a strange room. Then he remembered he was in the Railway Club, and with that memory, he was as happy as he believed he could be.

He rolled his head to one side. David lay sleeping in a small bed beside him. His blond hair was just visible through the hastily hung mosquito netting. Reuben lay there, wallowing in the feeling of security, happy to be with David again.

He thought about what they might do with their day. He would retrieve David's horse from the livery stable. Buy some provisions and new clothes for David. A good bath for David. He grinned when he remembered the filthy condition he was in when they rescued him. Despite the trauma of David's kidnap, he was still able to find some grim humour in that black episode. He thought about Mirambo and his wife. Two friends he would miss dearly. It was so sad. He owed it to them to make sure their children were returned to their grandparents. He thought about Hannah too. How she had despaired for him and David. He was touched by the compassion she had shown when she was in the midst of her own crisis. She would be so pleased to see them.

'Right!' he exclaimed suddenly. 'Up you get, Cole. There's a whole new day ahead of you.' He sat up and swung his legs off the bed, thrusting aside the mosquito net. 'David! Time to get up. We've got lots to do today.' He looked at the sleeping head and suddenly felt as though his whole body was collapsing inside. He blinked away the threatening tears.

'Oh, David, my son. I pray to God that I never, never lose you again.'

Hannah had just made her father comfortable in a chair on the lawn, adjusting the sun shade just so, puffing up the cushions and ignoring his pleas that she should not make such a fuss, when her maid appeared from the rear of the house.

'Excuse, Missy Hannah,' she called. 'Gentleman want see you.'

Hannah looked up. She wondered who it could be; it was far

too early for Major Webb to call. 'Must be Doctor Markham,' she said to her father. 'Bring him round here, Victoria,' she instructed her maid, using the name she had conferred on the poor girl with wicked enthusiasm.

Victoria disappeared and Hannah continued to fuss around her father until he put out a hand and stopped her. He looked beyond her towards the house.

'Well, bless me,' he said, with astonishment in his voice.

Hannah looked round and immediately felt her legs weaken. She clung to her father's shoulder with one hand, and he could feel the fierceness in her grip. Her breath faltered in her throat and tears welled up into her eyes. Reuben stood there with David. Both were dressed in new clothes and Reuben was grinning like a Cheshire Cat.

'Reuben?' she said weakly, unable to say or think more. Her hand went unconsciously to her breast as if its presence there would help her breathing. She felt her father nudge her gently from behind. It made her glance quickly at him. He was smiling and pushed her gently again.

'Go on,' he urged quietly.

Hannah looked back at Reuben, wanting to run to him that very moment, but her sense of propriety wouldn't let her. Reuben began walking towards her. Hannah's father nudged her again so she walked across the lawn towards him. Her pace was moderate, but her heart and mind were racing. They stopped and Reuben held out his hand. Hannah didn't want to offer hers because it was shaking so, but she did want so much to reach up and kiss him. Reuben, conscious that he was still holding his hand out, withdrew it, thinking that, perhaps, Hannah preferred it that way. Then Hannah suddenly put her hand out.

'Oh Reuben, thank God you are both safe.' She said it hurriedly, excitedly, her voice trembling. As he touched her hand he could feel the tremor in it. She dropped her hand quickly and clasped it behind her back. Her father watched as she entwined the fingers of both hands together, back and forth, in an effort to stop them shaking. 'We heard something this morning, but we dared not hold out too much hope.'

I'm being stupid, she thought. Why can't I say what I'm thinking: I heard some of the children were safe. I could have died when there was no news of you.

'Hallo, Hannah. This is David.' The laconic introduction told its own story. Reuben pulled David forward. David removed his new slouch hat, and his freshly washed, blond hair seemed to flash in the sunlight. Hannah just melted. She knelt before him and swept him into her arms. She clung to him possessively, in the same way she wanted to cling to Reuben.

David smiled self-consciously. 'Hallo, Miss Hannah. Papa has told me all about you. He said a lot about you.' He looked up at Reuben. Did I do right? his eyes asked.

Hannah held him at arms length. 'Oh, you're such a fine-look-ing boy.' She stood up. 'Come on,' she said. 'Let's go and meet my father.' She didn't let go of David's hand, but clung to it like a prized possession, afraid to let it go.

Mr Bowers wanted to get up out of his chair to meet Reuben and David, but Hannah wouldn't let him. He relented and sank back on to the cushions.

'Welcome back, Cole,' he said. 'Welcome back. I knew the good Lord would answer our prayers.' He looked at David. 'Young man, welcome to my home.' He held out his hand, which David shook vigorously.

'Good morning, sir,' he said to Bowers. 'I hope you are getting better.'

Hannah smiled quickly at Reuben. She was still holding David's hand. David relaxed and stood back a little from the chaplain.

Bowers chuckled. 'Of course I am. But if it hadn't been for your father here, I would have been in a right pickle by now.'

David seemed to grow visibly. 'We both would, sir. My dad likes rescuing people,' he claimed proudly.

Bowers showed a degree of surprise. 'So, you know what he did for me and my daughter?'

David nodded. 'He told me when we were coming up here.'

Bowers winked. 'And he's jolly good at it, too.'

'But not without help, sir,' Reuben put in.

Bowers expression altered slightly. 'And who helped you rescue me?' he asked enquiringly.

'I thought the good Lord might have had something to do with it,' Reuben answered humorously.

Bowers burst out laughing. '*Touché* Cole!'

'But with or without his help,' Reuben went on. 'I hope I never have to do anything like it again. I much prefer the quieter life.'

'Amen to that,' Bowers agreed. 'So what now?' he asked, changing the subject. 'Are you going back to your farm?'

'Naturally,' Reuben responded. 'Most important.'

'When?' asked Hannah.

'Well, tomorrow morning,' Reuben told her, looking up at the sky. 'It's too late to go back today. Besides, I wanted to see you both first; wish you a speedy recovery, sir.' He looked directly at Hannah. 'You too, Hannah. I also wanted you both to meet David. Perhaps more importantly, I wanted David to meet you.'

There was an implication in that which presaged an awkward silence. Hannah broke it when she said: 'Reuben, may I speak to you for a moment? Alone?'

Reuben shrugged. 'Of course.'

Hannah, still holding David's hand, asked him if he would mind keeping her father company for a few minutes. David agreed, naturally, and she let go of his hand. Bowers eyed his daughter curiously; his own, usually perceptive mind at a loss as to why she wanted to speak to Reuben alone. He watched them walk away and disappear round the side of the house.

'Now then, young David,' Bowers said to start the ball rolling. 'Why don't you tell me how your father rescued you?'

Hannah paused and took Reuben's arm, turning him so that he faced her. She was quite small beside him. 'Reuben,' she started without preamble. 'Why do you want to go back to your farm so soon?'

Reuben frowned. 'I have a lot of work to do, Hannah. The rising water is threatening to destroy everything I have worked for. I've got to stop it.'

'What of David?' she asked.

Reuben was puzzled. 'What about David?'

'Is he going back with you?'

'Of course. Why?'

Hannah didn't answer immediately. She wondered how much Reuben understood. 'Don't you think he needs a little time?' she asked eventually.

'Time for what?'

'Just time, Reuben. It's only a week since he was kidnapped. So much has happened to him since then.' She still held Reuben's arm and was increasing her grip on it. 'If you take him back now, he will have no time to adjust. He needs time to get over his ordeal.'

Reuben shook his head. 'David is a strong-minded boy, he won't have to adjust. He'll be busy helping me rebuild the farm. His mind will be too occupied to dwell on the past.'

'Oh, Reuben,' she said gently, and with compassion. 'How can someone as caring and thoughtful as you be so uncaring and unthoughtful? David has only you now. A week ago he had Mirambo and his family. It's what he's been used to. What you are planning for him is a very solitary life.'

'He has me.'

'Yes, he has you, but no one else. You're a man Reuben; an adult. He will be a child in a man's world. You cannot understand a child's needs as a woman does.' Hannah did not want to get angry, but she felt so desperately sorry for David. 'If he falls and hurts himself, you won't pick him up and help him, will you? No, he will have to be a man and ignore the pain.' She let go of his arm. 'And if he wakes up at night with nightmares about his kidnap, will you put your arms around him?' She shook her head. 'No, Reuben. You love that boy more than life itself. You've proved that. But now David will have to prove himself. And if he ever needs love and affection, real affection, you will never be able to provide it.'

'I will, Hannah,' he protested.

'No, Reuben, you will not,' she answered fiercely. 'You may think you can, but it isn't true, believe me. Men are not capable of that kind of love.'

Reuben became defensive. 'So you're suggesting that I give him up?'

'Goodness no, Reuben, I would never suggest that.' She stopped then. This was a defining moment for Hannah. Something she had unwittingly been leading up to, but afraid to admit it to herself. 'I just think that David should be given a chance to overcome the trauma of the past week. You go back to the farm, hire some local labour and leave David here.' She raised her hand before Reuben could protest. 'Not for too long, but long enough. Let him get to know us. Another family if you like.' She put her hand on his arm again. 'And if he needs someone, I'll be here for him. I promise.'

'That's kind of you Hannah.' Was he mocking her, she wondered?

'David needs to stay away from the farm, Reuben. And he needs more than just a father's love. I'm not trying to come between you and your son,' she told him, 'but I honestly feel David needs someone else.'

Reuben could see there was a great deal in what Hannah was saying and was mindful of his own misunderstanding of David's immediate needs. He realized a woman's insight often proved most penetrating and he was reminded of the promise he made to himself to bring a woman into David's life. Hannah's eyes seemed to dance all over his face while he considered what she had been saying to him.

'Very well, Hannah,' he said. 'I'll leave David here with you. But I'll stay at the Railway Club for a few nights before going back to the farm. I know David will also want to spend some time with me,' he added in riposte.

Hannah clapped her hands together and her face lit up with joy. 'Oh, Reuben, that's wonderful. I know we'll get along fine. My father will enjoy having him around too.' She clutched his hand, relinquishing the grip on his arm, and almost propelled him forward. 'Come on, let's go and tell David.'

David's reaction to the news could not have pleased Hannah more; he thought it was a terrific idea. Mr Bowers described it as 'splendid' and had mischievous thoughts about the little game he believed Hannah was playing.

'You will stay for lunch and tea, won't you?' Hannah asked. It was more of a command than a request. Reuben was grateful; he had been hoping Hannah would ask them.

'That would be nice,' he told her. 'We would love to stay.'

'And the day after tomorrow I shall invite everybody to a celebration.'

Bowers looked at Hannah with a puzzled expression on his face. 'What was that? A celebration?' he asked.

'Yes, Father, a celebration. We have so much to be thankful for: David's safe return, your good health. And it will give us a

chance to say thank you properly to all those who have helped.'
She sounded quite excited. 'Oh, it will be splendid, Father. And it
will cheer you up enormously.'

Reuben was smiling broadly at Hannah's enthusiasm. Her
father thought he hadn't seen his daughter look so happy for
some time. He looked at Reuben and David, then at Hannah. The
three of them were standing together as though it was quite
natural. Almost like a family.

'Yes, Hannah,' he agreed. 'I think it would cheer me up enormously.'

Major Webb needed no prompting to accept the invitation to
Hannah's celebration dinner. He even persuaded her to invite
Lieutenant Maclean explaining that it would help the young
adjutant to slip quietly into Nairobi's social circle. He did not
explain that his adjutant could be used to soak up much of the
table conversation while he, Major Webb, devoted as much time
as possible to Hannah.

Sergeant Ord was invited too, but stood on military protocol
and refused simply because he believed it was expected of him.
He had been surprised at the short shrift he had received from
the major at being so churlish. What Sergeant Ord was
unaware of, however, was that Hannah had foreseen the inevitable refusal and made no mistake in letting Major Webb
know that he would be held personally responsible if the brave
sergeant refused her invitation. So Bill Ord had put on his best
uniform and was present at the table when they all sat down to
dinner.

To complete the party, Hannah had invited Joseph Grundy.
His wife had declined because she was unwell. She had also
invited Seymour Pope, the Company's chief engineer, and his
wife, Jane. Hannah liked Jane Pope very much. Not only was she
very good company, but she also helped prepare the meal. It was
something she delighted in doing and excelled at. Although both
women had servants, they often cooked for their own pleasure.
And as far as Hannah was concerned, Jane Pope made cooking a
form of art.

Hannah sat at one end of the table while her father, who was
well enough now, sat at the other. Major Webb sat on Hannah's

right, and Reuben faced him across the table seated on Hannah's left, David sat next to his father and was flanked by Bill Ord who looked slightly out of place and uncomfortable. The fourth chair on that side was occupied by Joseph Grundy. Doctor Markham had turned down the invitation so, in his absence, Hannah had arranged for Lieutenant Maclean to sit round the corner from her father. The chaplain had spent many happy years at Cambridge University which was where Maclean had gained his degree, so she knew her father would enjoy reminiscing, which left Seymour Pope and his wife sitting between the two army officers.

There did not seem to be a square inch on the table which was not covered in food. Hannah had made a large jug of lemonade for David, but for the others she had provided carafes of South African wine. Because Sergeant Ord could not bring himself to drink the wine, Hannah had thoughtfully put a jug of ale on the table.

They worked their way through the meal, talking in desultory tones, swapping humorous anecdotes of past times. They touched briefly on the subject of David's rescue, congratulating Reuben and Sergeant Ord for their bravery, and remarked on the speedy recovery of Mr Bowers. The conversation inevitably swung round to the appalling weather they had been having at Nairobi and Jane Pope asked her husband why it had been so terrible.

'If only we knew,' he answered truthfully. 'I believe it has something to do with volcanic disturbances in the Rift Valley.' He shrugged. 'But Africa is a land of extremes, remember.'

'Aren't you being a little vague, Seymour?' she asked. 'After all, every country has its fair share of extremes.'

'I agree,' Reuben put in before Pope could answer. 'As a farmer I need a predictable climate. It's difficult enough in Africa, but it can be managed. I'm afraid the present weather has ruined my crop. I shouldn't want another year like it.'

'There will be many more good years than bad, Cole,' Hannah's father remarked from the end of the table. 'The good Lord will see to that.'

'Will he also see to the water spilling out of Lake Naivasha?' Reuben asked, good-naturedly.

'Nature will,' Pope answered. 'Once the level of the lake drops, the outlets will silt up.'

Reuben wondered if he had seen it. 'Have you been up to the lake?' he asked him.

Pope nodded. 'As soon as I received reports of water flowing into the valley I went up there with a small team of engineers. The rock up there is granite.' He cast around the table as he spoke, as if to reassure them all. 'It's tremendously strong.'

'There must be an enormous pressure behind it though,' Reuben suggested.

Pope nodded. 'Yes, but only because of the unnaturally high level of water in the lake. Once that drops, the outflow will reduce to a comparative dribble. In time it will silt up.'

'You sound very confident,' Reuben told him. 'But I suppose you have to be, particularly as the railway line runs straight across the Rift. That bridge would never withstand a major flood.'

Pope dabbed at his mouth with his napkin. 'On the contrary; the bridge is built to withstand flooding. We sank piles over thirty feet into the ground, down to the bedrock to support the trestles. When you build over an old watercourse like that it would be madness to ignore the possibility of flooding. You have to be prepared for every eventuality. Pity we can't say the same about our politicians.'

'Why?' Reuben asked.

'Damn Liberals tried to bring the government down at every opportunity because the line costs lives and money. I don't know what they expect.' He had the floor now so he pushed on with his diatribe against the Liberal opposition in Parliament. 'They waste no opportunity in putting question after question down accusing Lord Salisbury's government of throwing away money as soon as some unfortunate soul dies anywhere near the line. They claim we are building an empire on the bones of our dead sons. It's rubbish of course.' He moved his hands in a flourish. 'They just want to attack us at every opportunity.' He gave a mumbled laugh. 'It wouldn't surprise me if they attacked Nairobi Camp next.'

David dropped his fork. The sound of the steel clattering on the china plate cut through Pope's diatribe and stopped it dead.

Everyone looked at David. The two women smiled indulgently, Hannah thinking David might be a little embarrassed. Her expression changed when she saw it was quite the opposite; he had his mouth open and had gone a little ashen.

Reuben noticed the look of concern on her face and turned to David. 'What's the matter?' he asked his son quietly.

David laid his knife down and looked up at his father. 'I forgot to tell you something.' His voice was low, apologetic. He coughed nervously. Nobody spoke. 'When they took me away, I heard them say they were going to attack Nairobi Camp.'

Major Webb had been sitting casually in his chair. His arm rested loosely on the table. His face had the indulgent look on it in much the same way as Hannah. Now his body stiffened and he sat upright, his head coming forward as he leaned closer to the table. 'What did you say?'

David looked over at him. All eyes were fixed on Reuben's son now. 'When I was taken away, they kept us in a hut. This man came in with some others.'

'What others, David?' Webb's face had assumed a grave countenance.

David glanced quickly at Reuben who nodded softly. 'I don't know who they were, sir,' he told Major Webb. 'But I think one of them was the man called Snyder. When they came into the hut, there was another white man with them, but he went out straight away. There was also a tall man with a turban.' David's head dropped and his eyes fell away. 'He touched me all over.'

Jane Pope gasped. 'Oh Seymour, must the poor boy tell us this?'

Hannah was quick to realize her guest's sensibilities were surfacing. She pushed her chair back and stood up. 'Perhaps we should walk out on to the veranda, Jane. This will only be men's talk.'

Jane Pope's eyes flickered. 'Thank you, Hannah; if you wouldn't mind.'

The men stood up as the two women left the room. When they sat down again their eyes were riveted on David.

'Tell us what happened, David,' Webb prompted him. 'Tell us exactly as you remember.'

David continued with his story. 'When the tall man was touching me, he spoke in a language I didn't understand. But when he spoke to Snyder, it was in Swahili.'

'You understand that language?' Major Webb asked him.

'He understands it perfectly,' Reuben answered.

'Mirambo taught me,' David told him. He paused for the moment, recalling happier days at the farm. He had learned so many things from the Kikuyu. He felt so sad now that he was gone.

Reuben cut in on David's thoughts. 'What did the man say when he spoke to Snyder?'

David lowered his face and spoke softly. They all had to strain their ears to hear the soft voice. 'He said I was beautiful and Mwanga would be pleased. He said he was Mwanga's brother.'

There was a muttering sound round the table. Sergeant Ord shook his head in annoyance. 'Kabarega.' He remembered the tall figure he had seen through the telescope.

David glanced quickly at the sergeant and then lowered his eyes again. 'He said that in fourteen days Mwanga would celebrate their attack on Nairobi and take me to his heart.'

David was finished, but none of them realized because they were so absorbed by his story. The silence that followed was broken by the chaplain.

'Oh my goodness,' he muttered. 'The philistines.'

Major Webb sat back in his chair, his face showing clear signs of alarm. Of all the people in the room, he was the only one who was in a position to understand fully the importance of David's news.

'There have been attacks on the line before, Major,' Grundy said suddenly. 'Would this be any different?' There was a distinct sign of hope in his voice.

Webb dragged his eyes away from David and gave Grundy's question a moment's consideration. 'It would depend on the strength of the attacking force,' he said eventually. 'But we are now moving into Masai territory. They could raise a considerable army.'

Grundy shuffled in his seat. 'Major Webb, as company administrator I fully understand the political implications of building this line into Uganda,' he remarked ingenuously, 'but I fail to see what the Masai could possibly achieve by attacking Nairobi.

They have no country to call their own. They are quite nomadic.'

'You are correct on both counts,' Webb agreed, 'but wrong in your assumption that it is the Masai who would gain.'

'So who would?'

'The imperial German government.'

Major Webb's answer sent rumblings of protest round the table. Reuben thought it was about time David left. What they might be about to hear was not for the ears of a twelve-year-old boy. He asked David to leave them and join the ladies outside.

'It's a magnificent correlation,' Major Webb told them when David had left the room. 'The Masai fight the battle here in Africa while the Germans win it in England.'

'You have us at a disadvantage,' Seymour Pope protested. 'Well, myself certainly. Perhaps you would be good enough to explain?'

Webb noticed his young adjutant looking at him. The young officer was keenly aware of his commanding officer's insight into African politics. Webb weighed up the consequences of telling them what he knew against making a bald statement. He knew they were all intelligent men and decided not to abuse that intelligence. He would tell them.

'Gentlemen,' he begun. 'What I am about to tell you is confidential and is my own view of the situation. Although it is only my opinion, I would defend it most vigorously. So, I am relying on your discretion. None of what I am about to say must be repeated outside this room.' They all mumbled their assent. Webb continued.

'About ten years ago, the imperial German government financed an expedition into Uganda. It was led by a man named Carl Peters. I'm sure most of you have heard of him. He was a brilliant man; virtually colonized Uganda on his own. When you consider it was a country without real stature and generally accepted as British territory, it was really a unique achievement.'

'Carl Peters drew up various treaties, all meaningless of course, but important because he very cleverly drew them up with only the most powerful of the tribal chiefs. They included Mwanga, King of the Bugandans.' He made an empty laugh. 'He was practically King of Uganda itself. Well, naturally, we had to dismantle everything Peters had done. It took a great deal of time, but eventually the British were able to restore the status quo. I've no need to tell you that the Germans were furious. They encouraged Mwanga to take the law into his own hands and resist us. We chased him into the German Protectorate, but he started making trouble there. So we persuaded the German governor to throw him into jail, which he did.'

'Serves the bugger right,' Pope said.

Webb shrugged. 'That's what we thought. But when the Sudanese mutinied at Buddu, Mwanga mysteriously escaped from prison and returned to Uganda. He proclaimed Islam there and rallied a substantial Muslim army behind him. As you all know, Major Macdonald was sent into Uganda to quell the mutiny and put Mwanga's army to flight. He did this quite successfully.' Webb paused and finished off his wine. He put the glass down carefully and wiped the corners of his mouth with his napkin. He went on.

'However, Major Macdonald was ordered north to support General Kitchener in the Sudan. Although he had put Mwanga's army to flight, Mwanga was still at large. We then learned that the French were showing an unhealthy interest in Uganda. It was still vulnerable so we had to maintain a military presence there.' He leaned back, rattling his fingers on the table. 'So far, I believe, we have moved something like twenty thousand troops, two thousand baggage animals and several thousand tons of equipment into Uganda using this railway line. All of it shipped as far as the railhead.

'A large contingent of that army has been moved north to link up with Major Macdonald and Kitchener. Mwanga is aware of this and has become active again. He still has a large force of Muslim supporters. So, in order to provision the troops who are still in Uganda, as well as those who have gone north, it is vital we maintain a supply link between here and Mombasa on the coast. Mwanga knows that and is in a position to disrupt our supply route and lay siege to our army there. We are now convinced that Mwanga did not 'escape' from prison in the German Protectorate, but was sent back to Uganda by the German governor, acting on the direct orders of the imperial German government.' It was a powerful statement; one that left nothing to the imagination. Webb paused, letting it sink into their minds.

'Do you have proof of the Germans' collusion?' Reuben asked the major.

'No, of course not,' Webb answered immediately. 'But there is no doubt in my mind of that collusion because it is in their interests.' He leaned forward placing both elbows on the table and brought his hands together. 'The line they are constructing through their own territory is months behind ours. When the German governor visited our line earlier in the year, he conceded the "race" as he put it. Am I not right?' Grundy nodded vigorously at this. 'But we didn't believe it,' Webb said with undisguised urgency in his voice. 'They know we shall reach Uganda first. It means we shall be able to supply our forces directly. We shall be more effective in controlling insurgency. We shall be able to police Uganda properly and consequently protect our interests in the Sudan and the Lower Nile.'

'So how can an attack on Nairobi prevent us reaching Uganda without the German government showing its hand?' Reuben asked. 'That would mean war between our two countries.'

Webb faced Reuben and made a dismissive gesture with is hand. 'No. As far as the Germans are concerned, a military solution is out of the question. Only a war can stop us reaching Uganda now, but it has to be a different kind. What they will do is get public opinion in England to fight that war for them.'

Seymour Pope shifted uncomfortably in his chair. 'I'm afraid you are beginning to make frightening sense, Major.'

'I don't wish to frighten anyone,' Webb answered apologetically, looking round at all of them. 'But it is an inevitable conclusion. You see,' he continued, warming to his argument, 'public opinion in England is a formidable weapon. It has been used quite successfully in the past. Already that opinion has been roused by the Liberals at home. There have been a lot of deaths on the line. An attack on Nairobi would force the commissioner for India State Railways to withdraw all Indian labour until the British government could guarantee their safety.'

'Which it cannot,' Pope presumed aloud.

'No. And the German government is aware of this. They are also aware that Lord Salisbury's government is holding a very

slim majority in the House. If the Liberals can get the full
support of the public behind them, a vote of no confidence in the
government would win the day. That would force an election,
which Salisbury would lose; the Liberals would sweep into power
and the railway line would be scrapped. And we would lose
Uganda.' He stopped and was followed by a stunned silence. His
opinion had been put succinctly and with devastating effect.
Nobody spoke until Lieutenant Maclean began nodding his head.

'It really is very, very clever,' he observed. 'Quite brilliant.
There is nothing to connect the German government with the
Masai or an attack on Nairobi, which means they stand to win
the Jewel of Africa without firing a shot in anger. They would
appear blameless.'

Grundy sounded deeply affronted. 'They may appear blameless in the eyes of the world,' he said acidly, 'but we shall know
the truth and make damn sure we tell it.'

'With respect, sir,' Maclean pointed out. 'Against a Masai army
I do not think we'll be given the opportunity to tell that truth.'

Grundy regarded him with disapproval. 'We have two thousand men here in Nairobi, Lieutenant.'

Before he could reply, Webb answered for him. 'I have two
hundred soldiers all trained in the art of war, sir. They would
find it difficult to build a railway at short notice.'

'What do you mean by that?' Grundy asked defensively.

'The major means that two thousand men could not fight a
war at short notice,' Reuben observed.

'Certainly not with success,' Webb added.

Pope sighed deeply. 'It's an interesting corollary, Major. Is
there an alternative?'

Webb smiled ruefully. 'I have two hundred men and my duty
to do.'

'You could pull out. Retreat from such a one-sided conflict,'
Pope suggested. 'Or does that offend you?'

Webb became sardonic. 'It would offend the generals in
Whitehall. But seriously, we cannot talk of such things until we
know the exact nature of the threat.'

'So, what do you propose to do?'

Webb faced Seymour Pope who had asked the question. He
wondered how much ambition the engineer had and whether

that aspiration would stir some resolve in him when called upon. 'Whatever I do, Mister Pope,' Webb answered, 'I shall consider the safety of the civilian population in Nairobi Camp.' He pushed his chair back and stood up. 'Now, if you will excuse me gentlemen.' He looked to Lieutenant Maclean who was already on his feet as the others rose around the table. 'I will convene a meeting of all senior company officials,' he told them, 'once I have more evidence. If I think Nairobi is threatened, I shall not hesitate to lay the facts before you.' He turned to Reuben. 'Mister Cole, I would strongly advise you not to return to your farm until we can be assured of your safety and that of your son.'

Reuben chose not to tell Major Webb of his little agreement with Hannah; he simply agreed with the request.

'I will speak with all of you again' – Webb considered this for a moment – 'tomorrow perhaps. We should know a little more by then.' He thanked them all for their continuing discretion in the matter and went in search of Hannah. The sun had just set behind the hills throwing long shadows across the valley in which the camp lay sprawling. Hannah was sitting with Jane Pope. There was no sign of David.

'I have to leave now, Hannah.' He tipped his head forward in a small, formal bow. 'It was a lovely meal. Thank you.'

Jane Pope stood up. 'Well, if you men are finished, I shall go back to Seymour. Goodnight, Major.'

Webb smiled to himself, knowing Jane Pope's reason for hurrying back was simply to give him and Hannah a little time together.

'Is it serious, Kingsley?' Hannah asked when Jane had gone. The concern on her face was quite evident. Even in the fading light.

He laughed rather unconvincingly. 'No, of course not.'

'Oh, you are such a poor liar,' she told him. 'God help us if you are ever tortured for your secrets.'

'Would that you were my torturer, Hannah. My secrets would tumble from me.'

She blushed and drew her hand away. 'I must return to my guests.'

As she walked into the room, Hannah saw that they were all preparing to leave. They did their best to appear convivial, thanking her for a splendid evening. But the atmosphere had changed, and behind the smiles and good humour a curtain had been drawn to shut out the harsh truth. Hannah watched them leave and wondered just how much of Major Webb's light-heartedness was designed to keep something from her. She knew that beneath his veneer there was a very worried man indeed.

CHAPTER EIGHT

Reuben did not leave immediately. He waited until the others had left before asking Hannah if David could stay longer. She didn't mind?

'Of course not,' she said. 'He is more than welcome.' She sounded quite happy about it. Reuben was on the point of thanking her when she asked him what had happened after she had left the table with Jane Pope. 'Major Webb wouldn't say,' she told him. 'But I know he's awfully worried.'

Reuben looked at her, seeing the concern in her eyes and knew, somehow, the concern was for others, her father, David, her friends at Nairobi. When the time came, if it came, there would be a need for unwavering selflessness and resolute action. Sacrifice even. He wondered which of these qualities would be asked of her. He had no doubt that Hannah would not be lacking.

'Hannah, until Major Webb has talked with his own people, we don't know how seriously we have to take David's news.' He was making a bad attempt at showing less than moderate concern. 'Remember, David had a traumatic time. And his knowledge of Swahili isn't that good.'

Hannah stamped her foot angrily. 'Don't lie to me, Reuben. David frightened all of you. I could tell.' She flung her arm out, pointing nowhere in particular. 'I knew the moment Jane and I walked back in that room that you were all very worried indeed.'

Reuben was reminded of how perceptive a woman could be, but he battled on. 'Hannah, please, let's wait until Major Webb has learned more.'

She put her hand on Reuben's shoulder. 'Reuben, look at me.' He already was. 'What do you really believe? You were out there with Sergeant Ord. You know as much about the threat as anyone. So please, tell me, what will happen?'

He looked quite sad. But he told her. 'Hannah, I think we may have to leave Nairobi.'

Her eyes danced back and forth across his face. 'For how long?'

He shrugged. 'God knows.'

She lowered her hand and took hold of his, gripping both hands in her small palms. His own paws felt massive and cumbersome, but he felt they belonged there.

'What about you, Reuben?' she asked him. 'Will you leave? Give up your farm?'

He avoided her gaze. 'It may not come to that,' he lied tamely.

'But what if there's danger? Will you leave or stay and risk your life? And David's?' She had moved closer to him and he could feel her warm breath on his face.

'I don't know. I'll leave if I have to.'

Hannah's cheeks flushed with anger. 'Oh, Reuben, you're as bad a liar as Kingsley. You have everything in that farm, your whole life. David's life. Men like you do not walk away from that. You have fought so long and hard for it you are not likely to give it up and say goodbye simply because your life is threatened.' Her grip was tightening as she spoke. She seemed oblivious to it. 'You know you won't leave.'

'Whatever I do, Hannah, it may not be of my own choosing.'

'It will, Reuben Cole; whatever you do will be of your own choice.' Her voice softened. 'I've seen enough of you to know that.' She moved her head back in a gesture that mirrored his own defiance. Or was it pride?

His expression relaxed into a smile. 'Am I that transparent?'

She shook her head. 'No, Reuben, but I'm right.' She moved her hands up to her chest, unconscious of the fact that she was still holding his hands. The hairs on the back of Reuben's neck lifted. 'Something in me makes me feel as though I have known you a long time. David will be like you too.' It was the third time she had mentioned David, showing the same concern for him as she was for Reuben.

'There is something I want to ask you, Hannah.' He had to choose his words carefully, without letting her know what was running through his mind. He had to say this properly. 'If you had to leave Nairobi, would you take David with you?'

135

She didn't answer immediately. She could feel her heart beating beneath her ribs. She had to shut out the images that flashed into her mind, not daring to hold witness to an unimaginable event. 'It may not come to that,' she answered weakly. 'You said so yourself.'

'I know. But if it happens, will you take him with you?'

'If David wants to and if the time comes.' Her words were barely a whisper. She had moved closer to him and he wanted to put his arms around her and draw her to him. The urge in him was so strong and he sensed it was there in Hannah too. For a moment neither of them spoke. They just stood close, their arms the only barrier between them. Hannah's eyes searched deep into his soul. Reuben wanted so much to know if what he saw was the truth; the truth he so much wanted to believe. They were so close it was as if nothing else existed around them. The moment was there; he needed only to seize it.

A voice broke the stillness. It was David.

Reuben stood back from Hannah. 'Time to go,' he said.

They walked back to the house. David was on the veranda with Hannah's father. He had Reuben's hat with him, which he handed to him. Together they all walked to the front gate. Aubrey Bowers was reminded of his absent wife in the way Hannah stood beside Reuben and David. Something about their manner was so natural that he found himself wondering.

Reuben rumpled David's hair as Hannah put her arm around the boy's shoulder. David knew he was staying there that night, but not that he would be a guest of the Bowers for a few more nights yet. Reuben's touch on David's head was a show of natural affection that might have been a kiss had he been the boy's mother. Hannah's touch on David's shoulder was also a show of natural affection, and it remained so until Reuben had gone.

When the two of them turned round, Hannah could see her father smiling. She regarded him curiously. 'And what's amused you?' she asked.

Bowers checked himself and the smile disappeared. 'Oh, nothing my dear; nothing at all. Why?'

'Well, you were smiling.'

'Was I?' he asked, arching an eyebrow. 'I didn't realize I was, Hannah. It couldn't have been anything important.' He turned away so that she couldn't see the smile gathering on his lips again. 'The ways of the Lord passeth all understanding,' he muttered to himself and walked back into the house.

Major Webb rode furiously, his mind concentrated into one, single thought: the defence of Nairobi. Lieutenant Maclean and Sergeant Ord rode with him. When they reached his office, Webb opened his safe and took out a number of reports. Sergeant Ord's was among them. He cleared a space on the desk and set the papers down.

'Right, Sergeant. How many did you estimate were gathering on the Ndorobo Plain?' He shuffled through the reports as he spoke until his eyes fell upon Ord's report.

Sergeant Ord expelled a deep breath through his nose. It was loud and flared his nostrils. 'The camp looked like it held quite a number of *syrits*.' These were Masai army units. 'Difficult to judge, sir, but I reckon they could muster ten thousand.'

'You mentioned Kabarega.' It hadn't escaped Major Webb's attention that those ten thousand Masai, should they attack, would be more than a match for his army of two hundred soldiers.

'Yes, I'm pretty sure it was him I saw through the telescope.' He explained how he had watched the small group from his vantage point on the hill.

Webb scrawled something on the report. 'You said you saw two white men.'

'Yes sir. One of them was Snyder.' He shook his head. 'I didn't recognize the other one.'

'An envoy perhaps?' Lieutenant Maclean offered tentatively.

'Seems likely,' Major Webb agreed. He tapped the desk with his fingers, beating out a gentle rhythm. The two men stood watching him in silence. Suddenly he looked at the two of them.

'Right, the boy said fourteen days. You returned yesterday, sergeant, so we'll count today as day four.'

'Which gives us precisely ten days to prepare for an attack we are not even sure is going to take place,' Maclean said pointedly.

Webb glanced at Maclean. It was an unhelpful comment, but true nevertheless.

'What about Machakos?' Maclean asked, not really expecting

much in the way of an answer.

Webb shrugged. 'I'll go through the motions,' he replied. 'But where they will find reinforcements in the meanwhile. . . .' He left it unsaid. With all the rolling stock gathered at Mombasa waiting for troops from India, they had a snowball in hell's chance of a positive response from Army HQ at Machakos.

'Will we have to evacuate the camp, sir?' Bill Ord asked.

Webb's expression darkened. 'I hope to God it doesn't come to that.' The prospect of evacuation appalled him. It would be utter chaos, but he had to be prepared for it. 'I'll order all the rolling stock back to Nairobi. As a precaution,' he added.

'Shall I call a meeting of the Senior NCOs?' Ord asked.

Webb pulled a watch from his waistcoat pocket, flipped open the guard and checked the time. He closed the guard and put the watch back. 'Tonight, twenty-four hundred hours. In the sergeants' mess.' He ran his fingers through his hair then spoke to Lieutenant Maclean. 'I want you to prepare a complete inventory of our arms and ammunition. I want to know serviceability, readiness, number of fit men, walking wounded, everything. And I want you to send this.' He pulled a signal pad from his desk drawer and scribbled furiously. 'Quick as you can.'

Maclean left. Sergeant Ord asked if there was anything else before he went off to rouse the other senior NCOs from whatever billet they had chosen for the night.

'Yes. Who's out on patrol now?'

Ord thought carefully, trying to recall. 'Sergeant Jacobs,' he said at last.

Webb muttered under his breath. He knew Sergeant Jacob was a reliable man, but his remit was not specific. He could be out there for days yet. Whatever information he brought back, it could be too late. He made up his mind.

'I want you to go out again, Bill. Early tomorrow. I want a better idea of the number of Masai at Ndorobo. Go up to the railhead by train and ride from there. How long do you think it will take you?'

He figured it out. 'Day from the railhead to Ndorobo, day back.' Unlike his last trip he would not have the children with him. It would be a fast ride. He would take Taffy with him. 'Forty-eight hours from now.'

Webb grunted his satisfaction. 'Good. After I have spoken with the senior NCOs this evening, I want you to contact Cameron.' This was the engineer who had brought Reuben and the children back from the railhead. He scribbled out a note on regiment notepaper. 'Your authority.' He handed it up to Sergeant Ord, but held on to it as Ord stretched out his hand to take it. 'No heroics, Bill.'

Ord smiled. 'No heroics, sir,' he promised and took the note. Then he saluted and walked out.

When he was alone, Major Webb sat back in his chair and closed his eyes, his mind turning over the problems that now beset him. He had already made one tentative enquiry to Machakos H.Q. about troop support into Uganda and failed to receive any confirmation. The rolling stock had been sitting at Mombasa waiting for the arrival of troops from India. Webb had no way of knowing why the troops had not come. They were supposed to be on their way. He assumed an argument was raging back and forth between some office-bound colonel at headquarters and another in the field over where troops were required and who had highest priority. But whatever the arguments and suppositions, the fact was that no troops were forthcoming. Which meant the signal he had asked Lieutenant Maclean to send would almost certainly prove to be worthless.

Despite the semantics, Webb knew that if young David's information was correct, an attack on Nairobi would be little short of a massacre. He emptied his mind and began studying the reports on his desk. It was quiet in his office. All he could hear was the sound of his own breathing. The oil lamp burned brightly on his desk throwing out flickering shadows across the papers. His eyes fluttered and he forced them open, concentrating on the written words in front of him. He held each line until he was able to pick out the salient points and consign them to his memory, discarding the frivolous and meaningless. Plans formed in his mind, followed by vague images that began to coalesce into blurred pictures. They drifted in and out of his mind as his breathing became harsher and the words dimmed into an unreadable mess.

There was a sharp knock on the door. His head snapped up instantly as Lieutenant Maclean stepped into the room.

'The inventory, sir.' He slipped it on to the desk.

Major Webb realized he must have fallen asleep. He rubbed his eyes and yawned. The he stretched his limbs in an effort to force some life back into them. He wondered if Maclean had noticed and realized he must have been asleep for a considerable time.

'Thank you, Robert. Read it out, will you?'

Maclean pulled a chair up to the desk and held the inventory so that it caught the light from the oil lamp. He cleared his throat and Webb felt as though some terrible door was about to be opened.

'Two hundred and ten men, fourteen of whom are sick. Seven are definitely incapacitated for seven days or more. Each man, with the exception of ourselves and the senior NCOs, has a Martini-Henry carbine and eighty-five rounds of ammunition.' He glanced up. 'The standard allocation, sir.' He dropped his eyes back to the inventory. 'We have twenty spare carbines in the armoury plus twenty thousand rounds of ammunition, four Maxim guns, two Gatlings and the two Armstrong twelve pounders. We have two hundred shells for each Armstrong and forty magazines for each of the four machine guns.'

Major Webb looked thoughtful. 'How long could we sustain a battle?'

Maclean considered his reply very carefully. 'One hour. Intensive battle that is,' he added as if it made a difference. He put the hastily garnered inventory on the major's desk. It lay like an omen between them.

Webb looked at him. 'Normally we could draw munitions from Mombasa, but the Uganda and Sudan have seriously depleted reserves. I could put a requisition through. . . .' He let the words fall away.

Maclean watched Webb. He could see a man who had just been handed the responsibility of defending a small town with little hope, no, with *no* hope of succeeding, and losing his own life into the bargain. The flickering shadows in the room highlighted the lines of worry on his face.

Suddenly Webb took his watch from his pocket. 'I have to be at the sergeants' mess. Go through those reports while I'm away.' He sounded weary as he pushed his chair back and stood up.

'Wait until I come back, will you?'

Maclean moved round the desk as soon as Major Webb had left and lit a taper from the oil lamp. He lifted the taper to the lamp that hung from the ceiling in a cradle. It flickered into life. Then he sat down and produced a pipe from his pocket. He lit the pipe and sat in Major Webb's chair.

It was about an hour later when Webb stormed back into his office. He was brandishing a reply to his signal to Army HQ at Machakos. 'There is nothing, nothing,' he raged. 'Not one company, not one patrol, not one damn soldier within two hundred miles.' Maclean sat there, his face immobile. Webb jabbed a finger at the signal. 'Earlier intended troop movement cancelled. Use your own judgement should you wish to contact Macdonald.' His eyes were blazing. 'Macdonald? He's about four hundred miles away.' He went back to the signal. 'Will request urgently one thousand men be withdrawn from Peshawar. Imperative. Repeat: imperative you hold Nairobi.' He tossed the signal on to the desk in disgust. 'North India,' he said. 'By the time they reach Nairobi there will be nothing left.'

'If Machakos do not have the reinforcements available,' Maclean told him unnecessarily, 'they cannot help us.'

'I'm well aware of that, Lieutenant,' Webb snapped at him.

Maclean pressed on. 'So is the German government. With our troops dispersed all over Africa and India, their timing is perfect. They have us in a trap and there is nothing we can do about it.'

Webb seemed to sag visibly and dropped into a chair. He stared disconsolately at the young officer. 'I will call a meeting of all senior Nairobi officials and inform them of the relevant facts. I've no doubt they will have their objections and misinformed opinions. They will expect the Army to perform miracles.' He sat forward, bringing his hands together. 'But I think we have no alternative; I shall have to ask them to draw up a plan to evacuate Nairobi Camp and pray to God we never have to use it.'

Hannah went to bed that evening with her mother's letter on her mind. It was clear that her mother had no intention of returning to Africa. It was also clear that she intended that Hannah and Major Webb should be married in England. She thought about the possibilities of a wonderful wedding in Brighton, but soon she began to think about David, her promise to look after him and her gentle scolding of Reuben about a mother's love and understanding. She realized how at odds that was with her own mother's understanding.

She let her thoughts wander as she began to drift off to sleep. Images of Reuben's farm came to her and she could see David. He was standing in a doorway, calling to her. Reuben appeared over his shoulder and beckoned her. She had no awareness of what she was actually doing, but she ran towards them. She was laughing.

Then she saw her mother, sitting in a wooden, upright chair. She was wearing a beautiful embroidered gown and outrageous hat. She was shaking her head and frowning. Her father stood alongside her, grinning. He was wearing a morning suit of long tails and spongebag trousers. Her mother held a bouquet of flowers in her hand.

The vision faded and she was looking into the distance. Major Webb turned and waved. He was moving away. Then she was in the house with Reuben and David. They were laughing and she felt a strange peace.

Suddenly she woke. The room was dark except for the glow of the small oil lamp. She sat up and thought about the dream. Then she turned up the lamp and took her mother's letter from the drawer beside her bed. She read it through again and folded it carefully when she had finished. She sat like that for some time until a tear rolled gently down her cheek. She sniffed, wiped her face with the back of her hand and lay down, the letter still in her hand. She fell asleep, a much troubled young woman.

CHAPTER NINE

A brightening day held little interest for Major Webb as he considered emergency plans with his adjutant. Extra rifle practice had been ordered for the soldiers, battle orders prepared for his senior NCOs, tours of inspection completed and the stratagem of his command re-examined and reconsidered for about the third time. Although signals had flashed between his office and Army HQ in Machakos, the message was still abundantly clear: Nairobi had to be held at all cost.

His day raced by with unrelenting speed, denying him the chance to plan and prepare as fully as a commander should. And as the hands of the clock ticked round to evening he reluctantly readied himself for his meeting with senior officials at Nairobi.

He arrived at the Railway Club to find Reuben sitting outside on the veranda. David was with him. They both got up as Major Webb and his adjutant approached. Webb looked a little drawn as he stepped up on to the veranda. 'Good evening, Cole.' He paused and straightened slightly, the strains of the last few days clearly visible in his body language. 'I presume you are here because you want an answer?'

'I did what you asked,' Reuben replied laconically.

Webb looked down for a moment then returned his gaze to Reuben's face. 'Yes, well. I'm afraid the news is not good.' He said it with a touch of apology in his voice. He looked away, staring beyond Reuben into the club. 'I've arranged a meeting with the Railway Company's senior officers.' Reuben nodded. Everyone knew about the meeting. 'I wondered if you might sit in?' Webb asked. 'I could need you.'

Reuben arched his eyebrows. 'Me? What can a humble farmer have to offer?'

Webb's face remained impassive. 'You're nothing of the sort, Cole. And it's not your rustic skills that interest me.' He gestured towards the door. 'Please?'

The order was succinct and clear. Reuben spoke to David. 'You can wait for me here, David. Or go up to Miss Hannah's. I could be some time.'

David answered by screwing his nose up. He walked over to a chair and flopped into it without a word. Reuben knew he would wait.

The men exchanged glances. 'We're in the Victoria room,' Webb told him.

The Victoria room had originally been named after the Lake in Uganda, the prime objective of the Company. When the club's committee had convened to decide upon a suitable name for their committee room, it was discovered that there was not one single person within the Company they could elevate to that singular honour. And as the Company had been formed by the government to build the railway line, there was no deserving chairman or founder either. On hearing the name of the new room, one senior Company official congratulated the committee on naming the room after their sovereign lady, Queen Victoria. Feeling collectively embarrassed at making so obvious a mistake, the committee decided to say nothing and let everyone believe it was indeed Queen Victoria they had foremost in their minds when choosing the name.

The room was filled with cigar smoke and charged with an uncannily tense atmosphere as Major Webb walked in with Lieutenant Maclean and Reuben. The chatter subsided as each man looked in their direction.

Reuben knew only three of the men there: Joseph Grundy, Seymour Pope and Doctor Markham. The others were all introduced when they were finally seated round the long, oval committee table beneath a portrait of Queen Victoria.

Major Webb sat at the head of the table. On either side of him sat Reuben and Maclean. He looked at the people facing him expectantly. Sitting there were Sir Charles Ruskin, government administrator at Machakos. He had arrived barely one hour earlier on the first train into Nairobi in several days. Uangan Singh, representative for the Commissioner for India State Railways who had travelled up with Sir Charles, and Surajeh Patel, senior *jemadar*, or foreman, at Nairobi.

Major Webb began the task of explaining the nature of the crisis now facing the people, the Company and the countries they represented.

'Gentlemen, by now you will all be aware of the reason I have asked you to come to this meeting, that is, the threat Nairobi Camp now faces from the Masai.'

Doctor Markham puffed at the bowl of a huge pipe, his eyes firmly fixed on the major.

'The presence at such short notice of Sir Charles Ruskin and Uangan Singh imposes upon me the need to be unshakeably convinced of the facts and conclusions I am about to lay before you. To put the whole thing into perspective, it will be necessary for me to remind you of all the incidents that have occurred fairly recently during the construction of this line.'

He spoke then at some length of small, seemingly unconnected disruptions, which had occurred, and built up a picture of a project thwarted by a mixture of bad luck and unexplained disasters. He dovetailed the incidents neatly until he was describing attacks by bands of Masai *ruga-ruga* and the influence wielded over these people by the renegade Dutchman, Piet Snyder.

They listened attentively, each of them intelligent enough not to assume anything without considering all the relevant details and conscious of the need to allow the Major time to put those details to them. Occasionally one of them would ask a question which prompted Major Webb to reveal the nature of intelligence reports he had been getting; reports that led to the conclusion of a slow, but nevertheless a real isolation of Nairobi. He drew much murmuring when he expounded his theory of German involvement, but surprised them when he cemented that theory with the news brought to him by Reuben's son.

While he spoke, Webb noticed Sir Charles Ruskin nodding thoughtfully on several occasions, his expression showing knowledgeable agreement. But it changed to one of surprise and concern when the imperial German government was implicated.

'I have noticed no tension among my men,' Patel said

suddenly, glancing round at the others. He put the question to Major Webb. 'So how can you say these things are happening when my men have not noticed them?'

Webb held his intelligence reports aloft. 'Even with the benefit of these, Mister Patel, even with these, I was not aware of the real nature of the threat.'

'Are they so real, Major?' Sir Charles asked. 'Or is it the military mind overreacting?'

Webb wondered if he had asked the question for the benefit of the civilians seated at the table. Ruskin had a military mind and was well aware of the significance of intelligence-gathering and how important it was for the army to be kept well informed.

'It isn't an overreaction, Sir Charles,' he told him. 'All my information has been carefully considered by my immediate staff. The opinion is a collective one and one I strongly adhere to.'

'Major Webb, you come here with pieces of paper.' Uangan Singh sounded rather acerbic. 'Why do you not bring the men here who bring you these reports? Then we could ask them what they have seen.'

Webb thought it sounded like an opening for cross-questioning. Even his hardened soldiers might wilt beneath a barrage of words from some of the men who held the exalted positions of high office. To bring them here would be a betrayal. He spoke levelly, keeping his voice under control. He never expected this meeting to be easy.

'Those men who bring me these reports are out on patrol now, looking for further evidence of what we already know. Without their eyes and their assessments, we would be blind.' His hand closed into a fist and hovered just above the table. 'They will convince me, you, all of us here, of what action we must take.'

'Sir, there is one among us who has first-hand knowledge,' Maclean pointed out, reminding him of the reason he brought Reuben into the meeting.

Major Webb turned to Reuben. 'Perhaps you would be good enough to explain to these gentlemen what you saw.' He sat down.

Reuben sat up. He felt the men round the table were hostile to the major and wondered how they would react to his own account. To them he was almost certainly a man of no signifi-

146

cance, without political clout. They probably viewed him as some kind of roughneck brought in by Major Webb to support his claim with an isolated account of an incident or tales of terror from the bush.

He knew they were all probably accustomed to careful debate and prolonged argument. Lengthy discussions were always the order of the day and his own story would probably not accelerate their decision. Still, the major had asked him to sit in amongst the men who had the power to make that decision, so he would carry it through and add real knowledge to that power. He began.

'Major Webb has already explained to you what happened at my farm.' He expanded a little on the story, but still kept to the absolute truth. 'When I went after my son, it was with Sergeant Ord and his patrol. They had tracked Snyder up on to the Ndorobo Plain, beyond the Mau Escarpment. The trail led us to a Masai camp. It was huge, gentlemen, absolutely massive.' He made a circular motion with both hands. 'And it enclosed several smaller camps which contain Masai armies. They are known as *impis*. Sergeant Ord told me he had never seen anything like it before in Africa.'

'Could you give us some idea how big this camp is?' Sir Charles Ruskin asked.

Reuben wondered how best to describe it. Something that would convey the same meaning to all of them. He knew exactly how.

'It would dwarf Nairobi, Sir Charles.'

Doctor Markham took the pipe from his mouth. Sir Charles Ruskin closed his eyes and nodded as though it was something he had feared all along. The two Indians looked shocked. Even the two soldiers showed a reaction. Clearly, Reuben's comparison had the desired affect.

Major Webb took over. 'Gentlemen,' he began. 'Sergeant Ord and I have served together since I was a subaltern. He is a tremendously experienced soldier and one whose judgement I trust completely. It is his opinion that the Masai gathered at that camp will number ten thousand.' He had their undivided attention again. 'We know the Masai do not usually gather in large numbers. Unless it is to make war,' he added gravely.

There followed a long silence, which Joseph Grundy broke. His manner was edged with a little uncertainty, perhaps fear, but he was recognizably condescending. He addressed Reuben. 'Look, Cole, I was at the Bowers' home when your son started this scare. I must admit we were all genuinely sorry for your boy's ordeal, but to rely on a child's testimony when he had been subjected to such terror.' He paused for a moment, opening his hands in a gesture of disbelief. 'Well, really, aren't we putting too much' – he considered his words – 'trust, in his account? After all, the conversation he witnessed was in Swahili.' He shrugged. 'How do we know your son has a thorough knowledge of that language? He must have been very frightened when he was in that prison hut. Don't you think it's possible he misunderstood exactly what was being said?'

Reuben could see Grundy's ambivalence was tempered by fear and a reluctance to accept the unpalatable truth. Perhaps they all were. But they needed to concentrate on the facts being presented to them. So far, David's ability to speak Swahili fluently was not a proven fact. He needed to change that. 'Can any of you speak Swahili?' he asked.

Doctor Markham took the pipe from his mouth. 'I can.'

Reuben got up from his chair. 'Give me a minute or two,' he asked them. Then he left the room and returned with David. The boy was clutching his slouch hat to his chest and looked in awe of the surroundings. The light from the lamps pierced the thickening gloom of the tobacco smoke making it more like a scene from a Dickens novel than a meeting room in the heart of Africa. Reuben pulled a chair over from the wall and asked David to sit down. He nodded to Doctor Markham.

'Make no allowances for his age, Doctor,' he said. 'Ask him anything you like.'

Doctor Markham knew David well enough now to be able to put him at his ease. He smiled at him like an old friend.

'*Jambo* David,' he began.

David replied and soon the two of them were conversing rapidly in a tongue none of the others in the room could follow or understand. There was no hesitation between either of them. The men seated round the table watched in fascination as David coped with maturity beyond his years. The conversation lasted five minutes until the doctor raised his hands.

'Enough,' he said in English. 'This boy is a *fundi*, an expert.' He smiled at David, the genuine warmth and admiration showing in his eyes. '*Asante sana.*'

David grinned. '*Asante.*' Then he looked at his father. 'Good enough, mister?' he said.

Reuben found himself beaming in admiration. He felt tremendously proud of David. He wrinkled his nose at David who returned the gesture with a proud smile. He knew he had done well, but he didn't know why. He got down from the table and Reuben took him to the door. David cast a quick, impish look back at the assembled company and closed the big door behind him.

'Well?' Webb asked the doctor simply.

'Like a native,' Doctor Markham answered truthfully. 'I couldn't fault him.'

Major Webb looked pointedly at the company administrator. 'Does that answer your question, Mister Grundy?'

'I'm afraid it does,' he admitted grudgingly.

'Well,' Uangan Singh said suddenly. 'Now that we have all been reassured of the boy's ability to speak Swahili, perhaps we can now get back to the real question.'

'And what is that?' Webb asked shortly.

'If the Masai attacked, then surely your rifles and guns would be more than a match for their spears.'

Webb wondered if the Indian commissioner's representative was being deliberately naïve. Or was he, like others, avoiding the inescapable truth? 'Many of the more advanced and belligerent tribes in Africa, sir, are equipped with rifles now,' Webb answered directly. 'And if, as I believe, the imperial German government is behind them, you can rest assured their weaponry will be every bit as modern as ours.'

'Yes, perhaps,' Singh quipped. 'But they do not have the tradition and discipline of the British Army. I'm sure we could defend ourselves adequately against them.' He spoke as if the detachment at Nairobi were his own. 'After all, Lieutenant Chard defended Rorke's Drift against four thousand Zulus.'

Webb leaned forward, placing his elbows on the table. Maclean watched, a smile tugging teasingly at the corners of his mouth.

Webb closed his fingers together. 'Let me explain something, sir, about the Masai. They are the most formidable fighters on the entire African continent, including the Zulu nation. Their skills are legendary among European armies. They are superbly trained in the art of war. They are not like other tribes; their warfare is uncannily similar to ours. Nobody knows why this is so, or how they learned this type of warfare. They actually fight like the British, in line abreast. Most unreasonable of them, I must say.' That drew a chuckle from Sir Charles Ruskin. 'They may be simple, pastoral folk, but they live only to engage in battle. Forty years ago they laid waste to a vast, populated area on the shores of Lake Nyasa.' His fingers tightened as he spoke. 'They forced an entire armed garrison to flee from the sanctuary of Fort Jesus in Mombasa. I would say that if they have any masters, it is probably the British.' He relaxed and sat back in his chair. 'But we would be two hundred against ten thousand of them. Need I go on?'

Uangan Singh looked subdued. 'No, Major,' he replied quietly. 'You have made your point.'

Webb let him off the hook and looked round at them all. 'Gentlemen, I do think it's important that we understand the nature of the threat and the consequences of our ultimate decision. We need to consider not only the defence of Nairobi, but the dreams and hopes of all the people who are building a future here and a future for the British Empire. We must not let those dreams be trampled in the dirt.' Without turning he pointed to the windows. The sun had set behind the hills throwing a canopy of red over the land. 'A trained army will soon come over that escarpment and there isn't a damn thing we can do to stop them.'

It was a chilling thought and brought a vision to their minds of a gathering storm that threatened to roll across the land like a swarm of locusts, destroying everything in its path. Sir Charles Ruskin broke the inevitable silence.

'So what is it you want us to do, Major?'

Webb looked at each of them in turn. 'I want you to draw up a plan for the immediate evacuation of Nairobi.'

When Reuben stepped out on to the front veranda it was quite late. David had fallen asleep in the chair and his hat lay on the wooden boards where it had fallen from his head. An oil lamp had been lit and it threw a pool of yellow light round the entrance to the club. Reuben stepped out of the lamp's glow and picked up David's hat. The boy stirred and opened his eyes as Reuben put the hat back on his head.

'Come on David,' he said. 'Time we got you home.'

When Major Webb had dropped his bombshell, pandemonium had broken out. Everybody wanted to speak at once and he had some difficulty restoring order. Uangan Singh had described the whole idea as impossible, and Sir Charles Ruskin warned the major that the government would not hear of it. Grundy complained that it would set the Company back years and would probably ensure its collapse. He also said he would not be intimidated by a bunch of natives. But most of what they said was bluff and filibuster.

The arguments raged back and forth until, piece by piece, the harsh realities of Major Webb's argument began to break through, and they could see there was no real alternative but to evacuate Nairobi. After a considerable time the bare bones of a plan were laid and eventually they each accepted a particular responsibility.

Sir Charles Ruskin was to procure sufficient temporary accommodation at Machakos, which would certainly be in tented form, for the entire Nairobi work force. Uangan Singh would assist Sir Charles and be responsible for administering the refugee camp, while Patel was to organize the Indian workforce into a manageable and identifiable list from which Joseph Grundy could work.

Grundy himself would also hold the responsibility for the management of the rolling stock, which would be brought back from Mombasa for the evacuation. Lieutenant Maclean was tasked with drawing up a list of volunteers, together with their particular skills, who were willing to remain behind in support of the British East African Rifles.

Finally the meeting was closed and a further meeting agreed for the next day. Sir Charles Ruskin promised his wife would be sent for to assist with the evacuation of the women and children. It went without saying that Grundy's wife would work alongside Lady Ruskin.

Webb wandered outside. The evening air was warm and clear. He welcomed it. He saw Reuben placing the hat on David's head.

'What will you do now, Cole?' he asked.

Reuben looked over at him and shrugged. 'I don't know really. All I know is farming.' He shoved his hands into his pockets. He knew what the major was getting at. 'What if I offer my services?'

'Attach yourself to us?'

'It's a thought.' On his own he wouldn't make a lot of difference to the Rifle Company, but at least he would be a volunteer, in whatever capacity. 'I seemed to get along with Sergeant Ord. Perhaps I could be of some use to him again?'

Webb stared out over the camp, listening to the sounds of the night. A leopard coughing. Hyenas howling. Croaking frogs and men's voices drifting over the still air. Chattering and laughter, ingenuous and unaware of the danger.

'You certainly proved your resilience,' he told Reuben. 'And your bravery. We can do with men like you. Thank you.' He nodded at David. 'What about him though?'

David was watching them. Reuben knew he would want to stay with him all the time. He also knew it was out of the question.

'I'll ask Miss Hannah if he can continue lodging with her. For now.'

Lieutenant Maclean walked out on to the veranda. He was talking animatedly with Joseph Grundy. He stopped when he saw Major Webb. 'Are you going back, sir?' he asked.

Webb shook his head. 'Not yet, Robert. I promised I would look in on Mr Bowers.' The half lie rolled glibly from his lips. He did not even question the rights or wrongs of allowing himself time to see Hannah in this moment of gathering crisis.

'Well in that case, sir, I will get on with some preliminary work with Mister Grundy.'

Webb pulled his watch from his inside pocket, flipped the guard and checked the time. He studied it thoughtfully for a moment, then closed it up and pushed it back into his pocket. 'I'll be in my office in two hours.'

Maclean saluted, knowing he would be expected to be there when Major Webb returned. He said goodnight to Reuben and winked at David.

'We'll ride up with you, Major,' Reuben suggested when the two men had gone. 'Bit of company.'

He found himself wishing Major Webb had other things to do and guessed that Major Webb felt exactly the same way about him. Webb did not feel exactly the same way; he wished Reuben and his son had never come into his life. Nor Hannah's for that matter.

Hannah was waiting for them when they arrived. Her father had gone to bed. They both asked after his well-being and were reassured that her father was almost back to his old self.

'I'll get supper,' Hannah told them. 'Are you staying, Kingsley?' she asked. Webb felt aggrieved that he needed to be asked, but it was understandable. 'You must be famished, all of you.' She took David's hand. 'Come on,' she said. 'Let's see what Victoria has left in the kitchen.' Victoria always returned to her own, drab quarters in Nairobi Camp as evening fell, but without fail ensured there was sufficient food in the kitchen, already prepared, to feed an army.

The two men settled themselves in comfortable chairs. Major Webb filled a pipe and Reuben lit a cheroot. They sat for a while just contemplating the pleasure they derived from the aroma and taste of the tobacco.

'She's a fine woman, Major,' Reuben said after a while.

Webb could hardly fail to notice the admiration in Reuben's voice. He didn't like it. 'What happened that day?' he asked.

Reuben tried looking ingenuous. 'What day, Major?'

'The day you rescued Hannah and her father from the Masai.'

'I've already told you.'

Webb shook his head. 'No. You told me what you wanted to. What you thought was discreet to tell me. Hannah was attacked as well, wasn't she?'

'Did Hannah tell you that?'

'She didn't have to.'

Reuben had expected it, knowing it was inevitable. These things had a habit of coming out. So he told him.

Webb looked disappointed but felt a mixture of revulsion and admiration. He was appalled by the attack on Hannah and admired Reuben for what he had done.

'She owes you a great deal,' he admitted, trying to conceal his envy.

'Hannah owes me nothing, Major. I'm sure you would have done exactly the same if you had been in my position.'

Webb would have given his commission to have traded places with Reuben. An act of heroism like that would have drawn Hannah to him completely and irrevocably. He now felt that fate had conspired against him; Reuben was a threat to his hopes of winning her. He had seen how close she had become to Reuben and David. In fact, she almost doted on the boy. Webb's own courtship of her had been carefully nurtured and gently matured. Everything correct, nothing hurried. Some of it affected. But now, in the space of a few days, this man had entered her life and appeared to be held in the same esteem as himself. Webb liked Reuben, admired him even. But he found his presence an intrusion and an irritation. As a rival for Hannah's affection, he wanted to declare open war on him. But the present circumstances precluded that.

So, as fate had brought them together, so fate should decide. If they both survived the attack on Nairobi, he would challenge Reuben and beat him to within an inch of his life. But beneath that improbable thought lay a more sinister, uncharacteristic one. Somehow, by his own hand or that of the Masai, Reuben Cole could die a hero's death when Nairobi was attacked.

Hannah returned with David and saved Major Webb from himself. He immediately dismissed his own lack of conscience as a brief, mental aberration and promised he would not think of it again. He kept this up during supper where the conversation was slanted away from realities for David's sake.

Later, after Reuben had tucked David up in bed, the three of them sat on the veranda beneath a bright moon. The insects buzzed round the oil lamps and the sounds of the night drifted up the hillside. Reuben lit a cheroot and listened as Hannah fired questions at Major Webb. He did his best to answer them as honestly as he could and, inevitably, he had to tell her of the proposed evacuation of Nairobi camp. They could both see the look of utter astonishment on her face.

'How long will it be for?' she asked.

'Oh, only until reinforcements arrive from India.' It sounded trite, but lacked conviction. Webb knew reinforcements would never arrive in time.

'And until they do you propose to remain here with two hundred men?' she asked incredulously.

'It's my duty,' he reminded her. 'That's one decision I do not have to make.'

'But how on earth can you be expected to defend Nairobi with only a handful of men?'

Webb was beginning to feel uncomfortable; there were people in Nairobi who would swear he was mad to remain. They would probably accuse him of seeking personal glory and risking his men's lives in doing so, which of course was not true. They would forget he was a soldier and that his orders would be explicit. It was a decision he did not want to have to defend continually because he would inevitably lose his own standing, particularly with Hannah.

'Once the civilians have left, my task will not be so difficult,' he tried to reassure her. 'I can concentrate all my energies on dealing with the Masai.'

'How?'

As a question it was simple and direct, and Webb couldn't answer it. At least, he wanted to answer, but how could he tell her that he had no idea?

Reuben could see the major's dilemma. He took the cheroot from his mouth and blew a stream of smoke into the air. 'There might be a way,' he said. 'Depending on what form you think the attack might take.'

'That's always debatable, Cole,' Web answered. 'Military commanders do not usually have the enemy's confidence. Still, I'm prepared to listen. How would you do it?'

'Well, I'm not a military tactician, Major. But it's clear to me that they will have to cross the Rift Valley. The easiest route is to follow the railway line.'

'I have already figured that out for myself.'

Reuben went on, unabashed at Webb's little flash of temper. 'I suppose you must have done. But that's where you can stop them.'

Webb mimicked Hannah's bluntness. 'How?'

So Reuben unfolded his idea. And as Major Webb listened he began to realize the supreme effort it would require and the sacrifice involved. His mind was riveted on the extraordinary possibility of success and he listened with fascination as Reuben literally talked him into a corner. He felt humbled to think that this man, towards whom he felt quite alienated, was persuading him to make the singular most far-reaching decision he would ever make in his life.

And quite possibly the most shattering decision in the history of Africa.

Reuben finished. He put the cheroot back in his mouth and waited.

'You realize the enormous gamble we would be taking?' Webb asked him. 'And what we would lose if we fail?'

'If you try to make a stand here in Nairobi,' Reuben answered, 'you would lose anyway.'

Hannah sat motionless, her mind reeling from the enormity of Reuben's suggestion. 'There's no guarantee it would work, Reuben.' Her voice caught in her throat. Her fear was evident. 'You would have no control over it.'

Major Webb had discounted that possibility and was now thinking earnestly of the chances of success. The thought was as tempting as it was teasing. 'If we could evacuate Nairobi early enough,' he said, largely to himself. 'It would certainly give us time to prepare.'

'How long would you need?' Reuben asked.

He shrugged. 'Oh, two or three days. I'm not sure. Lieutenant Maclean would have to advise me.' It was clear he was now working out the rough details in his mind. He glanced up. 'You know, the evacuation shouldn't really impede us.'

'There's no reason for people to know. If that's possible,' Reuben offered.

'Oh, for goodness sake!' Hannah snapped. 'All you will achieve is a grand sense of panic.' She reached out and touched Major Webb on the arm. Her fingers closed tightly around the sleeve of his uniform. 'You cannot go along with this madness, Kingsley,' she implored him. 'You will not be able to keep something like this from everyone. All you will achieve is to transmit your own fear of what is coming. You'll probably end up killing more people this way than the Masai.'

Webb ignored her. 'It will be important to get everyone away as quickly as possible.'

Hannah lifted her head, tilting her chin in a small, defiant gesture that Reuben had seen before. 'Well, I think the whole idea is preposterous,' she declared. 'I for one will not be leaving Nairobi. I shall stay.'

Reuben looked astonished. 'You didn't object yesterday, Hannah. I warned you it might come to this.'

Major Webb picked up Reuben's involuntary slip. 'Well, seeing that you were informed of this before anyone else, Hannah,' he said quite stiffly. 'Why the sudden change of heart?'

'Because it has occurred to me just how bizarre this whole charade really is.' She sounded quite angry. 'There will be whole-sale panic. I just cannot go along with it.'

'Hannah, you have to go to Machakos with the others.' Reuben said it quietly but firmly.

'This is my home, Reuben. Give me one good reason why I have to leave.'

There was a fatalistic look in his eyes. 'You have no choice.'

Hannah's eyes widened in anger. 'Oh? I think I have the right to make that decision myself.'

'No, Hannah, it's not yours to make,' he snapped. 'You have to go to Machakos.'

Hannah squeezed her hands into tiny fists. 'I am staying,' she said firmly.

'No, Hannah,' Webb declared calmly. 'You are going.'

Hannah glared at him furiously. Then she made a noise expressing her contempt for the two of them and stood up. 'Then there is absolutely no point in discussing the matter further. Goodnight!' And she stormed off into the house.

Reuben jumped up and put a restraining hand on Webb's shoulder as he was about to rise. 'It's my fault. I'll go after her.' He was gone before Webb could stop him.

Hannah was leaning against the dining-room table. One hand stretched down to its polished surface for support. The other she held to her face. She had her back to him.

'Hannah, I must talk to you.' Reuben stood away from her, his arms held forward in supplication, his mind in turmoil. He so much wanted to take her to him and hold her tight.

'What can you possibly say now?' She spat the words out.

'It's about David. You promised to take him to Machakos.'

'I did no such thing,' she said angrily, spinning round to face him.

Reuben was suddenly bewildered by Hannah's reaction. The prospect of securing David's future against such uncertainty was quickly evaporating, and his dilemma would only serve as a wedge between them. There was no way he could leave his son to take his chances in the evacuation by himself. Hannah was the only one he trusted to look after David and her prevarication troubled him deeply.

'Hannah,' he said softly, stepping closer. 'I truly believed you would be taking David to Machakos.'

She stiffened. 'I cannot. Not without knowing.'

'Knowing what?'

She didn't answer. How could she? How could she tell him of her deeply unsettled feelings? That the thought she might never see him again troubled her beyond belief. That her feelings for him were so undeniable that the conflict between them and what she thought she felt for Kingsley Webb was tearing her apart. She thought that by refusing to leave Nairobi it might, by some peculiar turn of fate, mean that she would still be part of his world; part of him and David. But Hannah knew she was clutching at straws. Her obstinate refusal to leave was just an excuse to put off that moment when she knew she would never see him again. This madness would rob them all and she hated it. And in her hate and desperation she was hitting out at those who could not properly defend their actions or reasons. It was unkind and she knew it, but she couldn't help herself.

Reuben reached out for her, gently pulling her to him. He could feel the tension in her body. 'Hannah, I want David to be with you. He has grown so fond of you. If anything happens to me, he will be lost. Nobody should let a boy be punished as he has, so why punish him again?' He tightened his grip on her arms. 'Please, Hannah. You are the only person in the world he can turn to.'

She looked at him through tears of anguish. 'Reuben, why must I? Why do you ask this of me?' She turned her face away.

He pulled her gently again. 'He is all I have. Please.'

'I shall be needed here,' she said without conviction.

'No, you are needed with people like David.' She said nothing.

He put his hand on her chin and turned her face towards him. 'Hannah?'

She lifted her head. 'I will see David reaches Machakos and is placed in safe hands.' Then she shrugged off his grip and walked from the room.

CHAPTER 10

Aubrey Bowers had no reason to feel at peace with the world. So much had been promised, but now it seemed it was all no longer to be. Where he should have been cherishing the prospect of his wife's return to Nairobi, and Hannah's betrothal and forthcoming marriage to Major Webb, he now saw his world, and therefore his happiness, crumbling around him. His wife's decision to remain in England indefinitely had perplexed him. He had no desire to leave Africa, particularly Nairobi, but now his actions were to be precipitated by others. He worried for Hannah too. She had seemed so happy with Major Webb. Marriage between them had been a foregone conclusion by most people, including himself. But now his daughter was in torment and only a blind father would have been unable to see it. Reuben Cole had stepped into her life so dramatically it had rocked the foundations of her very existence. He had considered writing to his wife and insisting she return, in the hope that her presence would restore some balance, but he had dismissed the idea as churlish and unrealistic. Now it was academic in view of the events unfolding.

He got up from his favourite chair. The house was quiet except for the lilting sound of Victoria singing in the kitchen. The sun was low but he could feel its warmth through the early morning air. He had decided to go down to the small church, perhaps to draw some strength from the good Lord and pray for all their souls. He knew their future was in doubt and he needed wisdom and strength to guide him. He decided to ask Hannah to drive the carriage, something he would normally have done himself.

He felt stronger now. The last few days he had allowed himself to be lulled into a sedentary pace, but now the shock of everything was concentrating his mind and he had to disregard any lingering discomfort from his injuries that he might feel. There was the Lord's work to do.

He went out into the garden in search of Hannah. She was usually there in the early morning, just after breakfast, cutting flowers. The gardener told him he hadn't seen 'Missy Hannah' yet. Bowers went back into the house and to Hannah's bedroom. Her door was ajar and he could see her sitting at her dressing table. He pushed the door gently. Hannah didn't move. She was just sitting there motionless, staring at her reflection in the mirror, her mother's letter in her hand.

He knocked softly. The sound startled Hannah and she jerked her head round towards the door.

'May I come in?' he asked.

She smiled. 'Of course.'

He moved a chair away from the wall and sat down beside her. She didn't look at him.

'Something is wrong, isn't it Hannah?'

She glanced at him quickly and shrugged. 'No, what makes you think that?' She didn't sound very convincing.

He pointed at the letter in her hand. 'Your mother's letter.'

She looked down at it. 'Oh, no,' she said hurriedly, and put the letter on the dressing table. 'I was just thinking about, well, everything really.'

He leaned forward and took her hands in his. 'Has your mother given you her blessing?'

She tried to look at him but looked down instead. She bit her bottom lip and nodded.

'And now you are not sure.'

She shook her head. He held her hands tightly. She looked up, her eyes glistening. 'Is it that obvious?'

'No,' he told her truthfully. 'Except to me.'

She dropped her head again. 'I was happy. At least, I thought I was. Everything was so. . . .' She hesitated. 'Well, so right. Do you know what I mean?'

'Oh yes, I understand perfectly.'

She closed her fingers around his. 'What shall I do, Father? How will I know what's right?'

'Your heart will tell you that.'

'But I don't want to hurt anyone,' she answered imploringly.

He put his hand to her face, touching it like a fragile, delicate flower. 'Somebody will get hurt, that's inevitable Hannah. But you must never blame yourself. You cannot direct your love at the person you believe is the right one. Our Lord guides us along paths we neither know nor understand. We have no choice but to follow.'

'This is not the Lord's doing, Father.'

'Who can tell?' He dropped his hand. 'How long is it since we all believed our lives to be happily balanced? Our future mapped out so perfectly? Now look what has happened: your mother is obliged to remain in England indefinitely, perhaps for good. And if so it means I may have to return. Then what will you do? Marry Major Webb and live in India or return with me to England?' She looked at him, her expression deep and strained. 'I know, Hannah. Or will you remain here in Africa because you are in love with Reuben Cole?'

He sat back in his chair, his head nodding gently. Hannah was looking down at her hands, which were clutched tightly in her lap.

'But in the end, Hannah, the decision may never be yours to make. Some might say it's in the hands of fate. I would say it's in the hands of the Lord.'

'It still doesn't tell me what I should do,' she muttered.

He reached forward, taking her hands again. 'Look, I am going to the church this morning. I want you to come with me, drive the carriage. We shall pray together and ask the Lord to show us the way. Open your heart to him, my child, and he will listen.'

Hannah smiled briefly, reached forward and kissed him on the forehead lightly. 'Very well, papa, but give me a little while.' She sighed heavily. 'I'll meet you in the garden.' She picked up her mother's letter as he stood up to go. 'Did you know mother had given me her blessing?' she asked.

He nodded. 'She told me in her letter.'

'And what do you think?'

'I'm not going to tell you what I think. It would be wrong of me.' He winked at her. 'But I will if you make the wrong decision.'

Reuben stood at the edge of the crevasse and looked up at the towering rock face. It appeared to have suffered considerably more than when he had last stood there, almost certainly as a result of the tremendous pressure of water behind it and the earth tremors trundling out from Mount Longonot in the distance.

Lieutenant Maclean stood beside him staring at the vertical fissure that ran from its peak to somewhere below them. Water poured through the fissure and a fine mist ballooned upwards from the depth of the cavern. The second crack had reached the top so that it appeared as if a massive wedge had been hammered into the rock to hold back the awesome power of the lake.

'Oh my God,' Maclean uttered with deference. 'You were right, Cole; a sleeping giant indeed. Unimaginable power and destruction.'

A sergeant stood beside them who Reuben had only met that morning. He was studying the rock face thoughtfully. Maclean spoke to him. 'Well, Sergeant Hawk, what do you think?'

'Difficult to judge really, sir,' Hawk replied carefully. He had been in the army too long to commit himself. 'Couple of days at least I should think. Maybe more.'

Maclean looked up at the sky and then across the vast panorama of the Rift Valley. 'Two days?' His head began to bob up and down as he came to a decision. 'Right, Sergeant Hawk,' he said at last, 'bring the men and equipment up.'

They left the sergeant to organize his working party and walked to the top of the rising ground until they were out on top of the rock face. In front of them the ground stopped suddenly where it had been ripped open by the volcanic tremors. The shift in layers of granite and sandstone had opened up a gap that bore away from them like a giant furrow, angling downwards from the lake. They peered over the edge and it was like standing on the edge of a precipice. Reuben felt an uncanny urge to launch himself off into space. An urge he resisted.

They could see well into the crevasse. At the point where they were standing it was about thirty metres wide. As it ran away from them it narrowed until it petered out about three hundred metres away. The sides had crumbled to send an avalanche of rocks and trees to the bottom. And below them the spray rose from the cascading water beneath the colourful arch of a magnificent rainbow.

In the distance the railway line was clearly visible. The train on which they had travelled from Nairobi was like a child's toy. Beyond the line, far into the distance, was the legend of Mirambo's devil kingdom, shimmering in the haze so that it danced and moved. Reuben knew the water seeping from Lake Naivasha flowed beneath the railway bridge towards that place. If they released this sleeping giant it would rip the heart out of the valley and ram it into the choking bottleneck at Hell's Gate.

They turned to look at the lake. The ground sloped gently into the water. There was no indication on the surface that the water was bleeding away. A squacco heron picked its way carefully among the beds of papyrus reeds searching for food, ignoring the pied wagtails that bobbed from one lily pad to another. A flash of shimmering blue and red announced the fleeting passage of a malachite kingfisher, its scintillating plumage dazzling against a background of purple lotus flowers. A black crake poked its head from the reeds and then disappeared as quickly as it had come, leaving no sign of its presence.

Around the shores of the lake the flat-topped trees provided sanctuary for thousands of birds, and from somewhere among them the vibrant hammer of a woodpecker rifled like gunfire across the waters of the lake. The scene had majesty of its own, a regal quality that demanded their attention so they might forget, for a moment, the reason they were standing there.

Sergeant Hawk came up the slope with some men and began a detailed examination of the rock face. After a fairly lengthy process he was eventually suspended by ropes and carefully lowered over the side. Reuben and Lieutenant Maclean watched in silence as he scrambled from one fissure to another, supported by the ropes, carefully searching out cracks into which he could thrust his arm. Sometimes he would only manage to get his fingers in a crack, or perhaps just his fist, but he continued searching, moving like a fly over the cliff face. He was oblivious to the conditions as the water cascaded over him from the lake, so intent was he on the task at hand. When they finally hauled him to the top of the crevasse, he was like a drowned rat.

Maclean waited patiently until the sergeant had detached himself from the ropes. He removed his uniform and someone threw him a cloth. He caught it and began to rub himself down.

'Well?'

Hawk nodded confidently. 'It can be done, sir.'

As if in warning, Mount Longonot suddenly rumbled. They could all sense a measure of strain beneath the yellow sward of the valley. Reuben thought of the wedge of rock immediately beneath them and an involuntary shudder ran down his spine. He could imagine the rock weakening under the enormous pressure of the water, finally to crack wide open and send them all plummeting to their deaths in the crevasse. The men who would eventually be clinging to that rock face would also feel that fear, knowing they were so close to being crushed instantly to death.

Maclean started involuntarily and looked around wide-eyed at the mountain as it crackled and sent another shiver into the valley. 'Right, Sergeant, let me know the pattern of charges you intend to set.' He saluted and started off down the slope, anxious to get away from that forbidding place.

They rode quickly down from the higher ground. The heat from the valley floor seemed to charge up and meet them. In the distance Maclean spotted a patrol heading west. They were the only people in the entire valley.

And who else but fools would be there, he wondered, waiting for the gathering storm to shrug off its sloth and rise up?

Waiting for a cataclysm that no man would ever want to see.

David came running to meet Reuben as he stepped down from the train. He was excited and greeted him with the talk of going to Machakos. For a boy, it was a great adventure. When Reuben had explained the reason for going there, he had lied unforgivably, neither having the heart nor the desire to tell David the real truth.

He lifted David's hat and ruffled his golden hair. 'Now, what have you been up to while I've been gone?'

'Helping Miss Hannah,' David told him, straightening his hat.

'Have you been good?'

'Sort of,' David answered dismissively. He craned his neck and looked up at Reuben, squinting in the bright sun. 'Miss Hannah's waiting for you.'

They reached David's horse and Reuben swung him up into the saddle. David pointed along the track. 'There.'

Hannah was standing a little way from the line, just beyond the station limits. Reuben still had his hands on David's horse when he followed the boy's pointing finger. He dropped his hands without thinking and looked at her in pure astonishment. He could sense that familiar feeling rising beneath his ribs.

Hannah looked absolutely stunning. She was wearing a dress of white, embroidered cotton. Woven into the fabric round the neck of the dress was a simple ribbon of pink. Her bonnet was of the same colour but had a white, lace thread around it. Her gloves matched perfectly and she was holding a pink and white parasol.

'Go and fetch my horse, David,' Reuben ordered, his voice barely discernible.

David looked down from the saddle at his father. 'What?'

Reuben cleared his throat. 'My horse, David. Go and fetch it.' He smacked the rump of David's horse with the flat of his hand and walked towards her. The unsettling feeling inside him refused to move.

'Hello, Reuben,' she said when he reached her. 'Would you mind walking with me?'

He fell into step beside her. He had wondered if he would see Hannah again after her outburst the previous evening.

'It's nice to see you, Hannah.'

'I want to apologize,' she told him without preamble. 'My behaviour was unforgivable. I had no reason to refuse your request,' she explained. 'I'm sorry.'

He laughed. 'You make it sound so formal.'

'Do I?' She stepped sideways as two young black children went scurrying past, laughing as they chased each other. She watched them for a moment. 'I wasn't thinking properly yesterday. Perhaps it was the shock. You know; Major Webb's news.' She glanced up at Reuben quickly, and then looked ahead again. 'But today, well, I think it would be uncharitable of me not to take care of David.'

Reuben was so relieved he wanted to shout for joy. But instead, naturally, he simply thanked her. 'He will need somebody who is close to him,' he told her. 'And he really does like you.'

She looked back at him, her face shaded by the parasol. 'We do get on rather well, I must admit.'

'What made you change your mind?'

She looked away. 'Oh, I don't think I ever intended abandoning him.' She glanced downwards. 'I don't know Reuben. My father usually blames the Lord for uncharacteristic changes of heart.' She laughed gently. 'When they are his of course.'

Reuben was aware of her closeness. There was something quite special, personal almost, in the way they were walking together – unhurriedly, intimately. She smelt so fresh, as though she had just stepped out of the bath. And in amongst all the heat and the hustle and bustle of the rail camp, it was as if they were all alone.

'And what about *your* change of heart, Hannah?' he asked her. 'Will you blame the Lord for that?'

She stopped and faced him. 'Reuben, for the first time in my life I am truly afraid. Oh, not like the fear I felt when those savages attacked me. But this. . . .' She hesitated. 'This is different. It's as if my whole life is opening up into a picture that is so clear I can reach forward and step into it. Become part of it. It promises so much and yet I feel now that I will never reach it.' She put her hand on his arm. 'I'm frightened, Reuben. I pray to God for strength and seek wise words from my father. My faith tells me I must never weaken; never give up hope, but to fight and to pray.' She paused for a brief moment. 'I think that is why I behaved the way I did last night. Can you understand that?'

He took her hand and tucked it beneath his arm. They continued walking. Hannah made no attempt to remove her hand. David cantered up behind them with Reuben's horse in tow. He slowed to a walking pace, keeping behind them.

'Yes, I can understand that,' Reuben told her. 'We all experience a mixture of emotions. We all know what they are: love, hate, fear, jealousy, happiness and sadness too. We have the capacity in our hearts for all those things whether we understand it or not. But we sometimes forget we have tenacity as well.'

She leaned a little closer to him and smiled. 'You should be a preacher, Reuben. Perhaps I would learn under your guidance.'

'We would have to be together for that to happen,' he replied.

She put her hand to her neck and fingered the pink ribbon lightly. She coughed to mask the dryness that had suddenly afflicted her throat. Reuben guessed that his remark had struck a chord and unsettled her, so he switched the conversation to a more topical, if mundane, subject.

'Has Lady Ruskin arrived from Machakos yet?' he asked.

'I'm not sure.' Hannah seemed relieved to talk of something else. Her voice lightened. 'We've all had a message from Jane Pope asking us to attend a meeting this afternoon. Perhaps Lady Ruskin will have arrived by then.'

'I expect that will be about the evacuation,' he said. 'There's going to be an awful lot of work involved.'

She pulled a face. 'How do you evacuate two thousand people easily?'

Reuben just shook his head. 'You don't. You simply plan it and hope you can pull it off without too many problems.'

'I don't wish to sound unchristian, Reuben.' She lowered her voice so Reuben had to stoop a little to hear her. 'But I think it would be a lot easier if we were dealing only with Europeans.'

'Meaning?'

'Well, we are so much more disciplined. More practical.'

Reuben could imagine what Uangan Singh would have said to a remark like that, particularly as it was mainly Indian workers who were building the 'British' railway line.

'Well,' he answered, tongue in cheek, 'I'm sure the army will sort out any problems you have with the natives.'

She laughed and slapped him playfully on his arm. 'Oh, I'm sorry Reuben; I sound such a prude, don't I? Forgive me?'

He smiled. 'Forgiven.'

'Mind you, Reuben, it's as well talking about the Army helping, but Major Webb and his men are far too busy.'

'I'm sure he will detail some men to assist with the evacuation,' Reuben wondered out loud.

'And what about you, Reuben,' she asked, the humour gone from her voice. 'Will you help?'

He hesitated before answering. 'No, I shall be gone tomorrow.'

That stopped her immediately. The disappointment showed quite clearly on her face. 'What do you mean?'

He didn't want David to hear any of this conversation so he

dropped his voice a little. 'I don't want to leave at all,' he admitted. 'But you must understand that the longer I wait around here in Nairobi, the harder it will be for me to say goodbye to David.' The strain was detectable in his voice. 'I will be joining Sergeant Ord tomorrow as a member of his troop. I volunteered my services to Major Webb.'

He closed a hand over hers and she could feel the tension there. She herself was beginning to feel sad.

'You see, Hannah,' he went on. 'I want to stay here with David, but soon we will have to part, and that's going to kill me. I mustn't drag it out.' He was shaking his head. 'It has to be a swift break. By going like this, I can pretend I'm coming back. I hope I am. But if I remain here, I have to leave him. I don't want to.' He stopped then and just looked at her. There was despair in his eyes and he was no longer making sense. Hannah rescued him from his dilemma.

'You will come to dinner this evening, won't you? After my meeting?'

He nodded. 'Yes, of course I will.' He was thankful for the tactful diversion.

'Then be sure to bring David early so I can wash him,' she joked. 'I'm sure he will pick up plenty of dust and dirt now that he is going to spend the rest of the day with you.'

His mind relaxed and his face beamed. It was almost childlike. He felt quite pleased with himself now. His relationship with Hannah seemed so natural now, not at all affected.

'Yes,' he said thoughtfully, 'I must make the most of it.'

That evening they sat together on the small veranda talking against the background of noises that emanated from the bush. The nocturnal creatures uttered their weird and ghostly sounds, sounds that heralded an uneasy peace, like the calm before the storm. From where they were sitting, the camp was clearly visible in the moonlight flooding the valley. Lights burned from all places, twinkling through the canvas folds of the tents and from the open cooking fires. There was a sense of tranquillity out there; everything was in its right place, God was in his heaven and all was at peace with the world. They both felt content and neither wanted the idyllic evening to end.

Hannah had invited Major Webb to dinner but he had sent his

apologies. She understood why he had declined but it had left her with a shameful feeling of relief; it meant she would have Reuben to herself. Her father had an unctuous look on his face when he had been informed at the dinner table.

When the meal was over, he had made his excuses and retired to bed with a good book. It hadn't occurred to Reuben or Hannah how events had contrived to leave them alone, and the chaplain had no wish to interfere with God's work.

Reuben had spent some time with David before seeing him off to bed. Hannah had planted a huge kiss on David's forehead, which left him with a big grin on his face. Reuben had roughed his hair and kissed him lightly. It wasn't long before he was sleeping soundly and Hannah and Reuben were able to walk out on to the veranda alone.

They sat for a while, talking of the past, the present and an uncertain future. Reuben's chair creaked as he stood up.

'Time I left.'

Hannah got up from her chair. 'Why don't you come back tomorrow evening and see David?'

He took her hands in his. 'I've already explained, Hannah. It's hard enough knowing I may never see him again.'

'You could always come to Machakos, Reuben.' He could feel her hands tightening. 'You don't have to stay and fight the Masai until they kill you.'

He put his hands on her shoulders and pulled her gently to him. 'If there is no hope, no real hope, I may get out. I'm sure Major Webb will order a withdrawal if there are too many casualties.'

'Oh tosh, Reuben; you know you will never run away.' She said it in a spirited way but there was a hint of exasperation in her voice.

'He who fights and runs away,' he reminded her.

She glared at him, her eyes wide and on fire. 'Don't joke with me, Reuben. You know you will stay until the last man drops. You men all have boyish notions of heroism.' She had moved so close to him that he could feel the soft curves of her body. As she tried to speak again she choked back a sob.

He shook her gently. 'Hannah, please.'

Then suddenly, she was in his arms, willingly, passionately.

Melting into his body with a fierceness that threatened to consume him. He could feel the thrust of her hips wantonly searching him out, and the tears on her cheeks were running freely and unashamedly. Then she stopped as suddenly as she had started. She pulled away abruptly. 'Go now Reuben,' she pleaded. 'Please go.' She kept her face down, not daring to look at him.

He hesitated for a moment. Then he picked up his hat from the small table and stepped from the veranda. He was gone quickly as the night swallowed him up. She could hear the sounds of his horse's hoofs hard on the dirt road, and the tears fell freely from her face on to the wooden boards.

When he had gone and she could no longer hear him, she turned to go back into the house. A figure moved in the shadows and walked into the light. He stood there defiantly, watching her. Hannah gasped and clutched her hand to her chest.

'Oh God,' she whispered. 'How long have you been there?'

It was David.

CHAPTER ELEVEN

Sergeant Hawk's men began work on the rock face with an affected cheerfulness, their comic utterances a counter to their real fears and the daunting task confronting them. The work of setting explosives into the rock face would normally have been done with machine hammers, but the situation and the conditions meant they had to work by hand using steel chisels and sledge hammers. Their apparent good spirits did little to hide the dangers they now faced.

The men worked at the end of ropes, slung like bosun's chairs down the rock face. Water poured down on them continuously making the situation practically intolerable. Two men worked as a team; one holding the chisel, the other wielding the hammer. The chisel had to be driven two feet into the rock. It was hard, back-breaking work.

There were three teams working on the rock face. Those not actually engaged in setting explosives mounted guard or handled the ropes. Three teams working with little respite would each have normally been able to complete three holes in six hours. But changing the teams meant inevitable delays. Sergeant Hawk had hoped to complete twelve holes before nightfall, but at the end of the first day, only nine holes had been completed.

At first the weather had been kind to them, with clouds occasionally obscuring the sun, but the second day brought a clear sky and a burning sun. It meant that Sergeant Hawk was compelled to bring his men up more frequently to quench their thirsts, despite the water running freely from the rock face.

Lieutenant Maclean arrived early that morning. He had spent

his previous evening checking his mathematics, working by ability, guesswork and intuition, praying that Hawk's estimate had been right and his own figures correct; they had to set enough explosive charges to rip the heart out of Lake Naivasha.

Soon the men were taking water bottles down with them on to the rock face but found them an encumbrance, so they were forced to give up the idea. It meant each of them suffering their discomfort resolutely and labouring on until it was time to rest. Then they were pulled to the top by their comrades where they could plunge into the lake and later, rest beneath the shade of the trees. And as they lay there they could hear the sounds coming up from the precipice; the clink, clink of steel upon steel. Each man listened to the rhythm of the hammers and knew how the hammer blows of the sun were relentlessly punishing their comrades on the rock face.

They toiled on through the second day getting slower by the hour. Sergeant Hawk harassed and cursed them, but even he found the effort too much in the appalling conditions. In the end he gave up and simply coaxed and encouraged them. But by nightfall they had only managed to complete another eight holes.

Dawn on the third day saw the return of the cloud. In the bleak light they were roused from their sleep and urged to work by Hawk. Behind them the lake was awakening and bringing the wildlife out on to its misty surface. The men ate and washed quickly and were soon hanging from their makeshift slings over the precipice.

The wind returned and funnelled into the crevasse, building up against the rock face with a chilling fury. It swung them round on their bosun's chairs so they were being buffeted mercilessly, crashing continuously into the hard rock face. And when the rain suddenly burst from the sky, it fell upon them with staggering fury. They slipped and cursed and fought the wind and the rain. Hour after hour, struggling beneath the onslaught until, with the light fading quickly, the last man was hauled to the top. Mercifully, their gargantuan task was almost complete.

They slept like dead men that night. Nothing disturbed them. The guards patrolled watchfully as they slumbered. The nocturnal sounds of the lake mingled with others that night, and the only alien sound on the edge of the forest was the snoring of the men as they plundered the treasure trove of sleep.

Major Webb arrived the following morning. He looked tired, his face drawn, his expression betraying a man with so much on his mind. On the rock face Sergeant Hawk and his team were setting the explosive charges. Maclean was still there. When he saw Major Webb riding up from the valley with four soldiers he walked out to meet them.

Webb listened carefully to Maclean's account of their progress as they made their way back up to the rock face. He surveyed the granite cliff in a rather perfunctory manner. Not because he wasn't interested, but because he was relying on his adjutant's ability. They talked for a while about the morale of the men and their condition; what problems they had encountered on the rock face and when Maclean could expect to finish. Maclean then asked Major Webb how the evacuation was progressing.

Webb answered by turning away and asking him to walk for a while. He thought it best to talk out of earshot. 'We are only just beginning,' he said. 'Damn commissioner insisted all Indian nationals are evacuated first. Naturally the rumours are flying thick and fast but we have started to get them away. That's the main thing.'

'Have you deployed the men yet?' Maclean asked guardedly.

Webb stopped walking and looked out over the valley. 'They moved into position last night under the cover of darkness.' He glanced at his adjutant. 'Damn tricky, but they managed. All we must hope for now is that Snyder's spies didn't see us.'

'What about the twelve pounders?' Maclean asked.

Webb smiled. 'Those too,' he replied. 'And not too soon, I might add; the Masai build-up is just about complete according to the patrols.' He was silent for a while, deep in thought. Then he shook his head gently from side to side. 'Ten thousand of the bastards, Robert.'

Although they had been warned of the likely figure, it still unsettled Lieutenant Maclean. 'Against two hundred, sir.'

'Two hundred and fifty,' Webb corrected him. 'If you include the volunteers.'

'That's a great comfort,' Maclean murmured. 'How long?'

Webb became very grave. 'I wish we knew, Robert.' There was a deep sadness in his eyes. 'But if Reuben's son was right, we have another five days. Would to God we had more.'

Nobody knew what had happened to the days. They seemed to melt into each other. The people at Machakos were slow in building a makeshift evacuee camp, which gave the rumours time to gestate and multiply at Nairobi. Joseph Grundy did his best to mollify the effects of the rumours but the waiting only served to exacerbate the situation and increase the tension. Ill-founded speculation was also a root cause of quick tempers and bad judgement among those charged with the task of evacuating the camp.

And to add to Nairobi's problems was the directive issued by the commissioner for India State Railways, widely believed to be Uangan Singh's doing, that all Indian nationals were to be evacuated first. This decision had infuriated Lady Ruskin who was trying bravely to cope with all the procedural arrangements, and had expected it to be women and children first.

Another decision that drove a horse and cart through Grundy's plans was one of Major Webb's doing; he had commandeered a locomotive pulling two flat cars and a box car for his own use in what he described as 'expediting communication and transport'.

And Andrew Cameron, the Company's engineer who had waited at the railhead for Reuben and the children, was still working at the railhead with the platelayers. This meant another valuable train was in use. Consequently the rolling stock available was reduced to two locomotives pulling two passenger carriages and a box car each. The remainder of the stock had either broken down or been kept at Army headquarters in Machakos at their insistence.

When Joseph Grundy sat down at his desk and pencilled in the number of passengers each train would take, he arrived at the figure of six hundred. Then somebody insisted he make a tour of the camp to see the mountains of personal belongings piling up. When he returned from his small tour, he was furious and summoned Surajeh Patel, the senior *jemadar*.

'Would you leave your home without your personal possessions?' Patel had asked him.

'But dammit man, there's no need for them to take every

vestige they own,' Grundy complained.

'And if they leave most of their possessions behind, who will guarantee they will not be stolen – you?'

Grundy argued but he could see that Patel was not being obstinate; he was merely pointing out the obvious and there was nothing that he, Patel, could do about it.

When the man had gone, Grundy amended the figure to four hundred. Then Lady Ruskin appeared at his office.

'You do realize we require a train solely for the European element?' she informed him.

'Lady Ruskin, we are planning an evacuation, not an excursion,' he said acidly.

'Don't bandy words with me, Mister Grundy,' she answered back at him imperiously. 'I do not expect our people to share a train,' she fluttered a hand towards the window, 'with those people.'

Grundy shook his head. 'You are trying to impose an impossible restriction on me. I cannot do it.'

She almost stamped her foot in a show of frustration. 'Mercy me,' she cried. 'Is it so beyond your sensibilities that you cannot comply with modern decency? Or must I telegraph my husband?'

'Lady Ruskin,' he said carefully. 'It would mean that the women and children, your women and children, would have to leave Nairobi last.'

She shrugged. 'Be that as it may, but we shall leave with dignity and not in the manner of a coolie work force.' She then swept regally from his office and left him sitting there wishing he had never heard of Nairobi.

And so the problems mounted. Grundy was beginning to think he would never succeed. People came to him with claims that entitled them to first place on the evacuation list. Others said they would not go which meant a visit from Major Webb's special detachment to remind them they had no choice. The rolling stock kept threatening to break down permanently and Andrew Cameron was still working from the forward platelayers' camp a few miles from the railhead.

That was a puzzle to Grundy; how Cameron kept his platelaying gang going. He wasn't even sure that the men were aware of the drama unfolding at Nairobi. Cameron had insisted the men had been told, but he also revealed the men had been promised a bonus if they could get the line ten miles out of the Rift Valley before the job was brought to a halt. They had three miles and three days to go to the deadline. Their own evacuation, Cameron assured Grundy, would be swift and completed within a matter of hours when the time came.

But slowly and inevitably it was all falling into place, and the first evacuees were moved out with, according to Major Webb, six of the fourteen days, remaining. Soon, Nairobi Camp would be completely empty.

Major Webb rode into Nairobi Camp to a scene of bedlam. The narrow streets were crowded as most of the inhabitants, carrying large, makeshift bundles, moved their worldly possessions up to the railway station. There were some who had made handcarts and were now labouring in the heavy mud. Some had lost wheels and their clothes and pots were spilled ingloriously all over the ground. They looked pitiful as they scrabbled in the red clay, scooping their belongings up and piling them into the lopsided carts. Screams and arguments were constant companions to these little, personal disasters.

Webb watched disconsolately as he steered his horse through the camp. He felt utter dismay at the shutters covering the small shop windows, blotting out the sunlight and with it the dreams of the entrepreneurs. They would survive, he reasoned to himself, but how much would they lose? And where was that bundle that would be big enough to hold their worldly possessions?

He changed direction, trotting slowly through the Indian bazaar. It was empty now. The stalls were like dark sockets and fragile limbs. The body had been plucked of all its flesh, left to rot and decay. Here and there a flash of colour where the owner had left a small end of *Merikani* cloth. There was a broken chair and shattered clay pots; squashed and trodden fruit, signs of panic. Some had refused to go at first, but eventually the tingling crawl of fear had persuaded them to join the straggling queue of refugees heading up towards the railway station.

He turned into the European quarter. There was little

evidence of panic or fright, but he knew it had been there. He had felt it himself, undeniably, but he wouldn't reveal those feelings. He couldn't. But they were there, bubbling mercilessly beneath the surface.

Webb found Hannah at the Company offices, pouring over lists with Lady Ruskin. David was with them, looking totally bored. Webb knocked on the open door. They all looked up and Hannah's face brightened considerably when she saw him.

'Kingsley. What brings you here?'

He saluted and smiled. 'Good afternoon, Hannah, Lady Ruskin. Hallo David.' He stepped into the office. 'I would like to speak with you Hannah. Alone, if you don't mind.'

The two women exchanged glances. 'Of course, Kingsley,' Hannah replied and got up from the desk, curiosity colouring her face. 'David, would you be a good boy and help Lady Ruskin with these lists? You don't mind, Mary, do you?'

Mary Ruskin had that look on her face that said she understood completely. 'Take all the time you want, my dear. David and I will be fine.' She smiled knowingly at Major Webb.

Hannah followed him outside. She felt strangely tense and could sense that in him too.

'I need to talk to you somewhere quiet,' he told her.

'You mean now?' she asked unnecessarily.

When he nodded she looked around as though she might spot an empty doorway somewhere.

'The church,' she said suddenly. 'Let's go there.'

'Splendid.' He unhitched his horse, clutching the reins in one hand. Hannah took his other and they walked the short distance to the church. It was cool in there, and quiet. The bustle and panic of Nairobi seemed shut out, forgotten. They both knelt briefly before the altar, then sat together on a long, wooden pew.

'Well Kingsley, mysterious Kingsley. What do you want?' She was still feeling strange and her attempt at lightness was only to mask the feeling.

He half turned towards her, his face a mixture of apprehension and hesitancy. 'Hannah, when this is over, I shall be returning to my regiment in India.'

Hannah could hear herself breathing. 'Go on, Kingsley.'

'A signal came through yesterday advising me that. . . .' He hesitated, not sure how to frame the words. 'Well, let's just say that I shall be going back.'

Hannah could guess what was coming but wasn't sure she would be able to cope with it.

'I cannot go back without knowing, Hannah.' His eyes softened and he took her hands in his. 'Hannah, I love you and I know you love me. I want you to be my wife.'

It startled her. It shouldn't have done. She knew how much he loved her. So many times she had heard him say those words. But now, it seemed so sudden and her body trembled. She wasn't sure if it was through anguish or excitement. But the warmth and sincerity in his words touched her deeply, and she knew, for him, the waiting was over. It had to be now and he had every right to expect her answer. Hannah had believed for a long time that when this moment came, she would be so happy. But now, how could she be so sure of her true feelings?

'Oh Kingsley, I know you want me to be your wife.' Her voice faltered a little. 'But we have to wait.'

'No, Hannah, we don't. We can do it now.' His grip tightened and he leaned towards her. 'I want us to marry before the evacuation of Nairobi is complete. Before you go to Machakos.'

Her mouth fell open. 'But that's impossible.'

'It isn't my darling,' he argued gently. 'Not now; tomorrow or the day after I may be dead. I couldn't bear the thought of going to my grave without ever having known your true love.'

Hannah felt her pulse quickening. 'Kingsley, you mustn't ask me like this.'

'I must, Hannah. I have waited for so long. Would you deny me the love I have so dearly cherished and waited so patiently for? Something we have both longed for?'

His words were so near to the truth that Hannah was no longer sure how she truly felt. 'I promised my mother,' she said vaguely.

'Hannah.' His voice softened. 'Your mother wrote to me. I know she has decided to remain in England. She would not hold you from this.'

'It would not be fair to her or my father,' she protested.

'Or to me,' he replied.

She dropped her head and put her hand to her face. The tears were so close. 'Please, Kingsley.' She felt herself weakening, wanting to say yes, because she felt so desperately sorry for him. But was this a shield for her own true feelings, she wondered? Did she love this man enough to marry him but was unable to see that because of the emotive, impassioned way in which he was asking?

Suddenly she looked up in horror. 'Kingsley, I could become a widow before. . . .' She shook her head, fighting back the tears. 'Would you ask that of me?'

'Oh my dearest, I don't know.' He understood the social oblig-ations attached to widowhood, particularly as they were inspired by their own, sovereign Queen Victoria. Could he honestly expose Hannah to that kind of existence? 'Am I being selfish?' he asked.

She smiled and touched his face gently. 'Oh no, my love; you are being human.' She dropped her hand. 'Kingsley, I must be honest with you.' She wasn't sure how to begin really. 'Mother has given me her blessing. I said nothing to you because, well. . . .' She searched for the right way to tell him without sounding unkind. 'The moment was not right,' she said at last, ashamed of her own reluctance.

'Hannah, we could be married whenever we choose.'

She shook her head. 'Yes, but not yet. I know my father would be opposed to our union until later.'

He reached forward and kissed her lightly on the cheek. 'You are mine now, my darling Hannah.'

She turned to say something and their lips brushed. Suddenly they were in each others arms and Hannah's mind and feelings were in turmoil. She pushed him away, gently, quite breathless. 'Now we must go, Kingsley. We both have a lot to do.'

She stood up. He remained seated for a while, looking up at her, smiling. Then he stood up and made her kneel with him facing the altar.

'With my body, I thee wed.'

And together they walked arm in arm out of the church.

The train had stopped just before the bridge. Lieutenant Maclean was sitting with a group of soldiers on the ground beside the box car. An Armstrong twelve-pound field gun had been mounted on one of the flat cars. Where the other one was, Maclean had no idea except that it had been deployed when Major Webb had sent his men out under the cover of darkness. He scanned the horizon occasionally, as if expecting to see where the soldiers had been concealed, but there was little to see in the way of life except themselves and their horses grazing close by.

The hours passed slowly and quietly. A small herd of elephants appeared and eyed them curiously, lifting their trunks to catch the scent. Nothing interested them so they ambled away. In the forest beyond the high ground they could hear the sound of monkeys crashing through the trees; sounds far enough away to be mellow. There was the tap, tap, tap of someone clearing the dottle from the bowl of his pipe, striking it against the heel of his boot. Men laughed, played cards or dozed. Up high the buzzards quartered the sky, wheeling effortlessly in an undefined pattern in their search for carrion. Occasionally the clang of the firebox door on the train disturbed the peace. Steam hissed softly.

Then came another sound. It was a faint clack, clack, clack. Quiet at first, alien. Nobody took much notice although the sound carried quite clearly through the still air. A soldier, lying on his back with his hat over his eyes to shield them from the sun, sat up. He squinted against the brightness and put his hand up to shut out the sun's glare. He stood up, staring along the line, quite motionless. Then he turned and walked over to Lieutenant Maclean. 'Sir.'

He pointed along the track. Maclean glanced up and got to his feet, looking in the direction of the soldier's outstretched arm. The noise was louder now, but its rhythm unchanged. Others began to look, standing and peering along the warped, shimmering track melting into the distance. Then, through the watery haze, they could see the vague outline of a hand car.

'Get Major Webb,' Maclean instructed the soldier.

Major Webb had set up a small observation post on the high ground overlooking the valley. He was only about five hundred yards from the train and was soon scrambling up alongside Maclean who had taken up a position on top of the locomotive.

181

'What is it?' he asked a little breathlessly.

'I'm not sure,' Maclean told him. He squeezed his eyes until they were almost shut. The vague shape gradually became clearer and less distorted.

'Two people. Looks like one of them may be injured.' He looked round at Major Webb. 'Where's Cameron?'

Webb's expression was profound. 'Still up at the forward camp.'

'That could be him.' There was a hint of despair in Maclean's voice.

'We'll soon know,' Webb replied and climbed down from the engine. Dust billowed up from the ground as Maclean landed beside him. They mounted up and called for two soldiers to follow them. The four of them rode swiftly alongside the track.

It was soon evident that the man driving the flat car was indeed Andrew Cameron, but none of them recognized the prone figure lying beside him. Cameron was leaning forward working the driving crank, but the effort looked as if it was too much for him; it was obvious that sheer momentum was the only thing keeping him going. He saw them riding towards them and raised his hand. It was a slow difficult movement, and the effort unbalanced him, throwing him to the floor of the trolley.

Maclean reached him first. He jumped from his horse and ran beside the car, clambered on to it and pulled the brake on. The car stopped and Cameron turned his face up to him. He smiled weakly, his eyes hooding over as he spoke. 'Thank God. I didn't think we were going to make it.'

Maclean cradled the man's head in his arms. He pushed the wet hair away from the deep wound in his forehead. His shirt was covered in blood. Deep red streaks of it had soaked into the cotton twill of his trousers. Patches of it darkened the grey weave of his waistcoat. His arms were red and there was not one inch of white flesh visible on them.

Maclean pulled back the edge of Cameron's shirt carefully, gingerly exposing a wound that was still pumping blood. He looked up at Webb and the two soldiers, his eyes reflecting the horror he felt, and shook his head. He pulled the edge of the shirt back to cover the wound.

Webb unscrewed the stopper from the neck of his water bottle and poured a small quantity of the liquid into the palm of his hand. He touched Cameron's lips and fed him small sips of water. The engineer struggled to sit up, but his strength was ebbing fast. He lay back in Maclean's arms, gasping for breath.

'Take it easy, Cameron,' Maclean urged him quietly. He laid him back gently and looked over at the other figure. Whoever he was, the poor man was dead; probably one of the platelayers. There was a great deal of blood on the body, but the wound running along the back of his head to the base of his neck was enough to convince them that he had been dead a long while.

Maclean got up off his knees and released the brake. He began cranking the handle and the car moved slowly. Cameron's body rocked with the gentle motion. He opened his eyes and smiled weakly. Maclean avoided his stare and concentrated on working the crank.

They reached the train where willing hands took Cameron and laid him inside the box car. There were two soldiers in there with a Maxim gun. A medic attended his wounds knowing the poor man did not have long to live. His breathing was very shallow and his mouth hung open.

Webb knelt beside the dying man and brought his face very close. He whispered softly. 'Can you tell me what happened?'

Cameron's eyes fluttered. 'Many dead.' His chest heaved and he closed his eyes with the pain. 'My *jemadar*.' His head lolled. It was hopeless.

Webb leaned closer. 'Are there any survivors up at the forward camp?' he asked quietly.

Cameron tried to answer but his voice was unintelligible. He moved his head. Webb laid him down carefully.

'Rest now, my friend.' He looked at the others and nodded towards the door. 'If there any survivors,' he said to Cameron, 'we shall find them.'

He joined Maclean outside in the sunlight. He looked deeply sorry. 'He was a fine man. A good engineer.'

'But not a soldier,' Maclean reflected.

Webb considered the implications, not wishing to say anything for a while.

'There will be a train up at the forward camp. If Cameron had been able to, he would have used it. Unless the train was up at the railhead.'

Maclean knew what his commanding officer was thinking. 'And with the unlikelihood of there being survivors,' he offered, 'it means a train that Snyder could make use of.'

Webb began considering risks and chances of success. He made up his mind and looked up sharply. 'You will have to take some men up the line. If there are any survivors, bring them back. If you can bring the train back, fine.' Then he looked Maclean straight in the eye. 'If not, destroy it. We cannot risk leaving something like that which can be of use to the Dutchman and his damned Masai.'

The young lieutenant thought he could see a kind of sorrow in the Major's face. It was almost as though Webb was apologizing for sending him into battle first.

'I will set my field HQ beyond the bridge,' Webb said suddenly. 'Nairobi side.'

They buried Cameron and his *jemadar* and moved out. Maclean deployed his men along the train. The Maxim gun had been switched to the roof of the box car. Inside the car were six riflemen. The field gun crew were in position on the leading flat car and Maclean had stationed himself up front on the footplate. He had decided, after a lengthy discussion with Major Webb, to move up the line as far as possible and if necessary, use the field gun to destroy the train, which was still up near the railhead. Web had not been too happy about that because of the paucity of ammunition, but in the end he had agreed to it.

They had not travelled far across the valley when Maclean saw a patrol riding towards them. It was Sergeant Ord. Reuben Cole was with them. Maclean ordered the driver to slow the train and was leaning out over the weatherboard when Ord's patrol reached them.

'I'm afraid it has started, gentlemen,' Maclean shouted from the train. He told them about Cameron and his foreman. 'We have just buried them at the bridge.'

The train rattled steadily over the track as the patrol rode alongside at little more than a canter. They were heading north-west, up the valley. Ord's patrol had come from the west.

'We haven't seen any Masai yet, sir,' Ord told him. 'But we did engage some Wakamba just west of the escarpment. It could have been the same group that attacked Mister Cameron.'

'Were there many?' Maclean asked.

'Not at first. I thought we could handle them, but Cole spotted a larger group about a mile away. We had to disengage.'

Maclean called out to Reuben. 'Well done, Cole.'

Reuben acknowledged him by touching the rim of his bush hat. 'It's possible they are heading this way, Lieutenant. Probing forward perhaps?'

From what Sergeant Ord had told him, Maclean guessed that Snyder was using the Wakamba tribesmen to explore their forward defences, lamentable as they were, with pinprick attacks. It made it more imperative that Sergeant Ord and his patrol remain with them.

'I might need all the help I can get, Sergeant Ord,' he said.

Ord saluted. 'As you wish, sir.'

Satisfied, Maclean leaned back from the weatherboard and made a circular motion with his hand to the driver. The man wound the steam regulator open and the train picked up speed again.

They reached the platelayers' forward camp and could see immediately the utter devastation. Every tent lay flattened or burned. Wooden tables and chairs lay blackened and charred. Cooking pots had been overturned from their fires, washing lines torn down and the clothes scattered. Where once wooden huts had been were now only blackened and smoking ruins. There was also the sickening evidence of a massacre: dismembered bodies of men cut down in flight, their eyes staring sightlessly from dead sockets. Fear etched into otherwise expressionless faces and their mouths open in the rictus of death. And the vultures waddling through the devastation; their bellies heavy with mortal remains.

The train inched its way slowly through what was left of the forward camp, each man's face set grim as he looked upon the sickening, evil manifestation of Snyder's violence. They looked about them for signs of the attackers but there was nothing to be seen, nothing to be heard but an eerie silence. The fear that had visited that place of death hung over the land like an invisible cloak. The extraordinary sense of it was almost unbearable.

Then Reuben saw something. It was a dark shape, like a pool. It lay on the valley floor covering the yellow grass, settling like a mirage. Reuben stood up in the saddle. He called to Maclean and pointed. Everyone followed his direction. The driver couldn't see the dark shape but an overriding sense of danger brought his hand to the steam regulator and he wound it in a full turn.

Reuben continued to stare. The shape was moving, shimmering and blurring in the coruscating haze.

Maclean stared too. The shape took form and became distinctive, losing its optical illusion and merging into reality.

'Masai,' he said flatly.

It was a large number of advancing, well-ordered men. A Masai army. Like a long, black snake, it slid in disciplined formation along the valley floor.

The driver responded to Maclean's order to bring the train to a halt. Maclean climbed up on to the roof of the cab and stood pensively, his eyes glued to the column. 'Eight miles or so,' he said to himself.

He signalled the driver to move forward and dropped down beside him. 'Sergeant Ord!' Ord came up alongside the engine. 'I want an estimate of the size of that column. It looks like Snyder may have his entire army on the move.'

Ord wheeled away and signalled his men to follow, but before they had moved past the front of the train, a shot rang out. His horse whinnied and reared up, throwing Ord out of the saddle as it crashed to the ground and rolled over, kicking its legs wildly. There was another shot and a bullet clanged against the side of the boiler. It whined harmlessly out into the long grass. Another shot sent a bullet zipping into the side of the flat car. Maclean's men began returning fire from the train. Ord scrambled up on to the footplate beside Maclean as the driver opened the steam regulator to drag the train away from danger. Ord span round on the footplate and leaned out over the weatherboard.

'Over there!' He was pointing towards the western side of the valley. Running towards them and angling in towards the rear of the train were about two hundred men. Another shot brought a withering return of fire from the flat car. Among it was the unmistakable sound of the Maxim gun. The firing stopped.

'Wakamba,' Ord observed laconically.

'Probably the raiding party that murdered Cameron and butchered those poor souls at the forward camp,' Maclean said as he clambered up on top of the tender. 'Put a shell among that lot,' he bawled at the field gun crew on the flat car. Then he shouted down at the driver to slow the train. Almost immediately there was a deafening bang as the gun fired. The shell roared over the heads of the Wakamba and exploded about a mile beyond them.

A shout came up from the flat car. 'Can't get the depression, sir!'

Although the shell had soared over their heads, it had been enough to stop the Wakamba for a while. They had no way of knowing the problem facing the gun crew. After a few minutes they tentatively raised their heads above the long grass and began firing at the train.

Sergeant Ord called out to Reuben to come up alongside the footplate. As Reuben reached him, he was ordered to change places by the sergeant.

'I'm going out there to skirmish with those bastards. Come on man,' he clamoured impatiently, 'give me that damn horse.'

Reluctantly Reuben changed places with him and watched as he raced off, his patrol with him. They went out on a wide route to attack the Wakamba along the flank. Maclean ordered the driver to increase his speed and withdraw from the area. Apart from the obvious risk of losing their lives, he was also aware of the fact that the boiler might suffer irreparable damage. So the train began to accelerate and the Wakamba stepped up their rate of fire.

It soon became apparent that the Wakamba had a limited number of weapons, but what they lacked in firepower they certainly did not lack in courage. Their shoot and run tactics were bringing them dangerously close to the train, and because they were attacking on an intercepting course with the train it meant that Maclean was bound to encounter them. If he decided to retreat from the advancing Wakamba, he would simply run into the advancing Masai column.

The soldiers continued firing and the Maxim gun methodically pumped out its stuttering enfilade. Maclean was shouting orders and warnings to his men from the tender and firing at the same time. The Wakamba seemed oblivious to the hail of lead pouring down on them, and although they were losing men at an alarming rate, they were still running towards the train.

Reuben climbed up on to the tender then dropped down on to the flat car. Several men had come out of the box car and taken up positions along the length of the train. Although it was gaining speed, the train was still only chugging along at a running pace. Reuben dropped down beside the gun crew who were firing their carbines from the kneeling position. He could clearly see Bill Ord's troop skirmishing along the flanks. In the confusion and melee he saw a horse rear up as it was shot from beneath its rider. Almost immediately he saw one of the riders pick up the stranded soldier and scoop him up on to the rear of his horse. He then rode swiftly back to the train. Reuben could see it was Joe Hillier who had lost his horse. He was dropped by the train and his rescuer turned back towards the Wakamba.

As the train gathered speed it became a race between them and the attacking Wakamba who were narrowing the gap. It was already down to fifty yards and getting closer. The banshee howling of their war cries spurred the Wakamba to greater effort and they held their swords high above their heads as they hurtled towards the battle with demonic fury.

As the patrol kept harassing the Wakamba, so the Maxim gun kept up its rhythmic clatter, but they were only really parrying the attack. The Wakamba were close enough to the train now to inject real fear into the soldiers. Reuben was finding it almost impossible to keep up a rate of fire fast enough. He was constantly swinging his rifle from one target to another and re-cocking the gun in a blur.

Above the noise he heard a curse as someone's rifle jammed. Unthinking the poor man stood up to clear it. The Wakamba picked him off easily. The soldier cried out and tumbled from the flat car. As his body hit the dust beside the track, spinning and flailing like a rag doll, some of the Wakamba detached themselves from the attack and fell upon him, hacking the poor soul to pieces.

Suddenly they were beside the train. One climbed up on to the flat car and came at them like a demented animal. A soldier swung round and dropped him with a single shot. Before the dead man had hit the boards of the flat car, the soldier had turned and was firing on the attackers again.

The running Wakamba were now hauling themselves on to the train. Reuben began using his rifle as a club, swinging it at them as they tried to gain a purchase on the flat car. Some hung on grimly. Others fell to be cut to pieces by the spinning wheels of the train.

The box car had come under attack. The Maxim gun was no longer effective and the men were fighting desperately in hand-to-hand combat. On the flat car, Reuben found himself falling beneath the weight of the Wakamba. He lashed out with fists and feet, the gun now useless as a club. He saw a glint of flashing steel above his head and memories of David swamped him, and he cried out. A rifle butt was driven violently into the head of the man who had Reuben at his mercy. The sword in the man's hand clattered to the ground and the unconscious body followed it.

On the tender, Lieutenant Maclean was firing into a press of men who were trying to climb on to the footplate. The driver was fighting them off and Maclean was in danger of hitting him in his desperation. Although the narrow entrance to the footplate gave the driver and Maclean an advantage, there was always the danger they would be overcome by sheer weight of numbers.

Maclean sensed the train was losing speed. He slithered down the woodpile and screamed to the driver to hurl more wood on the fire. He took over the defence of their tiny platform as the driver kicked open the firebox door and furiously piled more logs into the gaping fire.

When the Wakamba gave up trying to board the footplate through the dangerously small gap, Maclean climbed back up on to the tender to continue his attack from the high position. The loss of speed had resulted in the Wakamba gaining considerable ground and the sight that greeted Maclean as he reached the top of the woodpile was hand-to-hand fighting along the entire length of the flat cars.

Reuben was clubbing the black savages mercilessly. Others were firing into the press of black bodies or physically wrestling. The struggle was fierce but the strength of the Wakamba was

189

overcome by the sheer tenacity and sense of self-preservation by Maclean's men. By clubbing, shooting and stabbing, they gradually overwhelmed their attackers. And as the train picked up speed, more and more of the Wakamba fell behind. Those who had gained a foothold on the box car had also met with fierce resistance and, little by little, the fighting subsided until, with the train gathering speed, the Wakamba finally broke off the attack.

When the shooting stopped, Maclean jumped from the tender to the flat car. The swaying motion of the speeding train made standing difficult and he had to crouch to prevent himself from falling. He steadied himself and took stock of the situation.

Several of his men were lying prone on the boards. Some were obviously dead, others wounded. Reuben crouched among them, recovering from the fierce struggle. He was covered in blood, but then, so were most of the soldiers. He put his hand up to Maclean to acknowledge him and staggered off towards the box car. Maclean went back to the footplate and instructed the driver to reduce speed. Then he returned to his men.

Reuben cleared the gap to the box car and swung himself over the guard rail. There were three black men lying there. They were dead. He pitched them over the side of the train and pulled the door open.

It was like a charnel house inside; blood smothered the walls and floor. A soldier lay dead, his head almost severed. Three Wakamba lay beside him. The smell of cordite was almost overpowering. The walls had been peppered with bullet holes, and massive splinters of wood covered the floor.

Joe Hillier was in there, sitting on the floor with a large splinter of wood embedded in his arm. He was carefully probing the wound. He looked up at Reuben and shook his head. 'God in heaven,' he said wearily. 'If that's what a few of them can do, what chance do we stand against ten thousand?'

Reuben left him in the care of his comrades and went back to the flat cars. The soldiers were gathering themselves together, mentally licking their wounds. Bill Ord's patrol was heading back towards the train. Reuben could see there were two missing. Joe Hillier was in the box car which meant the patrol had lost one man.

That loss saddened Reuben more than he could have believed. He had ridden with them for several days and had come to know them like brothers. Now one of them was dead and no doubt more would die. He pushed the thought to the back of his mind because to dwell on it would have robbed him of the will to fight, and he knew there would be many more losses to come.

It was simply a question of time.

CHAPTER TWELVE

The Reverend Aubrey Bowers took one last look towards the altar of the small church before closing the door behind him. His mind was now made up and he was pleased with that. Outside in the warm sunshine, sitting patiently on the pony and trap, was Hannah. His heart ached at his own decision and he dreaded the moment when he would have to tell her. It had to be now. He knew that. In one hour the train would be leaving for Nairobi with the last of the evacuees. They had not expected it to be so soon but the message had come through that it was now their turn. Hannah would protest, but he knew his decision was right; his duty clear.

The small bag he had so conscientiously packed with the frugal treasures of his little church lay beside the altar. Hannah would probably think he had forgotten it and make a small fuss. Then she would know. Ever since she had been a small child she had an uncanny way of knowing what was on his mind. He knew he wouldn't have to say anything. He walked towards the church gate, his eyes fixed on his beloved daughter.

As he walked, he prayed. 'Lord, I am your obedient servant. Grant me courage and release from the pain that must surely come.'

Hannah was looking out to some distant horizon, her mind fixed far beyond it. She heard her father's footsteps on the path and turned her head towards him. He paused at the gate, his arms hanging loosely at his side and a look of sadness etched deeply in his face. Her eyes took it in swiftly and she knew. She twisted in her seat, her hands clutching the side of the trap.

'Where's your bag, papa?' The question was irrelevant.

He took a step towards her and raised his hands in an urgent, supplicant gesture. 'Hannah, my dear.' He could not look her in the face, and for the first time in his life, he felt ashamed. He lowered his hands.

Hannah stepped down from the trap. 'You're not leaving, are you?'

He shook his head. 'I'm sorry, Hannah. I cannot.'

'But you must.' Her face showed the effect his decision was having on her. First, puzzlement. Then anger. 'You *will* go!'

He had breached the barrier and now felt calmer. He had to make her understand. 'No, Hannah, I am not going. This is my parish. I am needed here.'

'East Africa is your parish, Father,' she told him. 'Nairobi is just one small part of it.'

A wan smile flickered across his face. 'No, Hannah. We have always known, haven't we? The moment we came here, we knew this was the place. The rest was only pretence.'

'But your parishioners are no longer here.' She grabbed at his coat and he could feel the anger and desperation in her touch. 'They have gone.'

'No,' he argued. 'The soldiers are still here. And those who have bravely volunteered to remain. I owe it to them to show the same courage. They will have need of me.'

'But they are out there, somewhere,' she cried desperately, flinging her arm out. 'They will have no need of you while they fight. They won't even think of you.' She put her hand to her head. 'Oh, Father, how can you bring God to them when you are here in this empty shell? Will they come to you?'

He smiled and lifted her face gently with the tips of his fingers. 'My dear, dear Hannah, my sweet child. I shall go out there to them.'

Hannah reeled back in shock. She stood motionless for a moment and it was some while before she found the strength to speak. She knew her father's decision would be irrevocable and her pleas would fall on deaf ears, but she had to try and turn him away from this madness.

'You cannot. For once in your life you must think of me and mother first. It's only fair. You have to go to Machakos.' She almost spat the words at him.

'My duty is to the Lord and his work, Hannah.' He laid his

hands on her shoulders. 'If your mother was here, she would understand. She would have the strength to support my decision. You must too.'

'But what of me?' Tears sprang to her eyes. 'Oh Papa, I love you so much that if anything happened. . . .' Her words choked in a sob.

He pulled her to him and placed his hand on her head. 'My dear child, my life is almost run. You have yours stretching out before you.' His fingers caressed the soft tresses of her hair and he felt desperately sad for her. 'You must be strong. Your mother would expect it of you.'

'As she expects you to throw your life away?' she protested.

He pushed her away gently and tipped her face up to him. He brushed the tears away with the edge of his thumb. 'I have put my faith and trust in the Lord. If it His will, we shall be together again. He did not save me from those savages so that I might run away, and He will not desert me now.' He pulled a handkerchief from his pocket and dabbed at the tears on his own face. 'I know you will come to understand in time. Now, we should be getting back to the house. David will be waiting and you must not miss that train.'

As they rode back, Hannah was appalled at the emptiness that besieged her. It paralleled the emptiness and wasted streets of Nairobi Camp; as empty as her soul. Not everyone had left; some had managed to avoid Major Webb's team. But those who had chosen to remain could not fill the void or bring a spark of life in the wilderness that lay before her.

They pulled up outside the house and her father helped her down from the trap. He seemed almost content now, she thought, as though a great burden had been lifted from his mind. It was his fullness, the display of tranquillity that crushed the life from her and made her feel useless and spent.

She wandered into the house and called out. 'David, we're ready now. I'm afraid Papa isn't coming with us.' She stopped. 'David?' There was no answer. She went out into the garden and called for him there. 'David, where are you? Please don't play games.'

She went back into the house. His bedroom was empty. She went from room to room but he was nowhere to be found. She called again. 'David, come on. The train is due out and we must not miss it. Please David, I promised your father. We have to leave now.'

But there was still no answer. The house was quiet, almost lifeless. Her heart sank and she went back to the front door to call her father. It was then that she saw the note. It was propped up on the hall table. She picked it up. The paper shook in her trembling fingers. The words were simple and to the point: 'Miss Hannah, I'm sorry. Please forgive me. David.'

Lieutenant Maclean stopped the train after a few miles. Sergeant Ord's patrol arrived soon afterwards and Reuben was relieved to see Bill Ord at the head of it. He had been wounded in the arm but made light of it while the wound was dressed. In all, Maclean had lost four men, including the poor wretch who had fallen from the train. They buried their dead in shallow graves. The wounded, of which two were desperately ill, were left with one medic to attend their wounds. Those able to walk were instructed to take up defensive positions along the train.

After attending to their immediate needs, Maclean ordered that they all rest for a while. The driver kept up a head of steam in case they had to move off at short notice. Somebody produced a bag of Indian tea and, ignoring the scale and wood char that found its way into the steam, they drank it black and strong from a variety of small tins and mugs produced from the soldiers' ammunition pouches. Strictly against regulations, Maclean had observed drily, but who cared anyway?

'What do we do now, Lieutenant?' Reuben asked him, sipping the hot tea.

Maclean looked studiously along the track. 'I've been thinking about the train up at the railhead. We obviously can't go back up the line to destroy it; not with that damn Masai army on the move.'

'So, do we go back to Nairobi?'

Maclean shook his head. 'No, we can't do that. We'll have to destroy the track.' He looked up at the sky. 'It should be dark soon. We'll do it then.' He glanced over his shoulder to where Bill Ord was sitting with his men. 'Sergeant Ord, I want you to scout the area before dark. If there are no Wakamba about we'll remove some sections of the track. Then I want you to go back to the bridge, report my intentions to Major Webb.'

Maclean had decided to wait until well into the night because he wanted his men to get some kind of rest. He also figured that only fools and soldiers would be abroad at that late hour. When he was ready he moved among the men giving orders and posting extra guards. Sergeant Ord scouted the area and reported no sign of Wakamba or Masai. He then left with his patrol for the bridge.

The first guard died shortly after midnight. It happened so suddenly and unexpectedly that nobody could quite believe it. Maclean had been moving amongst the men when he had pulled a watch from his pocket and checked the time. It was just after twelve o'clock. Nobody had slept. Nobody could sleep. He was putting the watch back in his tunic pocket when he heard the shot. It was followed by a groan and a thud. Somebody shouted. 'Keep your heads down, lads!'

Maclean whirled round and dropped below the weatherboard. In the darkness he could see the crouching figures of Reuben and the driver.

'I've been a damn fool.' Maclean sounded very angry with himself. 'I did not expect anybody to move at night.' His voice was low and brittle. 'But Snyder could have used the train at the railhead to move some of his men.' He shook his head in self-admonishment. 'God, he could have pushed this far with no trouble.'

'But we didn't hear anything,' Reuben said. 'No train.'

Maclean glanced at him. Reuben's face was dimly lit by the firelight coming through the inspection glass on the firebox door. It gave him a macabre countenance.

'He could be a few miles up the track.' He shrugged. 'It's academic anyway.'

Two more shots rang out. One clanged against the side of the boiler while the other sailed harmlessly by. They ducked instinctively.

'We'll have to pull out,' Maclean said resignedly. 'Once those murdering bastards get a bead on us we've had it.'

More shots came from the bush, but this time they were answered by a return of fire from the train. Maclean nodded at the driver and motioned him to pull out. As the man opened the steam regulator it breathed life into the steam engine. It responded sluggishly. The couplings clanked and tightened, and then the wheels span. The whole train creaked as the slipping wheels began to bite. The driver showed anxiety on his face, which the others did not see in the darkness. He was concerned that the boiler might have been damaged. He coaxed the train along the track as though it had been sapped by a mortal wound. Steam could be heard escaping from all manner of places, and the train moved with agonizing slowness.

'I think we've taken several hits to the boiler, sir,' the driver called to Maclean. 'I'm having trouble maintaining steam pressure.'

Maclean grimaced. 'Just keep trying, man. Keep trying.'

The attackers were watching the train's sluggish efforts while they edged closer. They used the light from the moon whenever the fleeting cloud let the moonlight flood the valley. On the train the soldiers found it unnerving. The tension in the air was working on them, tapping away at their self-control, threatening to break it down and replace it with raw fear.

It was obvious there was something wrong with the locomotive as the train struggled to get up speed. And when the shooting came, each barrage was more telling than the last. The soldiers could feel the closeness of their attackers, but could not see them. They fired from the train but they were aiming blindly, shooting at shadows.

As attack followed attack, the confidence of the men out in the bush grew, and they showed themselves for the first time. Although everybody on the train was convinced it was the Wakamba again, the attacks this time were more subtle and more controlled. But it changed suddenly. The moonlight flooded the area and it was like a sign. Clear of their cover, the attackers ran, driven by confidence, towards the train.

And that was the moment some cool bastard had been waiting for. He opened up with the Maxim gun, peppering the attackers and slinging up shards of bush, dirt, shrub and blood. He scored several hits that immediately inspired his comrades on the train. They opened up with a stunning barrage. The effect was heartening, rippling through the train until the crescendo of noise was deafening.

On the footplate Reuben broke off from firing at the attackers and helped the driver hurl logs into the fire. The driver then stood up and began coaxing every last vestige of steam from the boiler. The injured train clattered its couplings again and the wheels dug in to drag it free. Then they were away, gathering speed and peace of mind at the same time until they had left their attackers empty handed in the distance.

'It never occurred to me earlier,' Maclean said when things had calmed down a little, 'that Snyder would use the train to move the Wakamba down the line. Not thinking clearly under pressure, you see.'

'Well, we're out of it now,' Reuben said tiredly. 'Thanks to whomever it was on that Maxim gun.'

'Yes. Good, solid thinking under fire,' Maclean admitted. 'Must recommend him.'

'Well, make sure it's tomorrow,' Reuben said lightly. 'He may not have much time after that.'

Maclean looked at him forlornly. 'He may have all the time in the world, Cole,' he said quietly. 'One way or the other.'

CHAPTER THIRTEEN

Reuben walked out on to the centre of the bridge. He felt apprehensive, nervous and alone. His emotions had broken free and were roaming at liberty through his body. This was going to be the day he would live or die. The day that could herald the beginning of a new life, bringing back the happiness he had shared with David at the farm. It was the beginning for everyone else too, for once this day was over, Africa's destiny would have been forged by an irrevocable act. And from that act, its future would be born.

He sat on the edge of the bridge. There was no safety rail, just a walkway about ten feet wide. The sun warmed his back as he let his feet swing beneath him, over one hundred feet above the swirling stream below. He thought of what he might have been doing had none of this happened. Somewhere on the farm, among the crops. Mirambo would have probably been toiling with him. He could hear, in his mind, the screams of laughter rolling down the sides of the valley as Mirambo's youngest children played. David would be there, with Mirambo's eldest, acting out some fantasy among the vegetation until called by their fathers to work.

Their life had been a mixture of idyllic nonsense and sheer, hard work; a blend of hot and cold that somehow managed to merge into an acceptable pattern. Tempering ambition while providing sufficient means to meet their dreams. Reuben had never regretted coming out to Africa. Even now he found it hard to accuse the country he had grown to love of negligence or desertion. It had given him a good life and he was about to defend it. And if necessary, die for it.

He looked down at the water below, then back up the valley to Lake Naivasha, unconscious of the height. He could just see the crevasse from where the water tumbled to run and swirl beneath him. It looked so quiet and harmless. To the right, standing sentinel over the valley was Mount Longonot. It rose nine thousand feet above sea level and was like a monolith, its towering, volcanic peak capped with grey ash from the spiralling column of smoke.

To the far left another craggy giant slept, the extinct volcano of Orengingai. It leaned threateningly into the valley. Reuben looked at it and cast his eye around the other peaks and slopes. Their colours changed from grey to brown, then to green and finally to a warm yellow as the rugged features softened into the cradle of the valley.

Behind Reuben was Hell's Gate, the narrow gorge through which the waters now flowed. It was frightening to imagine the power they were prepared to release into this valley and unimaginable to contemplate the effect of consigning that uncontrollable force towards the pillars of Hell's Gate.

His mind drifted, flitting from himself, David, this valley, the farm. He thought about Cameron and the bridge. It was a monument to men like him and Seymour Pope, men who wanted nothing more than to be allowed to build their railway in peace. Cameron had died because he had put his precious ideals before his own safety.

The bridge was a masterpiece. At the point where he was sitting it was a little over one hundred feet above the valley floor. Looking left and right the bridge seemed to go on forever although it was only about four hundred yards long. The cross-hatching of hand-hewn timbers was staggering, considering that each one had to be hauled into place by steam winches. It would have been exhausting, arduous and dangerous work. No doubt, Reuben thought lightly, Cameron would have enjoyed each moment, sweating over each timber and savouring it all until, at last, the masterpiece was complete.

He looked back along the line of the bridge and saw two figures standing there. One was small and elfin-like, and was wearing a hat that Reuben recognized. The other figure, a little taller, was dressed in large trousers that tumbled indecorously to her feet. She was also wearing a hat, but it was pulled down tight to hide her auburn tresses. Reuben got up slowly and walked towards them.

David pulled his hand from Hannah's and started walking towards his father. His steps were slow; hesitant almost. Hannah made an ineffectual attempt to stop him. She touched his shoulders but he shrugged her off. She let him go.

When David reached him, Reuben knelt on one knee, bringing his face level. He wanted to chastise the boy and demand that he run quickly for the safety of Machakos, to do all the things that would guarantee he would not bear witness to what was about to happen. But such was Reuben's inner joy at seeing him he could not say what was in his mind, only what was in his heart. He put his arms out and David clung to him. Reuben could feel the boy's tears mingling with his own.

He said nothing for a while. Then he pushed David gently away and held him at arm's length. 'Why are you here?'

'I wouldn't go,' David answered defiantly.

Reuben looked beyond him to Hannah. She looked funny in her large trousers. And helpless. She walked towards them. Reuben stood up and watched her. When she reached him she pulled David protectively towards her. Her hands were trembling. 'I'm sorry, Reuben.'

He looked at them both, shaking his head. 'Why, Hannah? Why?'

'He was on the veranda the night you left.' She couldn't look directly at him. 'He heard everything.' She lifted her head. 'I tried to persuade him you were doing the right thing.'

'Why wouldn't you go, David?' Reuben asked his son.

David couldn't face him. The defiance was melting away.

'Reuben, please try not to get angry,' Hannah pleaded. 'He loves you and believes in you so much. He won't leave you.'

'I cannot look after him, Hannah.' He looked over his shoulder, somewhere beyond the far side of the valley. 'You know what's coming.'

Their faces watched him. Please, please Reuben, they were saying. But what could he do? Nothing. He was faced with the fact that David was there and was his responsibility. The boy had burned his boats.

'I will look after him,' Hannah promised. 'We'll stay up on the escarpment. We have horses.'

Reuben glanced up to the top of the escarpment wall. It was about a thousand yards away and rose up from the valley in a gentle slope. It offered a commanding view of the entire valley. A grandstand seat for the spectacle to come. It made sense, he told himself. Hannah would know when it was time to run. With David beside her she would survive the dangers of the bush and reach the sanctuary of Machakos. He accepted it philosophically.

'I will walk with you for a while,' he said. David's face broke into a grin. Reuben put his arm around the boy's shoulder and looked into Hannah's eyes. 'Promise me that if you have to run, you will not hesitate. Promise.'

'I promise, Reuben. Believe me.'

Hannah was about to say something else when they heard the sound of a faint, shouted command followed by the unmistakable crash of the field gun. They all looked towards the direction of the bang and saw a smoke ring spiralling outwards from the high escarpment slope.

Reuben looked back across the valley. 'They're coming,' he said with a sad finality.

They stood on the bridge. Now was the beginning of that fateful day. Between the sleeping volcano of Orengingai and the rising flanks of Lake Naivasha, they could see the black shape of Snyder's army shimmering in the waves of convected heat. The shell from the gun exploded in a cloud of dust about half a mile in front of the column.

'They missed!' David exclaimed. He sounded disappointed.

'I don't think they are trying to hit them at that range,' Reuben told him. 'Let's go and find out.'

Major Webb had positioned the field gun on a rib of level ground just beneath the top of the escarpment. The area offered a commanding view of the terrain and a quick route to the top if it was deemed necessary. As they reached the gun they saw Lieutenant Maclean.

'Life is full of little surprises, eh Cole?' he called with humour.

Reuben acknowledged the fact. 'Best laid plans.'

'It won't be long now,' Maclean suggested.

'What was that shot for?'

'Give those at the front something to think about,' he answered, smiling. 'If we can hold them back a little it will bring the rear of the column closer. Tighten it up.'

'Major Webb's idea?' he asked. Maclean nodded. 'Well, let's hope the man knows what he's doing,' Reuben remarked, and walked up the slope with Hannah and David in tow.

Major Webb was sitting on a fallen log. There were no trappings of command. No tents. It made Reuben realize how desperate Webb's position was in terms of military support. And, more to the point, just how long he expected to occupy the position.

'Seems we are all getting a little more than we bargained for, Cole,' he said a little tritely.

Reuben sat down beside him on the log. 'Did you know about David and Hannah?'

Webb looked at him for a moment. 'Her father too. Stubbornness must run in the family.'

Reuben showed his surprise. 'Mr Bowers? Where?'

Webb looked out over the valley. 'Down there somewhere, moving among his flock.' He looked back at Reuben. 'It's like I said, Cole, we're getting more than we bargained for.'

Reuben wasn't sure he understood the Major's point, but chose not to dwell on it. 'How long?' he asked, just to make conversation.

Webb drummed his fingers on the stretched cloth of his trousers, his lips pursed in thought. 'An hour, maybe, perhaps less.'

They sat in silence for a while. It wasn't really the time for desultory talk. Hannah removed her cap. She had explained to Reuben that her unseemly outfit had been borrowed from her father because all her riding clothes were on their way to Machakos. She hadn't mentioned the fierce argument that had ensued. She was unaware of Reuben's eyes on her as she ran her fingers through her hair. From time to time she would stop and stare absently, as though she had thought of something and needed to stop in order to consider it. Then she would lift her hand and begin drawing her slender fingers through her hair again.

Reuben returned his attention to the bridge. The train on which he and Maclean had battled with the Wakamba was at the top of the escarpment. Reluctantly Major Webb had agreed they might need it, so it had been withdrawn to a safer position. Webb was a good soldier, but he was also a realist. It had the effect of leaving the line terribly exposed and empty as it cut neatly through the valley to climb the long, angular ascent to the escarpment summit, offering a tangible link to Nairobi and Machakos.

'Why didn't you cut the line?' Reuben asked. 'Snyder could push straight through to Nairobi.'

'He won't get through,' Webb replied with a surprising degree of confidence. 'I can promise you that.'

'You sound very sure of yourself.'

'Not really,' he answered. 'I plan to blow up the bridge.'

The statement was like a blow to the face. Reuben's head snapped round in astonishment. 'I don't believe it. Why not just dismantle the track?'

Webb shook his head. 'That can be replaced. I don't want to destroy the bridge, but if Snyder plans to use the train we left at the railhead, the bridge assumes a strategic importance. And if he succeeds, that bridge will be of enormous use to the German government.' He smacked a clenched fist into his open hand. 'And I'm damned if I'm going to let that happen. That's why I've instructed Sergeant Ord to blow it up.'

'Bill Ord? I thought Sergeant Hawk would be your man.' Reuben thought about the calm, self-assured explosives expert.

'He's up at Lake Naivasha,' Webb replied simply.

'I see,' Reuben muttered. 'And what about me, Major? Where would you like me to be?'

Major Webb looked carefully at Reuben, his innermost thoughts kept in check. 'You can go where you like, Cole. But I think Sergeant Ord would like you on the bridge with him.'

Lieutenant Maclean accompanied Reuben down to the bridge. He had set the charges himself and handed the matchsticks and striking board to Sergeant Ord. The fuse wire had been secured to the edge of the bridge timbers and looped away to the first sticks of dynamite about twenty feet below. He shook their hands, saying nothing, but in his eyes he said everything. Then he returned to his position alongside Major Webb.

Thus Reuben joined Sergeant Ord, the man who had become

his friend. He wished the friendship could have been forged in other circumstances and gone on for much longer. But the odds were that one, if not both of them, would not live to see the end of this day.

Snyder's army was clearly visible now. The soldiers watched its daunting advance and fidgeted. They checked their rifles a dozen times, scoured their ammunition pouches and some of them took to relieving themselves over the side of the bridge. Bill Ord kept glancing at the fuse wire to ensure some unseen hand had not dislodged it. Reuben paced nervously beside him.

The field gun fired again and its distinctive whistle followed the shell's rifling path through the air. It exploded extremely close to the Masai ranks. Another shot followed, dropping short. The column checked and swung closer to the line. Somewhere from the rising ground in the distance, flanking the southern edge of the railway track, a volley of fire could just be heard. The column moved deceptively, inching away from the firing.

Another shell dropped in front of them and the dust from the explosion mingled with the dust thrown up by the column of marching feet. The heat rising from the valley floor carried the fine powder upwards to be blown away by the breeze that fanned the valley heights. There were more rifle shots from the high ground in the distance. This time there was returning fire from within the ranks of the Masai. Reuben exchanged glances with Bill Ord, recalling their experiences at the hands of the Wakamba.

Another twist gave them a depressing hint of what was to come when a small group detached itself from the main body and stormed the high ground from where the volley of shots had come. They were repulsed initially by a crackling fusillade of gunfire, but more figures detached themselves from the column and joined the attack.

The shooting stopped and, for a moment, Reuben assumed with rising dismay that the riflemen had been overwhelmed. Then, emerging from the hill, he could see a group of horsemen riding away rapidly. The Masai broke off their attack when they spotted the fleeing riders who disappeared into the forest.

Suddenly there was more rifle fire, but this time it came from the northwest as Major Webb's men poured bullets into the

Masai's other flank. Reuben watched incredulously as a similar pattern emerged. Slowly, a picture was unfolding, a well-planned scenario. He realized now that Major Webb had planned only to contain the massed column, not attack it. He was harassing the main body to keep them in a controlled line, avoiding direct contact with the Masai by using hit and run tactics. With the odds stacked against him, Major Webb was doing exactly the right thing. For his daring plan to succeed, it made good sense.

He looked back towards the escarpment. High on the slope he could make out a solitary figure with signalling flags. The soldier raised his arms to beat out a message. The response was more firing, this time at the southern flank of the Masai. Reuben thought of the soldier with the signalling flags as a conductor, but it was Major Webb who was orchestrating and conducting the attacks from his elevated position.

The sight and sounds of the Masai became more distinct as they poured across the valley floor. They held their shields in front of them and their *simis*, their stabbing spears, above their heads. The rifle fire intensified as the Masai came within range of the bridge and the soldiers at the far end opened up. But now the fire was being returned. As the leading Masai reached the beginning of the natural defile through which the water flowed, they began to descend into what was little more than a shallow stream. The water provided a minor obstacle to their progress and they appeared to be in no hurry to wade into the stream. Some of them took up positions along the defile while others made for the bridge and began climbing the trestles. The rear of the column began bunching up on the slower-paced men at the front. Bullets rained down on the chanting lines of black skin, but they seemed impervious to the hail of lead and did not waver. As the main column closed up to the front, it tightened to present a thick mass of humanity beneath the soldiers' guns.

There was another explosion, but this time it was from the distant heights of Orengingai, and the ring of spiralling smoke betrayed the position of the second field gun. Major Webb had waited deliberately and patiently until the tail of the long column had passed beneath the volcano and the sweeping slopes of Lake Naivasha. Now the column was through, he was using the field gun to push the rear of the column closer to the front.

There were also the unmistakable sounds of Martini Henry rifles from behind the Masai. It looked very much as though Major Webb had kept some of his troops in reserve to continue harassing the Masai once they had passed beneath Orengingai.

Below him, to his right, Reuben could see men standing waist deep in the savannah grass firing across the water. The field gun opened up and hurled a shell towards the rear of the column. He wondered how long they could hold them. How long it would go their way. He knew that the sheer press of the Masai would soon overwhelm them and, as weapons overheated and jammed, Webb's plan would begin to falter. When the Masai finally came into contact with the soldiers, the losses would be considerable. But for now the plan was succeeding and Reuben was able to fire leisurely at the black army below.

A shout came up from the bridge, rising above the noise of the gunfire. Someone had seen the train. Reuben's heart sank when he saw the smoke streaming from the stack as the locomotive powered its way from the distant escarpment towards the bridge.

The firing coming up from below intensified as the Masai scrambled down the slope into the water. Reuben felt shockwaves as bullets thudded into the woodwork of the bridge. Smoke drifted up and he could smell the acrid stink of cordite in the air. He put his mind back to the moment and began firing again at the Masai wading into the water. Bill Ord was firing from the other side. At the far end of the bridge the Masai were gathering to storm the strongly defended position. Reuben swung towards them, firing over the heads of the soldiers. The Masai edged forward, four abreast, holding their shields in front of them. The hide skins offered little protection from the bullets and soon there was a melee of bodies draped across the railway line. But, inevitably, they pressed forward, gaining ground.

Below the bridge were small groups engaged in hand-to-hand fighting as the Masai moved down towards the water. Some of the more resilient of the Masai were using the lower timbers of the bridge to cross the stream. Inevitably this was drawing soldiers from defensive positions and from Reuben's lofty vantage point it did not look too promising for Major Webb's men now.

In the distance the train had grown in size and Reuben could see it was packed with Masai. He looked quickly to the high ridge and wondered when the Major would give the order that might contain the Masai horde for good. A bullet shattered the woodwork beside his foot, showering him with splinters of wood. He threw himself instinctively on the boards and crawled away from the edge.

Suddenly, there was a roar from the Masai column and the tail swung outwards, moving in a wide sweep to bring it level with the front ranks. It was an awesome sight. As the seething horde trampled over the bush, hundreds of small animals and birds scattered before it, panicked into flight. Columns of choking dust spiralled into the sky where the birds wheeled and circled in disarray. The ground seemed to tremble with the thunder of running feet and Reuben could feel it shuddering through the timbers of the bridge.

The noise was appalling. Below them the Masai crowded into the watery defile as bullets crashed into them bringing screams from the wounded and dying men. The distant field gun pumped away remorselessly, pouring death and smoke across the valley. On the bridge the Masai were forcing the soldiers back. Reuben was now firing continuously alongside Bill Ord. As the black men fell, so they were replaced by more. Reuben found the foresight of his rifle seemed to jump further each time he fired. The recoil pummelled his shoulder until he thought the pain would become so unbearable he might not be able to lift the gun. The noise and roar of the gunfire was ringing in his ears until the whole thing suffused into one so that he was aiming and firing like a man in a wild dream.

There was a surge of rifle fire from somewhere in the Masai ranks attacking the bridge. Sergeant Ord screamed for the soldiers to fall back and form a redoubt. He then shouted across to Reuben that he was going to blow the bridge. Reuben nodded and continued firing. He assumed that the soldiers defending the far end would be warned of Bill Ord's intentions somehow and they would have to make a run for it. He glanced back over his shoulder to make sure there were no Masai behind him.

Then Bill Ord fell. He went down like a weighted sack. Reuben's heart stopped for an instant and he felt that he couldn't breathe. For a small moment he was stunned. He had come to regard the craggy sergeant as indestructible and now he was lying face down beside the track, quite still. Reuben dashed forward to his friend's prone figure and knelt beside him. He was still alive but his skin was terribly pallid and his breathing very shallow. He was trying to say something and Reuben had to lean very close to pick out the words. They came in desperate gasps as Ord hung on to consciousness.

'Blow the bridge. Blow up the bridge!'

Reuben felt an uneasy panic rising inside him and he suffered the mortifying indignity of wanting to run. Suddenly he was scared and an unnerving, childlike fear took the strength from his body and turned the blood in his veins into a thin, trembling fluid.

Ord rolled on to his side and reached up for Reuben's collar. His fingers closed tightly around it. 'For God's sake, Reuben, blow up the bloody bridge!'

The passion and strength in that plea brought Reuben back to his senses. He laid his rifle beside the track and pulled the sergeant up into a sitting position. Then he levered him on to his shoulders and stood up. Ord's weight threatened to overcome him and he staggered dangerously close to the edge. He took control of himself and carried his wounded friend to firm ground where he laid him down. He looked into the pale face for what he knew would be the last time. Tears filled his eyes as he took the matchsticks and striking board from Ord's pocket and went back out on to the bridge.

At the far end the Masai had succeeded in gaining considerable ground and were well on to the bridge. As their dead and dying comrades fell, they moved them clear of the track, even though the soldiers had regrouped into a redoubt and were still firing at the swathe of bodies clustered around the fallen warriors. Beyond them the train was clearly visible, smoke pouring from the stack as it raced towards them. Reuben guessed there must have been five hundred or more men crammed on to the flat cars. Enough to get through to Nairobi and destroy what was left.

Below them in the valley the mass of black men had drawn into a huge rectangle and were well down the slope into the water, making tremendous strides against the barrage of fire coming down from Major Webb's men.

Reuben picked up his rifle and went to the edge of the walkway where the fuse wire had been attached. One look at the splintered chunk and his face turned cold. There was no fuse wire! Thoughts of David and Hannah flashed into his mind and he wished he could have been with them up on the escarpment and not here in what was probably the place he was going to die.

Then, above the noise and the dying, a tremendous explosion rent the air. The soldiers on the bridge stopped firing. The attacking Masai froze. Everyone turned their heads in the direction of the explosion. The effect was paralysing; high on the edge of Lake Naivasha the rock face cracked into a thousand pieces, shattered by the dynamite. For a moment, a small, indefinable moment, nothing happened. Then, like an exploding balloon, the enormous pressure from the water in the lake punched the rock into space, scattering it like a thousand pieces of fragmented paper. A huge column of water shot out of the gap as the force of millions of gallons ripped out the sides of the crevasse. Hundreds of birds rose into the air from behind the high ridge, exploding into flight as the ground reverberated with the shock.

Trees that had grown for years on the peaceful slopes toppled and disappeared as the water tore the ground from beneath them. Huge rocks tumbled into the maelstrom that belched out from the crevasse. Torrents of water erupted from the soil in jets as the mighty pressure opened up subterranean passages, and the fountains rose high into the air and fell in a fascinating display of cascading water.

The fighting below the bridge stopped. Such was the ferocity of the explosion and the staggering spectacle that nobody could fail to be stunned by it. Then the awful realization of what was about to happen settled on everyone and panic took over. But the soldiers knew they had a duty to hold their positions. They ignored the threatening catastrophe and began firing into the Masai again. From the sleeping giant of Orengingai, the field gun pumped shell after shell into them. Major Webb's plan was working again as the seething mass below fought to climb out of the deep valley, only to be forced back by the closing ranks of soldiers on the high ground.

Reuben knew the train would reach the bridge. He could not gamble on the possibility of it failing to get clear before the water struck, so he galvanized himself into action and swung himself over the edge. Using the timbers he climbed down to reach the swinging fuse wire. Firing had now resumed from the bridge. He could hear the bullets and the response ricocheting off the woodwork. He glanced up towards Lake Naivasha and could see the water pouring down the hill in a mighty, rolling wall. It pushed the earth and trees up before it, piling them into a huge, moving dam that smashed its way through all obstacles, pressed on by the cataract behind it. He tried to assess his chances of making it back to the top of the bridge after he had lit the fuse. The quickest way off would be to jump.

He reached the torn wire. It was hanging limply. He pulled the matchsticks and striking board from his pocket. His hands shook as he struck a match and shielded the blossoming flame. Then he cursed the gods loudly for his predicament and lit the fuse.

On the higher ground from where he was conducting the battle, Major Webb stood to bear witness to the cataclysm that was about to strike. He could see the soldiers firing into the Masai but the warrior nation was no longer intent on smashing through the stiff resistance being offered by his men; their only desire now was to flee, to run before the raging waters struck. He could see the train making good progress towards them but showing no signs of slowing. He guessed that Snyder was on the train and was gambling that he would clear the bridge before the torrent reached it.

He looked into the deep defile at the pandemonium. Shell after shell was falling into the mass from the field gun on Orengingai. The standing soldiers were pouring rifle fire into the Masai, dropping them like targets at a fairground. Further up the valley the wall of water was gathering even more incredible strength; the extreme edges of it were flowing up the narrower sides of the decline and curling in on themselves. Already the wall of water was about fifty yards wide and forty feet high. High on the edge of the lake where the rock had been shattered, the water poured through the gap with the sound of a fast-moving train. Its deathly roar crackled over the valley like a fanfare of trumpets heralding the approach of the apocalyptic horsemen.

On the train, in a strange parody of a demon rider, Webb could see Snyder quite clearly. He was sitting on the top of the locomotive, his huge bulk topped by a mane of flowing hair, like a Roman centurion leading his legion into battle.

The bridge blew up as the wall of water hit the Masai. The affect was appalling; the bridge shuddered under the explosion and sagged. The soldiers were already sprinting back to safety as another explosion shook the bridge. Incredibly it held for a while. Then the debris and water whipped the trestles away like falling skittles. Webb saw the telltale sparks from the train wheels as the driver applied the brakes in a futile attempt to halt it before it plunged into the precipice opening up before them. The bridge swayed and sagged, snapping and twisting the rails. The wall of water passed beneath the soldiers and he could almost smell the fear of those who had not yet cleared the tottering edifice.

The train reached the edge, still travelling at speed. Men were throwing themselves off in the hope of saving their skins, but the momentum of the train merely helped to propel them to their deaths. He watched the train drive itself over the edge as the bridge crumbled completely, and saw Snyder slip forward as the train plunged into the maelstrom below.

Hannah put her hand to her mouth to stifle a scream as the water hurtled through the depression towards the bridge. She had withdrawn to a higher point on the escarpment with David and they had watched everything with dread and alarm. When the attack on the bridge had begun, her first thoughts had been for Reuben. But now her thoughts were with the terrible battle being fought. Uncomprehending, she had watched as Reuben carried the stricken body of Bill Ord off the bridge and return to climb down between the crosshatching of timbers. David was getting increasingly nervous beside her and kept shouting for his father. Hannah had tried desperately to calm him down but the poor boy was becoming hysterical.

When the explosion came high up on Lake Naivasha, David started moaning and crying nervously. It increased Hannah's fears for all their lives and she could feel the tension draining the energy from her. She wanted to ride into the valley to Reuben, but she knew it was hopeless. She saw Reuben look round at the water hurtling towards the bridge, but he appeared to ignore it. David was screaming at him, his small voice lost in the distance that separated them, shut out by the roar of the gunfire and the rushing water.

They watched as the train hurtled towards the bridge and saw the soldiers running. Not able to drag their eyes away, they saw Reuben edge carefully along the timbers holding something in his hand. He kept checking the progress of the onrushing water. Then he stopped and something flared in his hand. The fuse wire fluttered and a flame blossomed. It changed to a stuttering shower of sparks and he dropped it. It swung away from him and he turned, once more carefully negotiating the timbers and making his way back towards the safety of the rising ground.

When the dynamite exploded, the bridge held for a while. Then some timbers moved and toppled into the river below. Hannah and David both jumped as another explosion rocked the bridge. Then the wall of water struck. David screamed so loudly that Hannah fell to her knees in front of him, begging him to stop. But, like David, she had lost her self-control and her hysteria crushed the boy's nerve until he was crying in terror for his father.

They huddled together, watching in stupefied horror as the water tore away the supporting timbers which were sucked into the raging torrent. In quick succession timbers canted over and were pulled down. The track twisted and ripped apart as the whole structure split asunder. Men slipped and plunged into the depths below. Others held on for agonizing moments before their strength deserted them and they fell like droplets of water into the tumult.

The train followed them, rushing to its death. Everything disappeared into the boiling cataract and the screams of the dying and frightened men rose above the crescendo of sound to make the flesh on their bodies crawl with the ice cold touch of fear.

Suddenly, everything was gone. There was nothing but over one hundred feet wide of bubbling water and debris flowing where, not long before, mortal souls had engaged in combat. The guns had stopped firing and the soldiers stood like statues as the river sucked the lifeblood from the valley floor.

On the far side, the remnants of Snyder's army gathered to

watch. There was a silent vacuum over the land as though the earth had given up its very existence to the cataclysmic devastation.

Lieutenant Maclean looked down on the scene of destruction, unable to comprehend for a while that they had been responsible for such havoc and death. He watched as some of the more fortunate soldiers dragged themselves clear of the rising water. Some of the Masai had struggled on to dry land too, only to stand beside the soldiers to bear silent witness to their comrades' deaths, all of them bound now by the same, Draconian catastrophe.

Suddenly, David shouted and tore himself away from Hannah's grasp. He ran up the slope to where his horse was tethered and climbed swiftly into the saddle. He dug his heels viciously into the horse and took off, his legs spread wide and his arms flailing as he plunged down the slope towards the tattered remnants of the bridge. Hannah scrambled to her feet and ran up the slope to her mount. She heaved herself up into the saddle, spurred the horse and went after him. She did not know what David was going to do but was terrified in case he plunged suicidally into the raging water.

Reuben opened his mouth in an instinctive shout as the timbers fell and pitched him into the torrent below. The water choked him and killed the shout in his throat. He coughed the water out and immediately sucked more in. A spasm of coughing besieged him, and his head whirled as pools of light spun behind his closed eyes. Suddenly he broke free from the strong undertow and swam to the surface. His head came clear of the water and he gasped for air in desperation, coughing and spluttering, fighting for his life. The water boiled over his head and he could feel himself being drawn down into its depths, spinning and tumbling once again. He kicked out in an effort to swim back up to the surface, his lungs bursting, but he seemed to have no strength to fight against the fierce drag of the swiftly moving water. He broke free again, briefly catching a glimpse of the sky before going under once more. He kicked and fought, determined to reach the surface and the sweet air above him. He felt his tongue thickening, filling his mouth, and he retched in another bout of coughing.

Then he was free, breathing pure air and being carried along by the racing water. He let himself be carried, conserving his strength, regaining his breath. His heart pumped wildly beneath his rib cage, forcing oxygen into his demanding body. His lungs cried out and he drew in deep draughts of air, holding his chin high and clear of the water. Beneath the surface of his own struggle, he could feel the panic rising. He fought desperately to subdue it, knowing that failure would only bring pain and death. And he wanted so much to live.

Another danger threatened him now. He knew the water was carrying him towards Hell's Gate. If he failed to swim clear of this virgin river, the tremendous forces piling up against the narrow gorge would crush the life from him. He started swimming for the edge of the water, barely twenty yards from him. Reuben knew he would be unable to swim directly for the edge because of the swift current, so he struck out at an angle. But each time he lifted his head to draw breath he could feel the strong pull drawing him away. He stroked harder, but the strength of the current as the water funnelled towards Hell's Gate was proving too much for him. He tried hard to put more effort into each stroke, but he was weakening and he knew that with each moment, the struggle would almost certainly be lost.

Then, above the noise of the roaring water, he heard a rifle shot. He stopped instinctively and immediately the pull of the water whipped him away. He had to stroke just to keep his position. He heard the rifle shot again and looked towards the water's edge. Sitting astride his horse and waving furiously was David. Reuben's heart soared and he struck out again, pushing himself to new limits.

David watched his father's uneven struggle, helpless from his position on the bank. His small body was tense with fear because he could see his father would not make it. He trotted his horse into the water but the animal backed off in fright. He held the reins firm and encouraged the horse, but could not make any progress towards Reuben's frantic struggle. Hannah rode up behind him, the sound of her horse's hoofs thundering on the soft ground.

'The rope, David!' she shouted. 'Use your rope!'

In David's fraught state he had forgotten the rope hanging

from his saddle. He gathered it up and rode downstream to head Reuben off. He rode fast, following the curve of the water as it swung sharply towards Hell's Gate, barely half a mile away. He coiled the rope loosely and tied one end to the saddle horn. He judged his moment carefully and rode into the water, pushing the horse well in until he could feel the strength of the water as it piled up against the horse's body, letting it wash up over his own thighs.

Reuben lunged for the rope as it snaked towards him. He felt its coarse fibres sting the back of his forearm as he made a grab for it. He snatched it and hung on for his life's sake. With this tenuous link to safety in his grasp, Reuben felt his strength suddenly ebb away. The water poured over his head and he felt the rope tighten. He struck out feebly, but his legs would not respond. He reached forward with his other hand, wrapping the rope around his other arm. Then he closed his fingers tightly on the rope and held on for all he was worth. Slowly his mind began to fade and eventually he blacked out.

Blurred images floated against the sky and he could feel something hard against his back. The images moved and brushed water from his face.

'Reuben?' Her voice was soft. He looked into her face and smiled. Then she was gone and David was on him, wrapping his arms tightly around his father, sobbing unashamedly. Reuben put his arms round David's back and let his own tears flow while he held him tight. They remained like that for some time. Then Hannah pulled David gently away. Reuben sat up. His head felt woolly and his body hurt abominably. A few feet from him the water raced by. He could hear the sound of it thundering up against the cliffs at Hell's Gate.

'Is it over?' he asked.

'Yes, it's finished,' Hannah told him. 'Everything has gone. There is nothing left.'

'Bill Ord?' he asked hopefully.

'I don't know, Reuben,' she answered honestly. 'So many people were dragged into the water.' She put her trembling hands to her eyes to stop the tears. 'Oh, Reuben,' she cried. 'It was horrible.'

The tension in her body was like a spring. Now it uncoiled itself and she broke, sobbing fiercely. David watched forlornly, his face puckering up. Hannah's voice faltered and cracked as she told Reuben how the bridge had gone and how so many people had died.

Reuben listened, trying to make sense of it all. He felt the truth descending on him like a dark shroud. He told himself it was a nightmare and he would wake up back at the farm with David and Mirambo. But this was the reality which made it all the more damning and hard to bear. He struggled to his feet and stood on trembling legs. 'Who will judge us this day?' he asked rhetorically, looking back to where it had happened. He put his arm round Hannah for reassurance. 'And what will they say?'

He climbed up on to David's horse and David swung up behind him. For a short moment they all looked out over the water. Then the weary trio began the long journey home.

CHAPTER FOURTEEN

'Why did Miss Hannah go away?' David asked. He studied his father's face intently, waiting for an explanation.

During the aftermath of the slaughter at Hell's Gate there had been a great deal of work to be done. Most people found themselves a task to which they could commit themselves. Hannah had chosen to work in the Railway Company hospital at Machakos. Although there had been many deaths, there had also been a great number of wounded. They had all been taken to Machakos, Masai included, where they were attended to by volunteers such as Hannah and the small nursing staff. Although the majority of their army had survived, the Masai had given up the fight. With their leader, Snyder, dead, the impact of the devastation in the Rift Valley had taken the spirit out of them and they had returned to their homelands.

In England the Liberals had brought tremendous pressure to bear on Lord Salisbury's government and whipped up a great deal of opposition to the railway line because of the events at Nairobi. The Indian Administration had brought themselves into the debate by taking a lot of convincing that the Masai uprising was over and no longer constituted a threat to the line's progress. Salisbury's government had survived the onslaught but it had been a tense and harrowing time.

Rueben had volunteered to work with the Railway Company until some semblance of order had been restored. One fateful decision taken by the Company was that the line would no longer cross the Rift Valley below Mount Longonot, but would skirt round to the north of the volcano.

Reuben had visited the farm with David, but such had been the devastation there that he knew whatever time he spent at

Nairobi, it would not jeopardize their chances of restoring the farm to its former glory. One piece of good fortune that had come from the flood was that the narrow mouth at Hell's Gate had been choked with sufficient debris to reduce the water flowing through it to a trickle. Because of the service he had rendered to both the Railway Company and the army, engineers had been promised to help him excavate a channel to take the water away from his land.

So peace and some kind of routine had returned to Nairobi Camp. Reuben had not seen Hannah for several weeks and his last inquiry had drawn a blank. Her father had told him that Hannah had decided to remain at Machakos and had no idea when she was likely to return. If at all. He had intimated that she might be joining her mother in England. Reuben couldn't blame her. He decided that the violence she had witnessed and suffered must have turned her against Africa. He tried to remain philosophical about it, but his heart ached that he would probably never see her again. He remained at Nairobi for a few more days after his last enquiry about Hannah and set out with David for the farm.

'I don't know,' he replied in answer to David's question.

'She didn't say goodbye,' David observed.

Reuben recalled how he had left David without saying goodbye when he joined Sergeant Ord's patrol. 'Some people find it difficult,' he offered as an explanation, wondering if he was apologizing for himself. 'They would sooner go without a fuss. Perhaps she will write to us one day.'

'Did you love her?'

Reuben laughed. The question caught him off guard. His laughter was a kind of defence. But he admitted it. 'Yes, David. I loved her very much.'

'Did she love you?'

'She may have done,' he said reflectively. 'Women are such strange creatures.'

'She didn't want to be evacuated to Machakos, you know.'

Reuben looked at him. 'I know she didn't. Neither did you.'

'She was glad when she found out I had hidden away.' He said it with a small note of triumph in his voice.

'Oh, was she now?' Reuben remarked lightly. 'And why was that?'

David grinned. 'She made me promise not to tell you.' He gave his father a sideways glance. 'But I don't suppose it matters now!'

219

Reuben's mouth turned down at the corners. 'No, I don't suppose it does.'

They continued with small talk as they trotted along in no particular hurry, towards the Rift Valley. In the distance Reuben could see two riders coming towards them. As they drew closer he could see one of them was Major Webb. A soldier was with him. They pulled up and Reuben greeted him.

'Bit out of the way, aren't we, Major?'

Webb saluted Reuben in acknowledgement. 'Something I had to attend to, Cole. It's finished now. You are returning to your farm I presume?' His expression was quite dour.

'Life goes on, Major. Must build for the future, don't you agree?'

Webb nodded. 'For us all. Mine lies in India.'

'You are going back?'

'I'm going back to my regiment as Lieutenant Colonel.'

Reuben was not surprised. Webb deserved his promotion more than anybody he had known. 'Congratulations. Bill Ord would have been proud of you.'

A sadness clouded Webb's face. 'I will miss that man like my own father.'

'Many of us will miss him.' Reuben did not want to dwell on Bill Ord's sad death. 'But he would have enjoyed it as if it were his own. Congratulations again, Colonel. You deserve it.'

Webb looked doleful. 'Yes, and thank you. Not just for your congratulations, but for everything else. You will get your reward.' He moved his head in a swift, bobbing motion. 'I must go now. Good day, goodbye and good luck to you, Cole.'

Reuben touched the rim of his hat and watched him go with a mite of curiosity. There was something about the man's general demeanour that did not exactly reflect the magnitude of the prize he had received. He wondered if it was because he was leaving Nairobi. Or maybe not. More likely that he was taking Hannah back to India with him, despite what Mr Bowers had said. It would make his reward even all the more remarkable; a fine woman and a career back with his regiment in India. He put the conundrum from his mind and began to turn his thoughts to other, more practical things.

They eventually turned off the road and began to negotiate the gradual slope as it dropped towards the farm. From there it was easy to see the remains of the rotted crop beneath the high water mark. Once again, Reuben felt terribly disappointed and cheated; five years of sweat and toil just about wiped out. He would have to begin again, of that there was no doubt, and he wondered now if he really had the heart for it. There was something missing. Or someone. It wasn't just Mirambo and his family either; it was as though the spark had gone from him.

'What are you going to do now?' David asked.

'What do you mean?'

'Miss Hannah said I should have a mother and that you should find one.'

'She told you quite a lot, didn't she?'

'Are we going to England?' David asked tentatively.

Although David's question was probing, perhaps impertinent, he knew that he was only repeating Hannah's words. 'That's what she meant, was it? About going to England?' Had Hannah known she might return to England? Was that it, he wondered? 'Have to rebuild the farm first, young man. Then we might think about going to England.' He pointed his finger directly at David. 'But no promises. Understand?' David nodded. Reuben dropped his arm. 'Right, no more questions about Miss Hannah, England or you having a mother.'

'But I'll be able to have a mother when we get to England,' David said, his face lighting up. Reuben didn't mind; at least it would give the boy something to look forward to. 'Race you to the farm, mister!' David shouted suddenly, and dug his heels into his horse.

Reuben called after him as he galloped away, but he was gone and out of earshot. Reuben smiled broadly and pushed his horse into a canter. As Reuben brought his horse down the slope he could see the front of his house quite clearly. He was still about half a mile away but he noticed a pony and trap outside. He saw David ride into the *boma* and jump from the saddle. He tethered the horse and walked out of the *boma* as far as the pony and trap. He studied it for a while. Then, quite suddenly, his arms flew up into the air and he ran into the house. Reuben negotiated the slope and rode his horse, as David did, into the *boma*. He slid from the horse and unbuckled the saddle, pulling it from the horse's back. Then turned and draped it over the side of the corral. At that moment, David appeared. He was running so fast that his hat flew from his head.

'Papa, papa!' he shouted excitedly. 'It's Miss Hannah. She's here!'

Reuben stood quite still, his hands still on the saddle. David ran up to him and grabbed his arm. 'Come on, mister, quick,' he insisted.

Reuben let David pull him and together they hurried towards the house. David beat him to the door and they literally fell in together. Reuben stopped and stared. Hannah was standing there, her hands clasped nervously in front of her. Her father was there too. He was smiling and got up from a chair as Reuben came in.

Hannah looked stunning. She was wearing the same white cotton dress she had worn before – it seemed so long ago. Her hair had been pinned behind her head but a wisp of it had broken free and hung down across her cheek. She looked apprehensive, nervous. She smiled lopsidedly at him.

'Hallo Reuben.' She twisted her hands together. 'I hope you don't mind us . . . I. . . .' she faltered.

'I thought you were going back to England.' He looked from her to her father. 'Did you two come here alone?'

Bowers shook his head. 'Major Webb would not hear of it.'

Reuben understood then why the major had looked like a soldier who had lost the battle even though he had won the honours.

'I saw him,' he said. 'He didn't tell me you were here.'

Hannah breathed in deeply. 'I told him not to,' she said rather sheepishly. Her face coloured a little. It brought a warm texture to her already beautiful complexion. 'I wanted it to be a surprise. No,' she said suddenly, correcting herself, 'that's not quite true. I didn't know if. . . .' She stopped and looked at her father, her eyes appealing to him.

Bowers saw the look in her eyes and stood up. 'I think it's time you showed me something of your farm, young David,' he said, deliberately ignoring Hannah's ineffectual plea for support. David glanced at his father then allowed himself to be ushered out of the room.

'I wasn't sure after so long.' Her face dropped. 'When I left.' She looked up. 'I thought you might have misunderstood.'

'Why did you tell David he needs a mother, Hannah?' He removed his hat and held it in front of him. He began rolling it by the rim.

'I didn't mean to pry. Besides, I don't think it's good for him to be without a mother.' She stopped. Then she raised herself to her full height. 'It isn't right; David should have somebody to care for him, the way a mother can.'

'We've managed until now.'

'That isn't true, Reuben. And David needs somebody even if you don't.'

He could see the defiance slipping back into her expression. Her eyes glistened. He felt unkind but was spellbound and wanted the magic to last a moment longer.

Suddenly she stamped her foot. 'Oh, blast you, Reuben Cole. If it wasn't for that stubborn streak you would have asked me long ago. I'm trying to tell you that I love you. I want to be David's mother.' She started crying and the tears fell from her face on to the cotton dress. She brushed at them fussily. 'Reuben, I want to be your wife.'

He walked over to her and lifted her chin so that her face tipped back. The tears clung to her upturned cheeks and he kissed her gently on the lips. 'I couldn't ask you to marry me Hannah because I thought you were going to marry Major Webb.'

'Well you were both wrong,' she said.

'Both?'

'Kingsley asked me before—' She hesitated. 'Before the trouble. I put him off. It was unkind of me, but I had to. He asked me again, several times. But this morning—' She stopped and dropped her hands to her sides. 'I love you, Reuben. I believe Kingsley has known that for some time. I dreaded having to tell him because I knew he would be heartbroken.' Then she smiled and her face brightened. 'I missed you terribly while I was at Machakos. And David. My father said I looked worse than the poor souls in the hospital. He said my nursing was honest but misdirected; there was another patient who needed me out here.'

'He has his uses then.'

'You haven't answered my question yet, Reuben.'

He was still holding her chin. He let it go and drew her to him. He had been deeply saddened by Hannah's absence and thought he would never again find the chance of real happiness. Now he felt a great release. It transcended anything he had ever known and unlocked a door to a future that held so much promise. One that he could share with the woman he thought he had lost.

'I didn't need to; I love you, Hannah. And if it will make you happy then, yes, David does need a mother. And yes, I do need a wife. And yes, I want you to be both.'

She threw her arms round him, enfolding him in a hug almost as strong as one of David's. He kissed her passionately and held her as if he would never get the chance again.

There was a noise from the door and Reuben broke off from the embrace. He saw David peering round the edge. He beckoned the boy over and scooped him up into his arms. David reached forward and drew Hannah in close so that the three of them were hugging each other. They were smiling, laughing and crying with happiness.

Hannah's father stood in the doorway watching them. His smile was celestial. Now they could put the sad memories behind them and find happiness. He wiped a small tear from the corner of his eye and gave thanks to God.

Author's Note

Hell's Gate is a story inspired by historical events. I have taken liberties with the date when Nairobi Railway Camp was first built, and I have woven my own, fictional characters into the plot. The railway line still stands as a monument to human endeavor, but my story is still simply a figment of my imagination.

Michael Parker